CROSSING *the* HORIZON

DEANNA EMBERLEY BAILEY

FORWARD BY KATHERINE PATERSON

CROSSING THE HORIZON
Copyright © 2015 DEANNA EMBERLEY BAILEY
Published by SHAKER MOUNTAIN PUBLISHING

Editorial Production: Diane O'Connell, Write to Sell Your Book, LLC
Cover Design: Lisa Hainline
Interior: Steve Plummer/SP Design
Production Management: Janet Spencer King, Book Development Group

For information, please visit www.crossing-the-horizon.com.

Printed in the United States of American for Worldwide Distribution

ISBN: 978-0-9907290-4-4
Epub editions:
Mobi ISBN: 978-0-9907290-3-7
Epub ISBN: 978-0-9907290-5-1

First Edition
10 9 8 7 6 5 4 3 2 1

Life is eternal.
Love is immortal.
Death is a horizon
and a horizon is nothing
save the limit of our sight.

—Reverend Robert T. Jennings, St. Francis
of the Fields Church, Louisville, KY.

This book is dedicated to our sons,
Solon Lawrence Bailey
(Solon)
William Theiler Bailey
(Liam).

You are always in our hearts and minds.
We will love you
forever,

Mom and Dad.

This story is a work of fiction, but it is based on real-life events and characters. Solon, Liam, and Amanda's names, as well as the names of their parents and grandparents, have not been altered. Other names and identifying details have been altered to protect individuals' privacy.

INTRODUCTION

WHAT HAPPENS TO us after death?
What happens to our loved ones after they die?
These universal questions have been asked since people have
lived. Hints of human hope of "afterlife" are evident in ancient
cave wall drawings and ritualized remains.

Remaining behind after the death of a loved one—and sur-
viving—is the hardest work I know. Hard to get up every day,
hard to find meaning in a life that feels empty, hard to feel ourselves changed—by undeserved tragedy—into sad strangers in our
own mirrors.

And yet—we do survive.
But how can we thrive?
How can this life left behind become tolerable, meaningful,
even joyful—ever again?

Those of faith will answer—Faith.
But even they will be tested beyond belief by this kind of grief.
And those with only questions, doubts, or certainty of zero—
will suffer the hopeless amputations of love lost.

But is love truly lost?
Or is it just beyond our vision, our reach, our yearning arms?

While reading Deanna Emberley Bailey's *Crossing the Horizon*, I have forgotten that the answers to these human questions are *not* known.

Perhaps the space beyond life *is* knowable—through a mother's intense love, propelled by pain, and carried by intuition into the next life of her children.

What saves this story—and saves us all—is human hope, humor, intuition and imagination, all woven into a compelling story of incredible love.

After reading "Crossing the Horizon," you can't tell me that this story is not true.

I forget that Liam and Solon are not alive—they are so vivid and full of life in their following adventures. And their story and their parents' journey can be a comfort and beacon of light and hope to all of us who have loved and lost.

Thank you, Deanna and Chris.

Respectfully,
Virginia Lynn Fry, MA
Author of *Part of Me Died Too—Stories of Creative Survival Among Bereaved Children and Teenagers.* (Dutton, 1995, Penguin Putnam 2000, revised 2005)
Director of the Hospice & Palliative Care Council of Vermont,
Bereavement Coordinator for Central Vermont Home Health & Hospice.

AUTHOR'S NOTE

April 13, 2006 marks the beginning of the end for me. December 25, 2009, marks the end. The end of life as we knew it.

On April 13, 2006, I was traveling down the beltway with my two young sons, having just left the gymnastics studio for home. The boys, tired from so much fun in the gym, were talking quietly in the backseat. My cell phone rang. These days, I won't answer my phone while driving. That day, I did. It was my mother. Through what I knew were tears, she told me my seventeen-year-old niece had just collided head-on with a bus and was at the hospital.

"Oh, no! How is she?" I asked.

"Not good. She's in intensive care and in critical condition."

My entire body began to shake as I pulled the car over and called my husband, Chris, to tell him the news. I was completely unprepared and could only imagine how my brother and his wife were dealing with this shock. Chris drove home from work, and met me there to be with our sons so that I could get to the hospital to be with Amanda, my brother, his wife, and my parents.

Amanda clung to life for five days, and during that time we stayed at the hospital, offering our presence and what little support we could, riding the roller coaster of emotion that came from not knowing if this beautiful girl would live or die. She took her last breath on April 18, 2006. We were all completely devastated, but none of us more so than my brother, his wife, and their two remaining children.

Amanda's death rattled the foundations of what I believed

about life. How could this precious girl suddenly be gone? Weren't the old supposed to die first? As I struggled to find a way to support my brother and his wife and tried to make sense of my own grief, I was flooded with questions about life, death, and my place in the world. It made me hug my two children even closer, grateful for the lives they continued to live and the joy and love we continued to share. I was sad beyond words for my brother and his wife, as well as for my nephews, who suddenly were left without Amanda in their lives. No prior warning. She was just gone from this world in an instant. For a long, long while, it was beyond my ability to believe that she died. It still is.

The pain and the shift in world view that I experienced after Amanda's death was new and scary. Many things changed for me. I had already been questioning whether or not to stay in my job in education. After Amanda's death, I decided to homeschool our sons the following year, in part because it was something I had always wanted to do and because I felt it would be good for them—for us. But I know in my heart that I also craved extra time with our boys after Amanda died so suddenly. I clung to them because I was afraid of losing them as unexpectedly as we had lost Amanda.

In the summer of 2009, after I was finished with a wonderful but intense year of homeschooling, I happened to read *The Lovely Bones* by Alice Sebold. Amazingly, this fictitious tale helped me deal with my grief from Amanda's passing. Though I had already believed in my heart that Amanda was with all of us in spirit, *The Lovely Bones* helped me actually picture Amanda active again in her afterlife. After reading the book, in my mind Amanda was just across some invisible barrier that prevented those of us who love her from seeing her. I could picture her watching over her Mom and Dad and her brothers, and maybe even watching over me. As a result, reading *The Lovely Bones* comforted me in a way nothing else had.

It was not long before tragedy struck our family again. On Christmas morning in 2009, Chris, the boys, and I were at Chris's father's home in Louisville, Kentucky, for the holiday. As far as the experts can tell, during the late afternoon of Christmas Eve, a fire began smoldering in the floor or wall space of the room adjacent to the second floor bedroom where Solon and Liam were to sleep. The enclosed fire smoldered throughout the night, starving for oxygen and spreading smoke throughout the spaces within the walls and the trussed floors and ceiling of the first and second floor of the home. On Christmas morning at 4:23 a.m., after the fire had smoldered and slowly spread for up to fourteen hours, the Sheetrock reached its high-temperature failure point of fourteen hundred degrees Fahrenheit. As sections of the Sheetrock collapsed, enormous amounts of superheated smoke poured throughout the home in all directions. Every smoke and heat alarm across the house (all of which had been programmed to call the fire department directly) screamed within thirty seconds of the collapse, waking us from deep sleep and plunging us into a most frightening Christmas morning reality. As fresh oxygen rushed in to feed the fire, it simply took off. There was nothing anyone could do to stop it. We rushed to escape.

But there was nothing we could do to save our sons. We tried. We tried as hard as any of us has ever tried to do anything in our lives. Within seconds of the Sheetrock's collapse, the boys were trapped in their room and suffering smoke inhalation. It was impossible for any of us to get up the stairs through the superheated smoke to help them. Given our sons' proximity to the origination point of the fire, the way the hot smoke so rapidly enveloped the home, and the speed with which that fire took off, there was absolutely nothing that could have saved them.

That was the end of life as we knew it.

The boys died so suddenly, so traumatically, with no chance for goodbyes, that Chris and I and everyone who loved them were left in a world of intense confusion, pain, and utter disbelief. How could it have happened? What had we done to make it happen? *Why?* In my racing mind, I continued to live in the fire, replaying the events and experiencing the same rush of hormones and bodily reactions I experienced so intensely Christmas morning as I tried desperately to save our sons. I struggled to get the images and sounds out of my mind. I simply could not believe the boys were gone and I could not get away from that damn fire. Although Chris and I began grief counseling within a month of the boys' passing, I had not even scratched the surface of my grief yet. I was still stuck in the fire, trying to find a way to save our boys.

Our grief counselor soon became concerned that I was suffering from post traumatic stress disorder (PTSD). So, in addition to ongoing grief therapy, I started individual trauma therapy to alleviate the PTSD symptoms. I learned how to use eye movement desensitization and reprocessing (EMDR) to stop the cascade of hormones my body released each time the fire came to mind, which it did dozens of times a day, whenever my mind was not otherwise occupied. I was told that stopping the cascade of hormones would give me a chance of escaping the panic and uncontrollable fear that overtook me every time I thought about that fire.

In a relatively short time, EMDR began to give some respite from my constant fire anxiety. When I was well enough, my trauma therapist recommended that, in addition to EMDR, I try to work to view the fire from our boys' perspective rather than my own, haunting recollections. She reasoned that if I could see the fire from the boys' point of view, I might be better able to understand and internalize the reality that their deaths had been quick. With the exception of their emotional turmoil, which I had internalized, the boys had not been in intense physical pain. They died of smoke inhalation and were dead before the heat of the fire affected them.

My trauma therapist recommended I do something creative while thinking about the fire from our boys' point of view. She offered a few ideas: write a song and sing it while playing my guitar. Create a piano piece. Create some artwork. Write in a journal. Whatever I chose to do, I had to do it one hundred percent from the boys' perspective, and not from my own. I had to put myself in their shoes. Take their perspective in that fire.

"Are you serious?" I thought. "I can't do that. They died!"

Further, my trauma therapist suggested that, after the boys died in my creative endeavor, I should push myself a little further by thinking about where their souls went after they died and incorporate that into my "project." She knew I simply could not fathom that the boys were completely gone. In my mind, there had to be a place for them. They simply had to be safe now, in some sort of afterlife. If they weren't safe, I couldn't bear to continue living.

I took six or eight weeks before I attempted to tackle my trauma therapist's suggestion. One day in April, four months after the boys died, I decided to begin writing about the boys' experience in the fire. Sitting at the computer, I deliberately chose to take the perspective of my oldest son, who I knew had passed out more quickly than his little brother. I figured taking that perspective would be less painful for me. I had been reliving and reliving my attempts to comfort and console my younger son before he succumbed to the smoke.

I began my story on Christmas Eve, knowing that at that point the fire was already smoldering and had not yet broken free. I wanted to recall our final, very happy evening together from the boys' point of view, and not just remember the horror of Christmas morning. I sat and wrote from Solon's point of view for four hours without stopping. The story simply poured out of me. As I wrote, I managed to get both boys through the fire and off to a place of safety. When I finished, I realized that I needed to write the next part from Liam's point of view and did so the following day.

Surprisingly, I discovered that writing from the boys' points of view did help me enormously. Not only was I able to take a different view of the fire, but I also felt incredibly close to my boys as I wrote. The writing became a therapy in itself. I continued with trauma therapy and grief therapy, and I wrote. For six months of two- to four-hour settings alternating from Solon's to Liam's point of view, this story of their life after death emerged. I did not edit or make changes as I wrote, did not worry about my spelling or punctuation, and didn't even reread chapters or spell check until months after I had finished writing the whole story. I just wrote and wrote for myself to try to feel a little better.

The story became, for me, much more than a way to get the boys out of the fire. Through writing, I relived the boys' personalities and felt their presence. I craved writing (for the first time ever in my life!). Though there were painful moments and I cried often, through writing I was able to revisit positive memories of our family time. I learned that my positive memories would help me through difficult times ahead. Writing also made it apparent how integral each of us—the boys, Chris, and I—were to each other's health and wellbeing throughout their lives. Perhaps most importantly, writing helped me to internalize the boys, to really feel and believe that they are not far away at any time, but rather, that they were right beside me and Chris in spirit as our lives continued in their physical absence.

Now, any time I feel Solon and Liam getting farther away, I reread my story, cry, laugh, and feel them nearby again. Thanks to this story, I believe that our boys are just across the horizon, safe as can be, still full of love, loved as they were on Earth, and forever connected to Chris and me and the many other people who love them. The story doesn't bring them back to life, or completely take away the pain of grief. Nothing ever will. It's only the beginning. But I am very relieved to have it to hold onto.

I did not write this story for publication, nor am I a writer by profession. I am sending this out into the world for one reason only: I want to help others who are suffering the wrenching loss of a loved one(s). With editorial guidance, I honed the dialogue and deepened my character and scene descriptions to better convey Solon and Liam's personalities. I added important details about Chris's experience in the fire and his relationship with the boys. The more I edited, the more painful it became and the more strongly I fought manipulating the writing any further. Sure, I'm aware the writing could still be improved with a more typical story arc and more skillful selection of words to convey the action. But because *Crossing the Horizon* tracks the path my mind followed as I navigated through intense grief, reflected on our lives with the boys, and discovered a way to feel them near once again, I've decided not to change the story further. Its current form reflects best how writing helped me heal, and I expect this will be best for readers working through grief, as I was.

I pray that, by sharing this story, other people striving to cope with the loss of a loved one will find hope along their path of healing.

Blessings,
Deanna

FOREWORD

WHEN MY FRIEND Deanna let me read the early raw manuscript that was to become this book, my immediate reaction was that her story must be shared. There would be many other wounded people that would need to read it.

I didn't know Deanna at the time of the events that open this book. I first heard of Chris and Deanna in the newspaper accounts of the tragedy. "How could any parent, how could any *human being* survive such a loss?" I wondered. When I met them a few weeks later, I was hardly able to open my mouth, for what words are there when we find ourselves face to face with unspeakable loss?

It was Deanna who found the words. Emily Dickinson's great poem urges us to "tell all the truth, but tell it slant." By telling the story from the boys' point of view—turning it into the kind of fantasy they themselves would have loved—she has made it not only possible for those of us who read it to bear the unbearable truth, but to share in the healing from tragedy that she began to discover as she imagined her sons' quest to comfort their devastated parents.

I am grateful she is ready now to share *Crossing the Horizon* with a wider audience, as I continue to be grateful for her friendship to me through my own time of loss.

—KATHERINE PATERSON, AUTHOR OF *BRIDGE TO TERABITHIA*

SOLON

I'M A BOY SCOUT. Well, I guess I should say I *was* a Boy Scout.

I learned everything there is to know about fire, or so I thought. I learned how to safely build campfires in the woods, how to start fires without matches, how to extinguish fires, how to be safe around the campfire, and much more. When I turned twelve, Mom and Dad started teaching me how to load the woodstove in our home, supervising me while I learned.

You could say I was extra cautious around fire. I knew that fire could help me do lots of things, as long as I respected it and played it safe. Oh—fire was wonderful in so many ways! It could heat our home, grill our food, and light our dinner table. But my favorite use for fire was making s'mores after an outdoor dinner. I loved to cook those marshmallows just to perfection and watch the chocolate melt when the marshmallow hit the graham cracker. Delicious!

Fire was my friend, until it appeared out of nowhere like lightning and killed my brother and me. It stole us from one of the safest places in the most wonderful life and sent us to another quiet, unfamiliar space far, far away.

It was Christmas 2009. We were with Mom and Dad at Grandpa Irv and GiGi's house in Kentucky. Though we had spent lots of time with these grandparents over the years, we had not been to Louisville to celebrate Christmas at Dad's father's house in nine years, so Liam and I were very excited and were having a great time with our Kentucky cousins. During the afternoon on

Christmas Eve, we decorated Christmas cookies and a ginger-bread house with our cousins, stuffing ourselves with sugar as we worked together to create our messy masterpieces. It was obvious this rare visit was special, because Mom, who was supervising, didn't even try to put a stop to our mess and just cleaned it up with a smile afterwards. We were having too much fun.

As the afternoon rolled on, Liam and Dad played soccer on the lawn with our youngest cousin, burning off some of his sugar high. I wasn't crazy about soccer. Give me a bike or a sled, and I'd be out the door in a flash, but all Liam needed was a ball, any kind of ball, really, and someone to play with. While Liam ran around outside like a madman with Dad and our cousin, I hung out playing on my Nintendo DS with my other cousin. You see, I had a certain attachment to technology. Mom and Dad worked to limit our "screen time," insisting it was better for us to run around outside and to create things on our own rather than sit in front of a screen that sucked us in. In my opinion, one hour per day Friday through Sunday was just not enough time with my DS, and I was relieved that this vacation seemed to be going differently. Dad and Mom were making enormous exceptions to our screen time limits, so I took advantage of it and stayed inside to play on my DS with my cousin and send emails on my iPod touch to my one of my best friends back home.

When it came time for dinner Christmas Eve, us four cousins sat at our decorated kids' table. Each of our places had been filled with wrapped, fun Christmas Eve gifts that were almost like party favors. We had a ball unwrapping the presents, running over to the adult table to show them our gifts, and playing together at our table before the lobster arrived. After stuffing ourselves to the brim, we forced dessert down anyway because, like the lobster, it was so unbelievably scrumptious.

After dinner, GiGi and Grandpa Irv read aloud "'Twas the Night Before Christmas" and the story of the Nativity as our whole family relaxed on couches and armchairs around the living room. Before these stories were read to us, I had even worked up enough nerve to sit at the piano and play some of my favorite pieces written by Burgmuller, Bach, and Nevin from memory for my grandparents, aunt, uncle and cousins. It was the first time many of them had ever heard me play, and they seemed thrilled. It was very late by the time we said goodbye to our cousins, kissed our grandparents goodnight, and hugged and kissed Dad before heading off with Mom to get ready for bed.

We climbed the stairs beside the house's front entrance and headed across the balcony that led to our room. Liam stopped in front of me and leaned his entire body over the balcony railing, hanging from his waist. Always the daredevil, he kicked his feet while staring down at the wooden floor in the entryway.

"Check it out, Mom!" Liam said, releasing his hands. Though it looked like he was having fun, I wasn't about to try that.

"Knock it off, Liam. It's late. Tomorrow's a big day."

Liam stood up with a grin and saluted Mom, and together we pushed open the double doors to Grandpa Irv's office. The office had been converted into our bedroom for the duration of our stay. Mom followed us in.

As we were getting our pajamas out, I said to Mom, "Are you sure Christmas is tomorrow?"

She said, "Yes, Sweetheart. Tomorrow's definitely Christmas. Why?"

I told her, "'Cause it feels like we just had Christmas." As we changed, brushed our teeth, and took our medications, Mom, Liam, and I talked about how lucky we were to have such loving grandparents and to be surrounded by so much love and care within our extended family. We agreed wholeheartedly that it had been a wonderful night. The three of us talked about the love of not only Grandpa Irv and GiGi, but also of all of our grandparents—Grandma Nancy and Opa, Nanny and Gary, and Papa Bill and Karen—reminiscing about some of our favorite things we had done with each of them. It was a long conversation, fueled with joy and enthusiasm for tomorrow, Christmas day. Liam and I agreed that we were very lucky to have such a wonderful family and fun-filled life. We climbed into our beds, content and eagerly awaiting morning.

When Mom kissed us goodnight and told us to sleep like pumpkins, like she did every night of our lives, she told us that she, too, was really looking forward to a special Christmas in the morning. We talked a little more, not wanting to say goodnight until she kissed us a second time sweetly on our cheeks and then closed the door and went downstairs to where she would sleep down the hall on the first floor.

After Mom left our room, I was so excited about the morning that I could hardly shut off my brain. I was really hoping I'd get a MacBook Pro laptop computer, either from my parents or from Grandpa Irv and GiGi. I know that it was a huge gift for a twelve year old to ask for, but I really, really wanted one. Using my plentiful seventh grade writing homework as a bargaining ploy, I had begged and pleaded with Mom and Dad for that new computer. Like a cellphone, I could carry that laptop everywhere with me, which meant I could do my schoolwork anywhere in the house and even bring it with me when we traveled. Unfortunately, my sometimes-copycat, ten-year-old brother, Liam, had decided he would ask for one, too. That really ticked me off, but Mom and Dad insisted that, like me, he was allowed to ask for anything he wanted. That didn't guarantee that either of us would get what we asked for, though. I thought about that MacBook Pro constantly as I drifted off to sleep Christmas Eve, praying my wish would come true.

At four thirty a.m., all of the fire alarms in the house started blaring. I was sound asleep, in a complete fog, and didn't really register the loud, repetitive sound. In fact, I didn't wake up at all until

I heard Mom screaming in panic for Liam and me to get down-stairs *right now* because this was a real fire. Before hearing that, I think I wasn't fully awake, despite the loud fire alarms and every-thing. Smoke alarms go off all the time when people are cooking a delicious Christmas breakfast, don't they? They certainly went off plenty in our home kitchen, like whenever Mom or Dad used the oven broiler or made us delicious oven-roasted French fries. Maybe in my sleep it just didn't register that there was a full-on emer-gency taking place. Or, maybe there was something else at work, keeping me flat in my bed.

Our room was pitch black. I couldn't see a thing. This was odd, considering we had left the light on and the door cracked in the bathroom that was inside this office/bedroom. Maybe Liam had turned out the light? But then why would it have been pitch black? Shouldn't there have been some moonlight coming in the window by the desk on the far side of the room? And where was that bath-room, anyway? There should have been plenty of light, and not total darkness.

Liam was yelling at me, screaming at me, really, but I couldn't see him. In his totally fear-filled voice, he was begging me to come to the door of the room where he was. Apparently he had gotten out of bed as soon as he heard Mom and had somehow found his way to the bedroom door. I was still glued to my bed.

I could hear Mom screaming at me, "Solon! Please. Get up. Come over to Liam. NOW! Come to our voices. Please. Get up! Hurry!" For some reason, I couldn't answer Mom or Liam and was having trouble getting myself to move. It felt like my feet were made of lead and the fog in my brain was just too thick to let the words through to my mouth. Mom kept yelling at me frantically. Slowly, and with enormous effort, I summoned the willpower and strength to get up. Right away, I stumbled and fell hard to my knees. I was lightheaded. Surely, that must have been why I fell. Already down, I got onto all fours and slowly crawled, across the room in the dark toward Liam's still screaming, terrified voice. I could hear Mom down in the entryway, still begging for me to get up. When I finally got to the door, with Mom and Liam still yelling and screaming for me, I bumped into Liam, who was lying on the floor inside the door.

"I'm here," were the only words I could summon, and they sure didn't sound like me.

It was clear to me that Liam was struggling to close the double doors to the room, which must have been overlapped the wrong way so that they wouldn't shut completely. Now that I was close, I could see smoke pouring into our room through the crack between the two doors. A light out in the hall flashed on and off every time the alarm sounded. I stopped there, thinking hard about this strange scene. It must have been a smoke alarm light that was flashing. That had to be what made this strange, pulsing glow through the crack.

I wanted to open those doors and get to where Mom was standing down in the entryway, but Mom was yelling, "Don't open the doors! *Do not open them!* Keep them closed! The smoke out here is way too thick and it's burning hot! It's pouring up over the balcony. You can't breathe it! Keep the smoke out of your room! Close the doors completely. You can do it. Stay down low. *Stay down!* Remember: smoke rises. Whatever you do, don't stand up!" Mom's voice was shaking.

Liam was crying and screaming, "I *am* down on the floor! Help! Help! Somebody has to come up and help us!"

I joined Liam in trying to get the doors closed but bumped into him again. It took all the effort and brainpower I had to form the words, but finally they came out, sounding incredibly odd and garbled.

"Move over, Liam. I'll do it." I'll never fully understand what happened next. I kept wondering why I couldn't move, think or talk normally. I knew how to close those doors when I was standing. So, not thinking about Mom's advice to stay down on the floor, I walked my hands up the door and stood up to close the doors like I had done so many times since we had arrived in Louisville. That was a bad idea. I got a face full of intensely hot smoke and took one breath, and then my head spun out of control. I immediately fell flat backward and my body and head hit the ground with a sickening thud, striking Liam on the way down. Liam screamed, "Ouch! Solon!" and started to cry harder.

I faintly heard Mom yell, "Boys! Don't push! Don't fight! This is an emergency! You have to work together!"

Then I heard Liam screaming at Mom, "I didn't push him! He fell on me!" He was crying even harder and freaking out.

"Sorry, Liam," Mom said. "I believe you. It's okay. It's going to be okay."

"Solon," Mom screamed, "are you okay? Answer me, Solon!" I tried to answer, but there was no way that I could have.

"Shake him, Liam. Is he moving?" Liam shook me and discovered my limp body. I couldn't talk, respond, or move in any way. Mom's voice was getting more and more faint with every passing moment.

Liam, crying hysterically, screamed, "No!"

"Is he breathing? Can you tell? Is he breathing, Liam?"

"It's dark. I can't tell. Get me out of here! *Help*!!"

Mom seemed to freak out then, and I very faintly heard her yell, "Liam! Stay there. I'm coming up. Stay where you are!" I could hardly hear her. Her voice was getting softer and softer. My brain seemed to be slowly shutting down.

Liam, lying beside me, was yelling in anger, "I'm scared! Help me!" Mom did not answer for what seemed like a very long while. Liam just kept screaming, "Mom! Mom!" at the top of his lungs. "Help me. Mom!"

Liam was panicking because Mom did not answer him and

yelled even louder. He was so close that he was screaming into my ear. With no reaction whatsoever from me, and nothing from Mom, he was completely freaking out. I can't blame him.

After a short while, I heard Mom talk to Liam in the faintest of voices. "I tried to crawl upstairs. I held my breath. I couldn't answer you 'cause I held my breath. I'm here. I can't get up the stairs. The smoke was burning me."

"You have to. You have to HELP ME! You have to come up!"

Suddenly, I could see again. Don't ask me what happened, 'cause I can't fully explain it in terms you'll understand, but I realized then that I was floating on the ceiling of the room feeling one hundred percent well and at total peace. I was floating there looking down at my body, which was lying face up on the floor beside where Liam was laying down on his stomach to avoid the smoke and screaming at Mom. Whereas before I couldn't see in the dark, everything was crystal clear as I looked down from the ceiling. I wondered aloud how I could see in this dark, smoke-filled room and how it could be that my body was down there and I was up here hanging out in the smoke, looking down on my body and feeling great. Nothing hurt. Some fire was starting to shoot through the entrance of the storage area beside our bedroom, and smoke had filled the room, but I couldn't feel a thing, not even any heat. I yelled to Liam to try to get his attention and tell him I was okay, but he didn't hear a word.

Mom yelled up, "I can't get past the fourth stair, Liam. It's way too thick. It's burning hot. I'm sorry. There's no way for me to get up there across that balcony. Stay in your room. Keep that smoke out. Don't try to come out or it could kill you."

At the mention of the words "kill you," Liam screamed louder than I have ever heard him scream. "NO! Help me! I'm scared!" He began wailing even more. Liam insisted that someone had to come get him out *now*.

Mom started continually telling Liam to hang in there. "Liam.

The firemen are on their way. I am scared, too. They're on their way. Someone's gonna come get you out. Hang in there. I know you're scared. I'm sorry! They'll be here soon. They'll have suits on to protect them from the heat. They'll be able to get upstairs to you even though I can't. I'm lying on the floor. I'm right here. I'm at the front door lying down below the smoke. I'll stay right here 'till they get here. Keep talking to me. I'm here. It's gonna be okay."

Liam cried louder and kept repeating, "I'm scared! Help ME!" He was shaking uncontrollably. Mom kept talking to him, trying to keep him calm, and telling him she loved him.

Liam started coughing and gagging, and then he coughed one last time and went silent. He floated up beside me to the ceiling.

I looked at Liam for a long while then. He didn't look like the Liam I was used to. He had the same shape and same general appearance, but he had changed. His skin, if you could call it that, was white and shining the brightest light. I could see right through him to the picture that hung on the wall behind him. I wondered if I looked the same way to him, if he, too, could see in the dark, and if he could see me up there next to him in this smoke- and fire-filled room.

Liam looked at me with those bugged out eyes he always gets when he is frightened and he cried out, "What's happened to us? You look so freaky. I'm scared! I want Mom and Dad." I looked down at my arm and, sure enough, it was white and shining, just like Liam's entire body was.

"Holy cow! Is that my body down there?" Liam asked.

"Yep. I'm afraid so. Can you see mine?" I never heard his answer because Mom was calling to us as loudly as I had ever heard her yell.

"LIAM! SOLON! Answer me! Are you okay? Please God! Help these boys! Hang in there, boys. Daddy loves you. I love you. We love you so much. It's going to be okay. Someone is going to come get you. The firemen are on the way. The alarms have already called them. They're on their way. They'll come get you out. I'm right here. I'm here. Hang in there. Please God, help them." Then I heard her yell, "Where the hell are the fire trucks?! What's taking them so lo—" She coughed and gagged.

After Mom stopped coughing and caught her breath again, she yelled up to us in a fainter voice that seemed to be fading, "Boys! I have to go outside to breathe. Smoke's thick down to the floor. I'll be right out front. I promise. I won't leave. I love you!"

A very short while later, I heard Mom yell up to us from further away. She must have been standing right outside the front door of the house. "Daddy just tried to climb up to get to you, but the smoke's too thick. He's gonna get on the roof and get you through the window. If you hear me, go to the window and meet Dad. Boys! Boys! Can you hear me?!" After another smaller fit of coughing, she screamed into our silence. "Go to the window and meet Dad!"

I tried to answer her, and Liam yelled at her with me. We yelled as loudly as we could, but I was sure she couldn't hear me, just like Liam couldn't hear me yelling at him when he was still alive and I was already up here. Mom's voice was becoming softer and softer, probably because she was moving further away from the burning house. "Oh God. Please. Please, God. Don't take the boys away from us. Why is this happening?!" She was screaming uncontrollably then. Though I couldn't see her, I knew that she was losing it.

"We need to get out of here, now," I said. "Hurry. We need to stop them, or they'll kill themselves trying to save us. You go meet Dad at the window. I'm going out front to comfort Mom before she totally freaks and darts upstairs anyway."

Liam refused to go to the window without me. He said, "Mom told us to work together, not fight. We need to stick together." Being my stubborn little brother, he wouldn't leave my side. "I am scared," he said.

I tried to go down and get back into my body so that I could bring it to the window and meet Dad quickly before trying to get to Mom out front, but there was no way to get back into my body and bring it to Dad. My body was dead and in the midst of tons of smoke, and a fire was beginning to take hold on the other side of the room. Liam watched, horrified. "What's going to happen to us?"

"I think we died, Liam. That's why nothing hurts now. Look at our bodies down there. That smoke's so hot that it's burning them, just like it would've burned Mom or Dad if either of them had gone any farther up those stairs. My body's down there in all that hot smoke, but I don't even feel it. I don't feel it at all. Do you? And look. The fire is shooting through the floor over there. That fire must be so hot, but we can't feel that, either."

"I don't want to die! I don't want to die!" I could tell from the look on Liam's face that he was crying, and so was I, but neither of us seemed to be shedding any tears.

"I don't wanna die either, but it doesn't look like we have a choice. At least we're together, like you said. Come on. We'll stick together. We'll be okay. Let's go to the window like Mom said and meet Dad. Maybe somehow we can convince him not to come in the room. It's way too dangerous."

We floated over to the window that we couldn't see when we were alive but could somehow see once we were dead and out of our bodies. Without even trying, Liam and I floated straight through the window as if nothing were in our way. We saw Dad scrambling up from the top of a ladder onto the roof, leaning his side against the shingles and gingerly stepping his bare feet along the gutter. His pants were on, but he was shirtless in the cold, dark night.

"Holy crap. Dad could slip and fall off!" Liam said, watching Dad use his lean upper body and legs to climb across the roof. We could hear Mom screaming in terror out front at God and the world.

"Dad! It's okay. We're right here. We're out!"

What was I expecting? He kept right on half-sliding, half-climbing across the roof, unaware that we were right beside him. When he got to the window, after a second he punched his fist through it. Black smoke poured through the hole like a furnace venting directly into his face. A noise came out of Dad's mouth quickly before he shoved his head into the rooftop, turning his face away with a cough. He went still for several seconds and held himself there for a while, struggling to breathe and recover. I wondered if the steady stream of smoke pouring through that hole was burning the back of his short, dark hair as he tried to avoid the heat.

"Holy cow," I said, looking at Dad. His whole face was bright red. It looked like it only took that brief moment of smoke to singe his face and make him unsteady. Grandpa Irv said something from the bottom of the ladder, and Dad moved away from the window hole and slowly started to work his way back across the rooftop, looking incredibly sad.

"Phew. That was a close one. At least we know Dad's not going in there now," Liam said.

I could hear Mom's desperate screams out front. If anything, her voice was getting louder and angrier. "Mom's out there losing her mind," I said. "We gotta go see if we can comfort her. She needs to know we're okay."

We found Mom alone out front wandering barefoot in circles talking to God, to herself, and to the firemen to hurry up and get there. Wearing only a sweater and her underwear, her long, dirty-blonde hair a mess around her angular face, she was crying and totally distraught beyond anything I'd ever seen. Liam and I went to her and began trying to tell her not to worry, that we weren't in any pain. She couldn't hear us and didn't seem to be able to see us, either. She just continued to walk in circles and look up at the sky above the house, clasping her hands and praying to God to help us. I can't say I'd ever seen her pray to God before. Then, suddenly, she became extremely angry, yelling at God, telling him that he couldn't take us, that she still needed us.

I said to Liam, "Let's try giving her one of our group hugs. Maybe she'll feel it." Liam stood on her left, and I stood on her right, and we wrapped ourselves around her, trying to hug her. Our transparent arms moved right through her as if she weren't even there. I wondered whether or not she could feel it.

Mom did seem to stop in place for a moment when we hugged her, and then she started repeating how much she loved us, over and over again, and how she didn't want to lose us. I told her how much we love her and Dad, and that we didn't want to lose them, either, but she couldn't hear me, of course. She couldn't hear Liam or feel him hugging her and crying out to her, either. Liam, heartbroken and sad, sat down on the ground and put his head in his hands, moaning and tearlessly weeping. We desperately wanted to help Mom feel better but couldn't find a way.

Quite suddenly, Dad ran around the corner from behind the house, running straight to Mom. His face was covered in black soot and his hand was bleeding. "Thank God you're okay," Mom said, throwing her arms around him.

"I broke the window ... " He paused. "I couldn't get to them."

Mom and Dad held each other and cried. "Oh my God. This can't be happening." I leaned into Dad and tried to wrap my wispy arms around him as he hugged Mom. They were both shaking uncontrollably. Liam joined me from Dad's other side. I was reminded of our family hugs that we sometimes shared in the kitchen, laughing, all our arms wrapped around each other in a giant mass of love. Liam and I wanted so badly to help Mom and Dad, to comfort them, but nothing we did seemed to work.

Out of nowhere, a black tunnel formed above us. I was scared that it might suck me up like a vortex into some sort of black hole or something, but Liam was the first to notice and point out a beautiful light at the end of the tunnel. It was a light like no other that I had ever seen. It was obvious that Mom and Dad had not seen the tunnel or the light. They just kept crying and hugging. In the distance, I saw what must have been a fire truck coming up the long drive into the neighborhood, red lights flashing. But the light at the end of the tunnel drew Liam and me toward it like a magnet. It was so welcoming that neither of us resisted moving in its direction. I had this sense that, if Liam and I could make it to the light, something magical might happen that would return us to our bodies, to Earth, to Mom and Dad and to all that we knew. Maybe then we could help them.

"Come on. Let's let ourselves go toward that light. Everything'll be right when we get there. I can tell." Liam agreed, so we let ourselves move toward the light with hopes of getting back home again soon.

What we saw as we passed through that tunnel along the way to that beautiful light was truly amazing. My twelve years of life on Earth were laid out in panoramic view along the left side of this tunnel. All of the highlights, the millions of fun and challenging things I had done in my life were there to see, almost in an instant. It made me realize just how amazing my life was, how full of love, challenge, friends, and family my life had been. In one moment, I saw Liam, me, Mom, and our aunts and uncles and cousins white water rafting through rapids in Wyoming, getting thoroughly doused by a giant wave that filled our boat and scared the crap out of us. In the next image, I was doing front flips from the diving board into a pool while Papa Bill and Karen watched with concern and Liam shouted, over and over again, "That was awesome! Do it again!" I even saw Opa John and Grandma Nancy bringing me through Fort Ticonderoga, Opa explaining in his animated way the details of the battles that had occurred there long before.

Liam and I had done so much in our childhoods; it was truly amazing to see it all displayed in one place. I wondered if Liam was seeing my life, too. "No. I'm seeing my own life on this side of the tunnel," he pointed to the right with a smile, "not yours." I turned my eyes back to scenes of my life. I looked at the image of the gravesite of my seventeen-year-old cousin Amanda and began to feel sad and confused. Amanda had died in 2006, five days after colliding head-on with a bus when she was driving home from school. Her death was incredibly tragic and shook our family to the core. But as I stared at this image of her gravestone, it gradually began to emit an incredibly warm, bright orange glow. I watched and wondered, and then Amanda's spirit body, all wispy and translucent, stepped out and reached toward Liam and I. As Amanda came forward, she repeatedly told us in her soothing voice not to worry. Everything was going to be okay. She was going to help us find our way in our "afterlife." Amanda had confirmed it. Liam and I were dead, just like her.

"Come boys. Let's head for the light," Amanda said.

"Can't we go back and see Mom and Dad?" I asked. "They need to know we're okay."

"No. I am afraid you can't go back now. I tried to do the same thing for my mom and dad in the hospital bed where I lay. They won't be able to hear you now. You'll be able to communicate with them, but not yet. We have to get through this tunnel and get to that light at the end."

"To where? When can we see them again?"

"You'll see. Don't worry. You're not alone. Trust me. I'll stay with you and help you make the transition. We need to move along to the light, where you'll meet up with your Guiding Spirit." Liam just looked at me, appearing confused, but somewhat relieved, probably because we had Amanda with us then.

Before long, Liam seemed to be enjoying himself looking at all the fun things he had done in his life and laughing his little laugh. I wish I could've seen what he was seeing on his side of the tunnel, but that wasn't part of the deal. I saw my life from my view, not his. Maybe I don't want to see life from his view, anyway. He could be rather mischievous and a pain in my butt at times. He was probably chuckling at some sneaky little trick he had played on me—like the time he set and hid my loud spy alarm in the closet beside my bedroom door hoping it would startle me into peeing my pants when I got up to use the bathroom at night. Fortunately, he failed. I tripped the alarm before even climbing into bed that night.

As much as I wanted to return to Mom and Dad and our lives, the light drew Amanda, Liam, and me toward it as images of my life kept appearing on the walls of the tunnel. As we approached the end of the tunnel it began to widen, and then it opened up into a large field with tall golden grasses swaying in the breeze. It was just the three of us, standing in this field with the beautiful light all around. Not another soul to be seen. The field felt lonely at first, and I was a bit nervous that something might jump out and attack, but then I realized that I had never felt so at peace in all of my life. Before I could stop him, Liam took off running across the field. He seemed to be running toward something that was running through the tall grass toward us, but whatever was running toward him was too short for me to see.

"Liam!" I yelled at him. "Be careful. Don't go far. Stick with me. Remember, Mom told us to work together."

When Liam returned a second later, he was carrying Spurs, our house cat. I wondered how on earth Spurs had ended up there. He hadn't been with us in Kentucky.

"Look." Liam held up the cat. "It's Misty. She saw us coming and ran into my arms." It was starting to make some sense. The cat, in fact, was not Spurs. Misty was Spurs's sister. She died when the neighbor's dog attacked her and broke her neck a few weeks after Amanda passed away. Our cousin Amanda and our dead cat were with us. It was getting stranger by the minute. Thinking we might soon encounter other dead people we knew, I wondered aloud at what point we would see Nana, our great-grandmother. She died at the ripe old age of ninety-five, when I was just five.

Amanda said, "You won't see your Nana here. In this field, you'll only see familiar beings that died sudden deaths around you. Nana lived a long, full life, so she's in some other place now. You'll see her somewhere else in your afterlife, but not here and now. If you look closely, though, you'll find others you know who died suddenly."

Liam was looking up at the sky and watching birds fly and squirrels climb the tree to his left. Those, Amanda told us, were the animals that had been killed around us. No doubt at least some of them were animals brought to our doorstep by our well-fed cats, who loved to hunt. Sure enough, Liam recognized the hairy woodpecker that one of the cats had left on our doorstep. It lay there dead for a few days before Dad noticed and buried it in the compost pile. A smile came onto Liam's face when he realized that this other life, this other place, this afterlife or whatever it was called, would have birds and little mammals around for him to enjoy just as he had during his lifetime.

"Look!" Liam said, pointing across the field. "There's a chicken coop way over there. Do you see it?" He pointed to the building at the far side of the field. With Amanda trailing us, we quickly made our way to the coop, which looked remarkably like our barn at home but was much smaller. When we peeked in the door, we saw three little chicks and seven hens. My mind flashed back to the time we'd raised hens with Dad and sold the eggs to the local store. We'd lost three chicks, and before the hens were old enough to lay eggs, seven hens were killed when an animal broke into the pen and attacked the growing pullets. Yep. Those were sudden, unexpected deaths, too.

"This is amazing and weird," I said to Amanda. "Lots of creatures that died prematurely near us are here. Do you see them all too?"

"No. I see only the ones that were in my life and died around me. I am not even sure that I see this field the way you see it. I see butterflies and bees and green grass. Let me try to explain as I understand it now. In our lifetimes, our spirits and bodies came into contact with different spirits and bodies. By spirits and bodies, I mean not just animals, but also plants and other living things. Now, here's the thing: when we die and come to this field, we can only see the spirits that we crossed paths with in life. Since most of the experiences in your lives and the spirits you crossed paths with were different than mine, you're bound to see things differently here than I do. Understand?"

Thinking that maybe I was beginning to understand, I looked over at Liam. We both nodded.

LIAM

I STOOD SURROUNDED by creatures from my past: Misty, who I adored and was so sad to lose during my life, as well as the birds, chipmunks, and mice that our two cats brought to the door. I was so happy to see all these little creatures again; I began talking to them and cooing at them like I used to do. After she rubbed up against me and let me hold her again, Misty wandered off through the tall grass.

I turned to Solon and Amanda and said, "This is awesome. It's so amazing here!" I ran off into the tall moving grass, following Misty. While I was following her, I noticed a football lying in the grass. It was green and blue, just like my Nerf football at home, the one Solon and I used to toss around with Dad or Mom outside our house. I picked it up and yelled to Solon, "Catch!" and threw him the ball. It landed in his hands, a perfect pass, if I do say so myself. Solon was game for tossing the ball around a bit, so we kept at it for a while. Amanda even joined us.

As we tossed and ran around, I hooted and hollered. "Nice pass, Solon!" and "Great catch, Amanda," and "Did you see that one? That was awesome!" I was feeling like I had during my lifetime after a good pass to one of my soccer teammates, or after kicking a homerun in kickball, or when I made 386 pogo stick hops in a row without stopping. In my lifetime, I absolutely loved using my body to jump, dive, swim, throw, kick, climb, and swing. Mom and Dad used to joke around that I had two speeds: intense and sleeping.

As Amanda, Solon, and I tossed that ball around, a strange

realization hit me. Wherever I was, I was having fun, but my body was gone. I was just a wispy sack of transparent fluff. No more legs and arms with muscles to move them. No more brain to coordinate it all. How odd. All of my throws in the afterlife seemed to just float through the air with little thought and absolutely no physical effort. Easy. Darn it! I missed my body and the challenge of using it well. I wanted that feeling of kicking the ball without knowing exactly where it would end up. It was more fun on Earth when I had tried to aim well and hit my target but didn't always succeed. I wanted my body back! Everything felt too easy. And there was another thing: since I had become a sack of transparent fluff without a body, I didn't imagine I'd ever be able to throw the ball around with my parents or my friends on Earth again. That just rotted!

As usual, Solon was bored with our game of catch long before I was, and he sat down in the grass. Amanda and I kept throwing the ball around for a bit longer. When we also tired of catch, I walked over to where Solon was sitting on the grass and noticed he looked incredibly sad.

"What's wrong?" I asked.

"Are you serious? We died and we're in this beautiful place, feeling at total peace, having fun with Amanda, but Mom and Dad are back there. Don't you miss 'em already?! Don't you wonder how they're dealing? We died! Don't you want to go back? And what about our friends? Don't you miss them too?"

"I sure do." Sadness flowed through me and I thought about our past lives. I wondered how everyone was coping back home. Then, I started to wish we were back in our old bodies again. I started thinking about how great it would have been to return to Louisville and wake up without a house fire and have a special Christmas morning with family, then return home to play, sled, downhill ski, and visit friends for the rest of Christmas break. I wondered if it could be done. Could we go back and redo it?

Could we somehow return to Earth to live again? That sure would have been great.

All of a sudden dark clouds rolled overhead out of nowhere, a harsh wind started blowing, and the grass started to sway violently.

Amanda came running to our sides, panicking and hurriedly explaining the situation. "We have to go. *Now!* Hurry, so we're not swept away!" She somehow grabbed each of our hands and began running across the field. Solon and I took off with her, the grass whipping at our transparent legs and the sky becoming even darker. Amanda's high-pitched, alarmed voice scared me.

As we ran, clinging tightly to each other, Amanda explained. "This is your afterlife. You *cannot* return to live with your mother and father or your friends. *Stop thinking about it!* It's over! Any time you fantasize about going back to live again, a violent storm like this'll form. Hopefully it'll bring you back to your senses fast, 'cause if you keep dreaming about going back, the storm'll pick you up and send you to awful places. Believe me, you don't want to be carried to one of those dark places in your afterlife. It's really bad! Besides, you'll be able to go back and visit the people you knew in life and see what's happening there now, but there's absolutely no way to go back for good to your past life. Ever. You died."

She tried to console us as she ran, holding tightly to both of us. "Don't worry. You might be able to communicate with people you love, but any time you dream about going back, really being alive again, you risk ending up in a place you don't want to visit. Trust me. You have to accept that you're dead. You can't go back. The afterlife is amazing and truly wonderful. Consider it a new adventure."

As we ran, Solon and I began asking questions. "How? How can we talk with Mom and Dad? They need to know we're okay. We have to tell them we love 'em and miss 'em, that we wish we were still there." Oops. That was the wrong thought. An enormous gust of wind picked us up and threw us through the sky toward the edge of the huge field. Landing hard, I screamed, scared that we would soon find ourselves in a land filled with three-headed monsters and demons ready to attack us.

Amanda yelled out, "Hurry. Right now, think of something you both loved to do in your lifetimes, something that connected you to each other. Think hard about it, but don't say it out loud. Each of you should do it in your own mind. Silently agree on something." Was she nuts? How could Solon and I "silently" agree on something?

Amanda continued, "When you both think about the same thing, you'll find your way out of this mess. Do it now! Think hard. Think fast before you're carried off. *NOW!*"

We continued running as fast as we could toward the edge of the field, which was much closer then it had been when we'd taken that little flight. Still clinging to Amanda and Solon, I started frantically trying to think of all of the fun that Solon and I had together sledding, skiing, building Legos, listening to music, dancing to our iTunes music, and playing Guitar Hero. My mind was jumping from one great activity to the next.

"Don't just think about it quickly. Visualize it, really picture it in your head," yelled Amanda. I couldn't understand how she knew that we were thinking too quickly.

I thought about our trips down the sledding hill with Dad behind the house on our toboggan. I thought about all the Legos that Solon and I loved to build with for hours in the family room. My Lego castle came to mind. I had so much fun building that castle all by myself after my tenth birthday. Mom sometimes helped me uncover hard-to-find pieces in the pile of bricks, but I built that castle by myself, and it was huge. Sadly, the whole thing crumbled before I died when I tried to move it. I was so proud of that castle and I was crushed when it broke. I had not rebuilt it yet.

As we continued running across the field, I saw a large, bright and glowing castle appear from out of nowhere near the end of the golden grasses. This castle, which was nothing like my Lego castle, had many turrets and a moat with a bridge leading up to its massive front entrance. It was enormous and intricate, almost white in appearance, and as bright as the sun. Oddly, it was brighter than anything I'd ever seen in my lifetime, yet I could stare at it without hurting my eyes. And it was beyond beautiful; it was so amazing and inviting that I couldn't take my eyes off of it.

"Where'd that castle come from?" Solon yelled to Amanda as we continued to run. So somehow, we'd done it. He could see a castle, too.

"Where? What castle? Where is it?" Amanda yelled over the wind. "We need to get there, quickly. I don't see it. Only you two can see it. You have to get us there, fast! Focus on the castle and run like the wind."

Solon and I pointed at the castle and ran as fast as we could, dragging Amanda with us. As we approached, we headed straight for the bridge that crossed the moat and ran up to the front door. Solon reached out his hand, prepared to grab the brass handle that was glowing a sort of crimson color. "Wait!" I said. "It's glowing. It might be hot."

But it was too late, and his hand was already on the handle. "Nope. Not hot," he said. "Give me a hand, would ya?" With great effort, together we were able to pull open the enormous door a crack. At that moment, we turned around and watched the field evaporate behind us and felt the wind suddenly die to a light breeze.

Amanda stood at the doorway and told us she wouldn't be going in. She couldn't see our castle, much less enter it. We hovered at the doorway, uncertain, and not wanting to leave her. She was our safety net, the one that could help us make sense of our new surroundings. We stood there, nervous and undecided. We didn't know whether to go in or stay there with Amanda.

Amanda, noticing our hesitation, said, "You'll be safe here. Don't worry. This is your portal to lots of great adventures. It's your space to learn how to find your way around in your afterlife. You'll have help when you get inside, I'm sure. I did when I entered my enchanted space. A spirit greeted me and helped guide me. This is all new and probably a little scary, but remember: you'll be okay as long as you don't wish to go back to your past life to live. That'll cause all kinds of challenges and make the beauty of your afterlife crumble around you. Believe me, you should do everything possible to avoid going to the scary spaces the storms could take you."

"But how can we do this without you? How will we know where to go or what to do inside? Why can't you come?" I asked.

"My afterlife portal's very different. Remember, I can't even see yours, and that field we just left, I didn't see it the way you did. I didn't see the animals that you saw because they weren't part of my life. This castle wasn't part of my life, either. That's why I can't see it or enter it."

That made me wonder. "Solon. How can you see the castle? That Lego castle was mine. Did you help me build it or something, 'cause I don't remember whether you did or not."

"I helped you find a few pieces for it, but I wasn't thinking about your Lego castle. I thought about all the trips we took to Alison's house for piano lessons. You used to sit on Mom's lap and listen when I played. That was before you grew up, got bored at my lessons, and refused to sit still and chose to play outside, kicking soccer balls and jumping on pogo sticks. Well, guess what? When you'd sit quietly, I loved having you listen to me play because it made me proud. You know, when I first saw this castle on the side of the field, I was thinking about the day I was working on the duet "The Enchanted Castle" while you sat on Mom's lap drawing castles even though you were already bored with sitting for my lessons. That day I remember thinking that you must have thought that piano piece was really peaceful, like I did, because you actually sat still the entire lesson! Nope. I definitely wasn't thinking about your Lego castle, but I guess since we were both focused on castles, this castle appeared. What does it look like to you, like your Lego castle, or different? To me, it's nothing like your Lego castle."

"It doesn't look like the Lego castle at all," I said.

Amanda spoke up. "From what my new friends here tell me, you're both seeing the same castle. The image came to you through your connected spirits here in the afterlife. And, Solon, 'Enchanted Castle' is a fitting name for the castle in front of you now," she said. "This castle will help you see what's happening back home. If you follow the spirit's advice in the castle and don't take the wrong path, you might even be able to communicate with your family and friends and use the castle to travel to other places in your afterlife."

I said, "This is just too strange. We need to walk into the unknown and try to find our way in a totally foreign castle, of all things. I miss my life. I miss Mom and Dad and everyone else. Now you're gonna leave us too and just say, 'good luck boys.' It's so unfair!"

"You'll be fine," Amanda said. "All of this is unfair. Our deaths were unexpected and unfair, too. Think about it. Our families back home are doing exactly what you're doing now: trying to find their way in a strange new world, a world without us that they never planned to live in. Their lives have changed entirely, and they have to find a way to new meaning in life and work hard to adjust to being alive without you. That's totally unfair, for sure. Well, just like them, you two need to find your own way in this afterlife and work hard to adjust to being here without the people you know and love. You are absolutely right. It's unfair, but you'll be okay.

"You can do it," Amanda continued. "Take your strength from your parents, just like you did when you were alive. Just like my mom and dad, your mother and father poured themselves into caring for you, raising you to confront the challenges that life presents, and loving you throughout. They helped you learn to take risks—physical, academic, musical, and more—risks that helped you discover what makes you happy and fulfilled. Rely on what they taught you. If in this Enchanted Castle you see something that you want to explore, go ahead and try it out. If you think doing the thing you chose will help you in your afterlife, keep working at it, just like your mom and dad taught you. Trust them. Even though they're not here, their spirits still live in you. I have to go now. Go on into the castle and have fun."

"Can't we just come with you instead?" I said on the verge of tears, wary of what lay beyond that castle door.

"You need to do this. You'll be fine. Stick together, and don't worry so much. I'll see you again. Promise."

And with that, Amanda took off running. When she reached the end of the bridge over the moat, she disappeared.

I turned to Solon, who was still holding the shining crimson handle as he looked back at the place Amanda had been. "Did you see that? She disappeared into thin air! What now?"

SOLON

"THERE'S NO WAY around it now," I said, yanking on the shining, crimson handle. The door wouldn't budge. "Gimme a hand, would ya?"

Liam grabbed the handle. With both of us pulling hard, the door slowly began to creak open. When we had created an opening large enough for one person to scrunch through, I cautiously slid across the threshold first. What lay before me was a complete surprise. We weren't in a room inside a castle, but rather we stood at the edge of an enormous, undulating field of green grass. The fence surrounding the field looked exactly like the one Dad used at home to contain our sheep or chickens, or to protect our garden, but this fence was much, much longer—long enough to surround this entire field.

The scene that lay before us was unbelievably beautiful. Every hill of the rolling grass was bathed in the amazing glowing light that we had seen at the end of the tunnel and in the first field we encountered with Amanda. I turned around to see Liam right behind me. Once again, he was staring with those bugged-out eyes, looking startled.

"What the heck?!" Liam quipped. Clearly he was as surprised as me to walk through a castle door and end up in a glowing field. How many castles do you know with entire fields inside them? There wasn't a single wall within view. Somehow, we must have traveled somewhere entirely new when we stepped into the castle.

"What now?" I asked. A different voice altogether answered me.

"What would you like to do?" The voice was loud, but soothing and friendly and not the least bit scary. I had no idea where it came from because I could hear it all around us, as if it surrounded us, yet it wasn't too close, and it wasn't far away, either. We stood there looking around, trying to figure out where the voice had come from. I certainly had never heard a voice like that before.

I whispered, "That might be a spirit, maybe the one Amanda said we'd meet that could help us out. Think we should talk to it?"

"I can hear you, Silly Solon. Just be polite, ask for help and I might be able to oblige."

Liam and I looked at each other as if to say, "This is soooooo weird."

Liam leaned over and whispered in my ear, "What should we ask?"

"I can hear you too, Littlest Liam."

Again, Liam and I looked at one another, only this time we were smiling at our odd situation. How did the spirit know our names and, better yet, how did it know some of the nicknames Dad and Opa Jon had called us? Shoot. How could Liam and I have a private chat if this crazy spirit could hear anything and everything we whispered to one another and then plop itself in the middle of our conversations? I had to find some way to talk to my brother without being heard. Liam and I had lots of practice whispering at home and at school, but this spirit even heard us whisper softly to each other. Hmm . . . maybe, just maybe, in our afterlife I could think hard about a question to ask without actually asking Liam aloud and see if he could read my mind. But then would the spirit be able to hear me, too?

I thought hard: *What should we do now? Ask this spirit to help us find a way to tell Mom and Dad we're okay?*

Liam looked at me, startled. He scrunched up his eyes and lifted his eyebrows, one cocked higher than the other, as if to say something without saying it aloud. Liam was well practiced at this form of non-verbal communication. It was his way of communicating with me when we were busy scheming up some plan behind Mom or Dad's back but were within earshot of them.

I thought hard: *If you hear what I am thinking, words and all, nod your head.*

Liam nodded and looked at me, surprised. His eyes were directed straight at me, so he knew I hadn't moved my lips. Clearly, he was as amazed as I was that he could hear my thoughts. He scrunched up his shoulders and turned his right hand over, palm up, as if to say, "How'd you do that?" Liam always was expressive and communicated with every part of his body, even if he wasn't talking aloud.

I thought hard: *Try just thinking really hard about what you wanna say. Think really hard about the words without saying them. I want to see if we can talk without saying anything aloud.*

Liam went silent. He was busy thinking, looking at me, and repeatedly raising his eyebrows, but I wasn't hearing anything. Then, all of a sudden, I heard him yell without moving his mouth: *I AM GLAD WE'RE TOGETHER! DID YA HEAR ME THAT TIME?*

Ahhh! I raised both of my hands to my ears and held my head. Man, that had been way too loud! His words were echoing in my head.

When the echoing finally died down, I thought: *Turn down the volume! That hurt. As always, you're yelling. Yes. I heard you. I am glad we're together, too. Whatever you did worked, but that was way too loud!* I paused, thinking. *I have no idea why the other things you were thinking before didn't work, but, whatever. Try it again, but don't yell this time? Yell, and I'll kill you.*

"TOO BAD. YOU CAN'T KILL ME. I AM ALREADY DEAD. REMEMBER?"

Ouch! His words were a little softer that time, but they still reverberated in my head.

"Very funny. Somehow you have to find a way to speak quietly. It hurts!!" I thought.

"YOU'RE COOL!" He countered, still not getting it.

"Gee. Thanks. That was a little softer, but it still hurts. Keep working on that some other time, okay".

Oh well, I thought to myself. At least we seemed to have found a way to communicate without that spirit hearing our every word. I became rather excited. It would be so awesome once Liam was able to do it without yelling into my head. Sending someone your exact thoughts without writing or talking would have been so handy in our past lives. I couldn't help but imagine all the fun we could've had in school with our friends without our teachers hearing anything we said! Eager to use our newfound abilities, I started another conversation with Liam.

"Should we ask the spirit for some kind of help now?"

Liam simply nodded his head. That wasn't very helpful, but at least his voice wasn't echoing in my head again.

"What should we ask it?" I braced myself for his yell.

"HOW CAN WE GET BACK TO EARTH?"

"No way! Are you nuts?! How do you propose we politely ask that? It might offend the spirit. Remember, Amanda said we can't think about going back to our lives on Earth, and if we do we'll end up in some bad part of our afterlives. Asking could start another windstorm or something even scarier. What then?"

"SO HOW CAN WE GET BACK TO TELL MOM AND DAD WE'RE OKAY WITHOUT ASKING TO GO BACK?"

"I don't know."

Loud Liam and I both sat there at the edge of the field thinking.

We had to find a way to let Mom and Dad know that we were not hurting. They must have been back there on Earth, probably still in Louisville, freaking out because we died in that fire. Somehow Liam and I had to find a way tell them that we were okay. Could we communicate with them without going back to Earth, I wondered? The spirit told us we could be polite and ask for what we needed.

"Liam, we could try asking how to communicate with people on Earth while assuring the spirit that we want to stay here in this lovely afterlife because we feel remarkably at peace and loved right where we are."

"OH, YOU'RE SUCH A SWEET TALKER. YOU DO THE TALKING. BUT DON'T BLOW IT, OKAY. YOU KNOW HOW MUCH I HATE SCARY THINGS, SO MAKE SURE YOU'RE CAREFUL WITH YOUR WORDS."

I waited for my head to stop hurting and then asked my question aloud, "Can you hear me, spirit?"

The answer, "I sure can," surrounded us.

"Liam and I want to tell Mom and Dad back on Earth that we're okay and they don't need to worry about us. We want to stay here in heaven because we feel so at peace here, but we need for our family and friends to know that we're not hurt, that we're okay. Could you please help us figure out how to do this?"

"Well said, young man. Communication with the living is not difficult. Most people who die and move on to their afterlife want to assure their loved ones that they're all right. You can do this quite easily if you set your mind to it. You don't need me to teach you. It seems you and Liam have learned how to communicate with one another without talking out loud or gesturing, and you do so without me hearing you. Is this true?"

"Yes, Ma'am." Why did I think this spirit was feminine? I wondered.

"Woah, now. Who says I'm a ma'am?' What makes you think

I even have a gender? Just because people do doesn't mean I do. You both have a gender because you were once living people. I've always been a spirit with no gender attached."

"Is there a name we can use to talk to you then? What should we call you?" I asked.

"Just call me your Guiding Spirit."

"Okay. How can we tell Mom and Dad we're okay?" I asked.

"You'll learn to communicate with them in the same way that you've learned to work together to get to different places here and the same way that you've learned how to communicate with each other without me hearing. Use the resources available to you and follow your intuition. The way to communicate with them will come to you as you move through different places in your enchanted castle."

"So you can't give us any hints about this, where to go next, or how to talk to people who are still alive?"

"Continue on your path. Focus on your goal and you'll find a way to communicate with your loved ones on Earth. Most importantly, just like your Mom and Dad used to say, have faith in your abilities and set your mind to it. You can do anything you set your mind to."

"But where should we start in this big empty field?" I asked. "Can you at least tell us that?" The Guiding Spirit never answered me. "What should we do next?"

"Trust your intuition," the spirit repeated.

Liam and I stood there looking at each other in silence, puzzling over what to do next.

"Some Guiding Spirit that is, it's not guiding us much now, is it?" I said to Liam.

"I heard that, wise guy," the Guiding Spirit said.

"Sorry," I said.

"Oops. We are going to have to watch ourselves, aren't we," I thought so that Liam could hear me without the Guiding Spirit chiming in.

Liam and I stood at the edge of the field, uncertain of what to do or where to go.

"Well, I guess we need to figure this out on our own," I said aloud. "So where should we start, Liam?"

"This field doesn't seem to have anything in it that'll help us. Maybe we should try to go somewhere else in this enchanted castle. Remember, Amanda said it would take us to other places in this afterlife. There must be more to see besides this field. Maybe in some other place we'll find some sort of phone or something that will let us tell Mom and Dad directly."

"Good idea. But how do we get out of this field and find another place?"

"I bet there's a gate along the fence somewhere. Maybe if we find a gate, we'll find a new 'room' in the castle," Liam said, looking hopeful.

We began to walk around the fence, careful not to touch it for fear it might zap us like Dad's sheep fence would. As we walked, we talked about hiking with Mom and Dad.

"Remember our hike in the Presidential Mountains last fall?" Liam asked. "That was awesome! Coming back down the trail, I saw that black bear. Remember that?"

"How could I forget? That's all you talked about for the next fifteen minutes after the bear ran away. You wouldn't shut up about it and thought you were out-of-this-world special for having spotted it."

"Well, it was cool."

"Yeah, it was cool. I agree, but boy did I get sick of listening to you brag about seeing it."

"I wasn't bragging! I was just excited," Liam said. "You should have been, too."

"I was, until you went on and on and on about it. That got old."

"Sorry. I like to talk about the things that excite me. Geez." We walked quietly.

"I remember hiking Camel's Hump with Mom and Dad," I said. "In fact, I remember taking tons of hikes. Mount Hunger, Mount Norris, Mount Philo, Mount Moosilauke, and trails in Acadia, too. We sure hiked a lot."

"Look!" Liam was pointing off in the distance. On the other side of the green field a mountain range had appeared where none had existed before.

"That looks like the view from our house on Earth!" I said. "Look. There's Camel's Hump and the whole mountain range that we could see from our deck." Then it struck me. "I bet that's it! Somehow that's going to help us to communicate with Mom and Dad. We have to get there," I headed across the field and straight for Camel's Hump.

"Wait up! It's way too far. It'll be a day or two hike just to get to the mountains." Liam was exaggerating, but he was right. It was clear that it would take a while to get there if we walked. Liam continued his protest. "What if we go all that way and it's not the answer? What if it doesn't help at all and we've wasted two days trying to get there? Then what?"

"We need to trust our intuition like the Guiding Spirit told us. My intuition tells me this is part of the answer. What about yours?"

"Ugh. My instincts tell me it's gonna kill me to go that far!" He stopped walking.

"Nice try. You're already dead, little brother," I joked. "Let's go. You can do it."

Liam let out a huge sigh as we began walking in silence in the direction of the mountains. Along the way, my thoughts drifted to life on Earth. I wondered what was happening back there now that Liam and I were no longer alive. Was everyone we knew and loved in total shock and missing us already? I wondered if our friends knew. I hoped that Mom had called them to let them know what had happened before they found out from the news reports. She would know that Liam and I needed her to do that, wouldn't she? I wished I could tell everyone that I was doing just fine and that I was at peace, except for this nagging need to be sure that everyone knew that Liam and I were okay and together still.

We walked in silence for hours it seemed, yet we weren't any closer to those mountains than we had been when we began. When Liam and I stopped to discuss that, I expected Liam to throw a fit and say he would go no further, but instead, he just said, "Hey! Check it out. Let's hitch a ride on those eagles." He pointed at the small rise to our left, smiling. Atop it stood two large eagles.

"Don't be silly. Birds can't lift us. We're too big. Remember, they've got hollow bones."

"Oh, I bet they can!" Liam said. "We're spirits now. Remember? Wispy spirits without bodies. I bet we're light as a feather. Remember how when we tried to hug Mom and Dad our arms passed right through them?"

"Right. Maybe we weigh nothing at all." I thought about that. Without my Earth body it would be impossible for me to do so many of the things I enjoyed during life. Would I ever give hugs again? Play the piano? Make marzipan cake in a kitchen? Play guitar hero, or my DS? Ski? Ride my bike? How could I do those things without a body? Sure, my wispy body seemed to be able to pull open doors, race across fields, and throw a football, but boy did I miss the familiarity of my old body, how it moved, and how it felt. In that moment, I wished I could have my body back again.

My thoughts were interrupted when Liam let out a small whistle, like he used to when he tried to lure small animals or birds his way. It never worked on Earth. The animals and birds ran or flew off every time. I didn't expect it to work here, but next thing we knew, the two eagles flew to us and landed right smack in front of us. Liam followed his instincts and did what he always wished he could do on Earth. He climbed up onto one of those eagle's backs, lay down on his belly, and wrapped his arms around its neck. Before I knew it, his eagle was lifting off and flying away toward the mountains.

"Liam! Come back! Don't leave me here alone," I yelled, not at all pleased to be standing by myself in the still-unfamiliar place.

"Hop on the other eagle and follow us!" Liam yelled to me from up high.

Hesitantly, I climbed aboard the other eagle and wrapped my arms around its neck like Liam had. My eagle took off, trailing Liam's by what seemed like a mile. My thoughts raced. What would happen if I fell off? Would I fall all the way to the ground? That would surely hurt. Would I learn to fly alone somehow by flapping my transparent arms? I suppose anything was possible for a spirit, but it was all so new to me. The only thing I really understood was that Liam and I had to stay together. Mom had said so. But who knew where we were headed?

LIAM

Totally cool! We'd flown in airplanes many times in our lives, but we were always protected from the wind in air-conditioned cabins. Here, flying on an eagle surrounded only by open space felt absolutely incredible. My eagle lifted me up in the light that bathed me in comfort. My arms, firmly wrapped around the eagle's neck, seemed to shine even more brightly than before. As we cruised along, I enjoyed the rustle of wind in my hair, feeling carefree, blessed, and totally at peace. I turned around to see Solon on his eagle behind me, gradually closing the distance between us. When they pulled up alongside us, our birds slipped into rhythm and pumped their wings in unison. Solon and I looked at each other and smiled.

"Do you feel as good as me?" I asked.

"This is amazing. Absolutely amazing! But where are we going?"

"I have no idea. I'm not worrying about that now," I answered. Geez. I wasn't in the mood for Solon to spoil my fun ride.

"How'll we get back to help Mom and Dad? I still picture them scared to death like they were when we were trapped in the fire," he asked. Without an answer, I rode on in silence. I sure was enjoying my ride and didn't want to think much about what we'd left behind on Earth.

Solon spoke again. "What can we do? There must be some way to send 'em a message."

"Think about what we've already learned in our afterlife," I said, hoping to shut him up so I could enjoy my ride. "Maybe you'll figure something out."

We rode on silently, taking in the unfamiliar but beautiful sights. This sensation of flying made me feel invincible, free of all concerns, and comforted, as if I were back safe at home, snuggled up against Dad listening to a bedtime story with Solon.

Solon broke my train of thought. "We're safe here, sort of," he said. "As long as we don't think too hard about going home." Shoot. Now he'd done it. The fear I had felt in that first field of our afterlives when we had been thrown around by that wind came back. Not a pleasant thought.

"How'd we avoid getting sucked up by that wind and taken to some awful place?" I said, "Remember?"

"We thought of something we did together, and when we both thought of the same thing, the castle appeared."

We flew silently, each in our own world, thinking. The air around us cooled as the eagles flew higher, still following the landscape that was rising as we approached the base of the mountains.

"And," I said, "In the castle, we learned to talk with each other without saying a word."

"Hey!" Solon said, "Maybe we can communicate with Mom and Dad without talking, send them our thoughts somehow. If we both think hard about something we want to say, maybe they'll get the message."

"From here? You seriously think it'll get to 'em from here?"

"Maybe."

I thought about that. Maybe it would work. What did we have to lose?

"Let's focus only on one of them to start," I said. "You know, 'cause to make the castle show up, we had to both think about the same thing." Solon didn't say anything.

We flew over the summit of Camel's Hump, the mountain we had seen on clear days from home. The view from the top was stunning. To my surprise, on the other side of these familiar-looking mountains the landscape gave way to a blue ocean that stretched as far as my eyes could see. This was nothing like the landscape on the other side of the Green Mountains back home. There was no ocean west of Camel's Hump on Earth. Just Lake Champlain.

"Check it out!" I yelled as the eagles began descending along the backside of the mountains until we were flying side by side about five feet above the ocean. Nearly skimming along the surface of the water bathed in this amazing light was absolutely exhilarating. "This is totally cool!"

"Let's both try picturing Mom," Solon said. "Then maybe we can send her a message."

"Okay."

For a few seconds, nothing happened. Our eagles continued flying straight across the ocean. I thought hard about Mom, trying to picture her face, her long hair, anything I could to make her image more clear in my mind. Still nothing.

"Maybe we need to think of Mom in a specific situation," I said.

"So let's imagine her reading to us on the couch in the family room," Solon suggested.

We both were silent again as we glided above the ocean deep in thought. All of a sudden, I felt my stomach drop down to my feet as both eagles shot upward like a speeding elevator ride at the fair, giving me the familiar sensation that I was leaving my stomach below. I held on to my eagle's neck so tightly that I worried that I might choke it. The higher we flew, the more nervous I became. What would happen if I fell off this high above the ocean? The thought of landing in the cold water, unprotected, surrounded by large swimming animals that could eat me frightened me. I looked over at Solon, whose face had turned whiter than white. He looked as terrified as I felt.

I screamed, "Hold on! Don't fall off! We have to stick together!"

As soon as I said that, the eagles changed course out of nowhere, descending as rapidly as they had risen. I felt like I was back on a roller coaster at Six Flags Riverside as my stomach lurched up and down with every change in direction. Beaks pointed down, these birds shot straight toward the ocean at an alarming rate. The surface of the water was coming at us faster than my eyes could take in. Solon yelled out to me, "It's gonna be okay. Just, whatever you do, hold on tight to that eagle. We're gonna crash into the ocean soon. I love you, bro! We're gonna be okay." It was as though Solon had taken Mom's place by trying to ease my fears.

"Hold your breath when we hit the water and kick like crazy to get back to the surface," I screamed, remembering what it felt like to plunge deeply into water.

As the eagles careened toward the water, I closed my eyes and inhaled what, in my life, would have been a last huge breath of air before we crashed through the water's surface. To my surprise, the massive impact did not hurt like it would have on Earth from that height. In fact, I felt nothing at all. I opened my eyes and saw Solon beside me. His eyes were as wide as I imagined mine to be.

"That was wild!" We exclaimed, almost simultaneously.

"Where are we?" I asked, looking around. We were floating on the ceiling of a church, but not one I remember ever seeing before. It was huge, with seating for five hundred people or more. The space was relatively empty, except for a string quartet and a French horn player playing softly at the far side of the room. They seemed to be warming up, just as Solon and I had warmed up with our instruments before concerts. The quartet's music was so beautiful that it made me want to cry. I wondered if we were still in our afterlife or back on Earth. The inside of the church and everything in it were misty, every object's outlines slightly blurred. While we watched, people gradually filed into the pews, everyone with solemn looks and downcast eyes. The quartet played on.

Solon spoke up, "Looks like some sort of service is about to start. Let's stay put and just watch for now. Where'd those eagles go anyway?"

"I don't see 'em." I scanned the room frantically, but couldn't find the eagles anywhere. "They're gone!" Then I was nervous. "How will we get back?" Solon didn't answer, probably because, like me, he had no idea. I thought about how different things looked with their grainy appearance. That only worried me more.

"I'm scared," I said. "This doesn't feel like our afterlife anymore. Are you sure we haven't landed back on Earth? It sure looks like it, you know. What if we get stuck in some sort of in between? Or end up in that dark place in our afterlives? I liked that feeling of total peace, you know."

"So did I."

"Let's go back." I wasn't sure how we'd get there, but boy, was I ever eager to feel that safety and peace again.

"Relax. Just watch for now. We'll find a way back. Maybe we can call the eagles back when we need 'em," Solon said, wishfully. This didn't calm my fears, but I certainly wasn't going to dart off alone and try to call the eagles back.

We kept floating on the ceiling, side by side, watching intently as more and more people dressed in dark clothing streamed into the church. The big room was nearly full, except for a few empty pews at the front. I recognized no one. Then, a door at the side of the church opened and more people began to file in. They entered in pairs, looking distraught, as if they were marching to their death, or something. I didn't recognize any of them at first, but then I saw our aunt and our cousins appear.

"Look!" Solon said, pointing. We kept scanning the faces of people entering. Almost all of them were familiar to us: members of our extended family, aunts and uncles, cousins, and all of our grandparents. A pastor walked through the door with Mom and Dad following, holding hands. Instantly, I was overcome with intense yearning to race over to them for a huge hug.

"What're we gonna to do?" I asked. "How can we tell 'em we're here and we're okay? We have to think of something!"

Dad was wearing a dark suit. Mom wore a black dress with grey scarf draped around her neck. They were staring at the wooden floor in front of their feet and looking sadder and more disturbed than I had ever seen either of them, except maybe the night of that nasty fire. Solon and I watched in silence. Seeing Mom and Dad and knowing they couldn't see us was incredibly frustrating. They had absolutely no clue Solon and I were right there, floating on the ceiling, wanting to comfort them.

"Just watch for now. Something'll come to us," Solon said.

The pastor lead Mom and Dad to the right side of the church where about 25 fire fighters stood in uniform with somber faces. Some of them were crying.

As Mom came closer, it became obvious that she, too, was crying. Her eyes were bloodshot and puffy and her nose was running. Carrying a fistful of tissues, she was leaning into Dad, his arm around her. Mom walked up to each firefighter in turn and hugged him. Dad walked right behind her, shaking each fire fighter's hand. From this distance, I faintly heard Mom and Dad say, "thank you," to each of them. The hugs and handshakes from our parents brought even more firefighters to tears. Mom was crying hard by the time she'd made it to all the firefighters, and Dad looked like he was barely able to contain his emotions. He put his arm around Mom again and the pastor slowly led them to seats in the front pew. They sat down beside Grandma Nancy and Opa Jon, surrounded by the rest of our extended family.

The piano began to play. Turning toward it, I saw Alison, Solon's piano teacher, working the keyboard. Her music was so sorrowful, I, too, started to cry. The entire gathering of people sat quietly and listened as she played.

"This is our funeral," Solon whispered to me. "Look. There's the program. It says, "The Celebration of Eternal Life for Solon and Liam Bailey' right on the cover."

"Do you think they can see us?" I asked. I really wanted them to be able to see us, to know we're okay.

"Think about it," Solon said. "We can't really be at our funeral. If we were, we'd have been swept off to some ugly place by a fierce wind already. Somehow we can see the funeral, and it certainly feels like we're here, but remember, we're just spirits now. I think we're watching it without being in it, if that makes any sense." Solon tried to explain what both of us were struggling to understand.

"But how're we supposed to talk with Mom and Dad from here?" I asked. "That's what I wanna know."

"Well, they look a little busy right now, don't ya think? Just watch and listen. Maybe there'll be some clue. Keep your eyes peeled, okay?"

We continued to watch the service. It was filled with piano music, many of the same pieces that Solon played in his lifetime, and music from the quartet with the French horn. That was the instrument I used to play in our school band. The music was nice, but for me, the most painful part of the service was listening to Grandpa Irv, Opa Jon, and our aunt speak from the heart about how much fun they had with us and how much we would be missed. That was torture. The additional Bible verses and poems shared by our other aunts and uncles were beautiful, too. I felt myself start to cry again.

The pastor shared with the congregation his thoughts, readings from the Bible, and prayers. It seemed that everyone relaxed into his soothing voice. I noticed that Mom was no longer crying as hard, but she and Dad looked just as sad and stressed.

A solo vocalist stood up and sang the verses of "On Eagles' Wings," and everybody in the church sang the refrain:

> And he will raise you up on Eagles' wings,
> Bear you on the breath of dawn,
> Make you to shine like the sun,
> And hold you in the palm of his hand.

Solon turned to me, shocked. "We just rode eagles here. Do you think they were bringing us to God? Is God here, in this church? The hymn says God held us in the palm of his hand. Let's look for God," Solon, studying different parts of the church, seemed convinced we would see God. I was beginning to feel hopeful again. Maybe the eagles would return and help me escape my sadness.

I looked all around, searching for any sign of God's presence. I looked to the pastor and, feeling drawn to him, slowly drifted away from Solon toward this man I'd never met, curious, but not scared. Somehow, I felt safe near him. The pastor is God's messenger, or God's communicator, right? I was safe near him, right? And maybe I would find God closer to the pastor. As I floated closer, I saw to the pastor's left two small tables draped in ornamental cloths, each one covering something boxy. My curiosity got the better of me, and I floated over for a closer look.

"Wait!" Solon said, nervously, "Don't get too close. You might distract him." Solon stayed right where he was on the ceiling, but I felt drawn toward the pastor and toward those little tables so I slowly kept inching closer as the pastor spoke. I willed my eyes to see through the ornamental cloths, and to my surprise, I suddenly had X-ray vision. Cool! Yet another new ability I could have used in my life! On one table sat a little wooden box with my name, "William Theiler Bailey," engraved on top. Solon's whole name,

"Solon Lawrence Bailey," was engraved on top of the box on the other table.

"We were cremated! Our ashes are in those boxes!" I said, pointing at the tables while I floated as fast as I could back to Solon's side. "That sure is freaky."

"Well, just imagine what happened to our bodies after we left 'em. The heat and smoke were so intense. Mom and Dad probably had no choice but to cremate us," Solon said. "Holy crap. Imagine how they feel now. We went through one fire, and then they had to send our bodies through another! We have to talk to them somehow. They have to know we're okay now. Oh my God!"

I suddenly felt nervous about our behavior, of all things, probably because I had just been floating next to a pastor. "We'd better be more polite here. No more 'holy crap's,' and 'oh my God's.' We're in church!"

"Fine," Solon agreed. "But, geez. What a mess!" We floated silently on the ceiling, watching as the service unfolded. By the time the pastor said his final prayer and the ceremony ended, we hadn't seen God, hadn't said "boo" to Mom or Dad, and we had absolutely no idea how to get back to our afterlives. Oh, how I hoped we wouldn't be stuck in some sort of in-between that left us missing our family but also missing the peace we felt in the light of our afterlives.

Mom and Dad left the church first before everyone else in the congregation even stood up. The pastor accompanied them to the side door, and Solon and I floated along behind them. They climbed into a sedan at the front of the church, then got out and moved into a limo parked behind it. They slammed the door, closing out the throngs of people who started streaming out of the church. Clearly, Mom and Dad needed to be alone.

"Now what?" I asked.

"Let's go with 'em," Solon said, moving toward the limo. "Somehow we'll find a way to communicate with them. I know it!" He was about to float through the limo window when I caught a glimpse of something above us.

"Wait! Look up!" I said, pointing skyward. "The eagles are circling! We can go back now. We might not be able to get back again later," I said, begging him to return to the safety of our afterlives.

As if in a trance, Solon raised both hands in front of him with his palms facing up. I followed suit, not sure why we were drawn to do this. The eagles descended and landed at our sides.

"Climb on," I said, excited by the prospect of riding my eagle friend again. When we were both lying on our eagles, I saw the limo pull away as the eagles rapidly ascended into the heavens.

Before long, we were flying over an ocean, headed toward the backside of the mountains we had flown over a short while ago.

"Well," Solon said, "It seems we're learning to put our faith in things unseen." I looked at him. What on earth was he getting at? He continued, "We weren't sure if the eagles would come back for us, but by trusting we'd be okay, we got through it. They came back for us."

"But we went there to talk to Mom and Dad, and that hasn't happened. Right?" I asked, disappointed and a bit irritated with Solon's upbeat attitude after our own funeral.

"No. But we found a way to see what's happening on Earth. We didn't know how to do that before, did we?"

"Are you thinking we'll be able to go back again and see anytime we want if we have the eagles to take us over this ocean?" I asked. "We haven't proven that yet, have we? Maybe it won't work next time. How do you know?"

"Whatever. I don't know. I'm just suspecting it's true. Have some faith, would ya! We'll figure this out, and someday we'll be able to comfort Mom and Dad, and maybe everyone else who misses us. Imagine how great that'll be."

That would be great—if it ever happened.

Before long, we were back in the beautifully lit green pasture on the other side of the mountains. The eagles landed, and we dismounted and thanked them for the ride with a little pat on top of each of their heads. They flew off, and we stood there in the enormous green field wondering what to do next. I wasn't scared. The field and its beautiful light were too comforting. I was definitely not scared. Just puzzled. Solon and I looked at one another.

"What now?" I asked. "This is crazy-weird. At least we're back. It feels so good to be back."

"Let's sit down and think about everything we know about this afterlife and try to come up with some new ideas about how to communicate with Mom and Dad."

"Good plan, lads," echoed all around us as we settled our transparent bodies in the soft grass. We looked at each other and smiled.

"We're not alone," I said, feeling a little relieved.

"Nope. We sure aren't." Back in the field, the Guiding Spirit heard our every word again. Solon and I sat quietly, admiring our surroundings and picking at the grass. I was mulling over whether or not it could be helpful to have our Guiding Spirit listen to us as we tried to figure out how to help Mom and Dad back on Earth. Maybe, I reasoned, if the spirit overheard us, the spirit would drop a hint or two that would help us. Maybe we should just ask for help again, or maybe I could beg a little, put on my pouty little face, curl out my lower lip and flutter my lashes and outright beg, "Please? Pretty Please?" Like the time I really wanted to have my birthday party at the Pizza Putt so I could race my closest friends through tunnels and slides in the indoor playground. But Pizza Putt was an hour-long drive from home and was way too far for a party. I was hopeful, but begging hadn't worked then. We ended up at the local bowling alley, which turned out to be tons of fun, too. I sure did crack up Mom and Dad and lighten the mood whenever I performed my little begging routine, though only to a certain point, I guess.

"Well, we know we just found our way back to Earth, sort of," Solon said, thinking. "We weren't swept off to any terrible place. How did we do that?" We sat quietly for a long while. Eventually, Solon said, "I think we just rode the eagles to a place where we could see Mom and Dad on Earth. But I don't really think we were there. Maybe we watched it somehow, but without being there. It looked so grainy and different than things look on Earth, and it definitely did not look like everything looks here. And we weren't swept away by a storm. We couldn't have actually been on Earth."

"Don't be so sure about that, young man," the Guiding Spirit called out.

Not wanting the spirit to hear him, Solon pushed his thoughts silently to me. *"Oyo . . . a giant hint. Sounds like we really were on Earth watching our funeral. I wonder why it looked so different."*

"BECAUSE WE WEREN'T IN THE AFTERLIFE ANYMORE BUT WE'RE DEAD, DUH!" I thought back to Solon.

"Be nice."

Solon looked at me. "So, the eagles took us to Earth to be with Mom and Dad. When we wanted to leave Earth, they helped us get back to our afterlife, too. If we were really on Earth, though, why didn't a windstorm sweep us away?"

"Your goal." The spirit was dropping huge hints now.

"That's it," I said. "Our goal was to talk with Mom and Dad, not to go back to our life again. When we were with Amanda, that's what made the hurricane winds come, when we longed to go back to our lives. Wanting to communicate doesn't mean wanting to be back in our past lives. See the difference?"

"I guess that's true. You're probably right. So . . . we think we know how to actually really go back to Earth and see Mom and

Dad now. I still wonder how we can communicate with them when we get there, though. Any ideas?"

"Not right now. Maybe we'll get back there again someday and figure something out. Maybe your idea of pushing our thoughts into their heads will work when we're beside them next time. Remember, we didn't even try this time." I looked around. "The eagles are nowhere to be seen, though. I guess we'll have to wait."

After a long while, Solon said, "Let's hike up the mountain. At the summit, we'll be able to see over the other side to the ocean. Maybe the eagles will show up again as we hike."

"Yeah," I said. "And if the Eagles don't appear out of thin air, then we'll just walk down the other side of the mountains and go for a swim in the ocean. Sounds nice but, *are you crazy*? It'll take us days to get there. I like hiking, but that's way too far!"

"Yeah, but you love Mom and Dad, and right now we need to figure out how to tell 'em we're okay. We can do it. Just like when we hiked in life. We just need to keep putting one foot in front of the other. We'll get there."

"Fine," I said, starting to walk in that direction. "I expect those eagles to show up again so I can hitch another ride. Flying was awesome!" *That's my secret reason for not wanting to hike. I really want to ride those eagles again!*

SOLON

WE HEADED ACROSS the field toward the mountains. Walking in silence, side by side, I couldn't help but think about home and about everyone we left behind when we died. Here in this open field alone with Liam on a hike, facing a mountain range that reminded me of our view from home, it was tough not to long to be back on Earth again. Every time I thought too much about home, I saw dark clouds starting to form over the mountain and quickly forced myself to think about something else so my desire to go home wouldn't send Liam and me into another windstorm. After a few close calls, I suggested, "Let's talk about something that has nothing to do with wanting to go home. It's too quiet. I miss our past life."

"Me too. Hiking has a way of making me think about my life. So . . . what should we distract ourselves with?"

"I don't know. Maybe this hike's a bad idea," I said, stopping. "It seems a little dangerous, doesn't it? We don't wanna start one of those hurricanes again.'"

"Let's just talk about something else," Liam repeated, continuing to float across the field, "like some of the silly things we did in our past lives. Maybe that'll keep us 'safe.'" Liam's idea was a good one. I caught up with him.

"Okay. You first," I said.

"Give me a sec."

We continued to walk across the field, and all of a sudden Liam started to laugh hard.

"How about your joke? The effect of kale on global warming?" he asked.

I laughed. That was hard to forget. Our family had just finished dinner around the dining room table, and we were considering ice cream for dessert. Somehow we started talking about the gas-producing foods we ate, and which ones were the worst and which ones don't seem to have any effect at all. Somehow the topic of kale came up. Kale was well known for its gas-producing effects in our family. This joke popped into my head and I blurted out, "We need to make a bumper sticker that says, 'STOP GLOBAL WARMING: EAT LESS KALE.'" Our entire family went into such a fit of hysterics that I thought for sure I could make a business from that fine bumper sticker idea. This made everyone laugh harder, and we joked around about what the sticker might look like.

"No problems with kale in this afterlife, though," I said. "We don't even need to eat, much less fart!"

"And do you remember those hysterical family names we heard on the car radio?" Liam asked. "Remember? We were doing errands with Mom, and when she heard that joke, she laughed so hard that she had to pull over to stop laughing. How'd that one go again?"

"Hmmm . . . that's a little more complicated. I think the father's name was 'Beek Painin D'Az'". We laughed but kept walking.

"Oh yeah, and the son was 'Heesa Painin D'Az,'" Liam chimed in, chuckling.

"And his sister, 'Sheesa Painin D'Az,'" I said. We were both laughing pretty hard then.

"Yeah, but my favorite was the dog. You remember?" Liam asked.

"What?"

"'Toto Painin D'Az.' Get it? Like the Wizard of Oz?" Liam put his arm around my shoulder, trying to give me a little squeeze. It felt good to walk together and talk about fun stuff from our lifetimes. I was loving Liam's company and so thankful that we were together, joking around like nothing had happened. We walked along telling funny jokes we remembered, and then we invented ridiculous stories about adventures we might have in our afterlives. Thankfully, the weather remained calm the entire time.

After walking through the field for what felt like days, we finally began to approach the wooded base of the mountains. I wondered to myself when we would come to Dad's electric fence, or, well, the fence that looked like Dad's. Maybe there was no fence on the backside of the huge field. I began to look for a trailhead but couldn't see one in either direction.

"Ugh," Liam said. "I'm so sick of walking. There's just no way I'm gonna bushwhack through those trees to get over that mountain. When we get to the trees, let's walk one way or the other 'til we find a trail."

"Fine. But let's rest first." I was getting tired too, or maybe just bored from walking so much. I sat down in the grass and pictured a trail on the mountainside. I knew in my heart that a trail must exist but wondered which way we should turn to find it.

Liam interrupted my thoughts. "Let's lift up our hands to see if the eagles'll come back? It worked outside the church."

"Yeah. But the eagles were already flying over us when I called them. I don't see them nearby, do you?" I asked, looking above us.

"No." Liam raised his arms to the sky anyway and called out, "Here eagles, eagles. Come to Solon and Liam now. We need your help. Please. Come carry us home again." We waited silently, searching around the sky. Liam's attempts to summon the eagles had clearly failed. No birds appeared.

"Nice try. Looks like that didn't work. Which direction do you wanna head now?"

"That way." Liam pointed to his left, maybe because in that direction we would reach the trees a little sooner than if we turned right.

I slowly got up out of the grass, and we started walking in that direction. We walked in silence for a while, and, as we came closer to the trees, I could see the electric fence. "Great! Now we have to figure out how to get over that. Do you think there's a gate somewhere so we don't get zapped?"

Liam thought for a moment, and then said, "Wait. You remember how Dad's electric sheep net fencing worked, right? If we could unhook the clip that attached the fence to the electric power, it would stop the current from flowing, right? I wonder if there's some way to detach the electricity from this fence."

I thought about that for a second and then realized that we were making one big assumption. Just because it looked like Dad's sheep net fencing didn't mean it really was electrified in this afterlife. After all, was there even electricity in heaven?

"You know, this fence might not be electrified. We think it is 'cause we know Dad's was. And think about it. Do we even know that spirits can be electrified? I say one of us should try touching the fence and see if we get shocked. If it isn't electrified, we can just push it down and step right over it the way we did at home when we knew the fence wasn't on."

"Oh. Sure Solon. This is your great idea. Go right ahead and touch it. I'm not doing that! It hurt like heck to get electrocuted by Dad's fence! Are you crazy?"

"Yeah, but Liam, there are some things you just gotta do, even if they're hard and they might be painful. We have to get through this fence somehow if we want to climb the mountain and get back to Mom and Dad. What do you suggest?"

"I already made a suggestion. You touch the fence, and then we'll know, smarty."

I started to get upset. If I was going to touch that fence, there was just no way I was doing it alone.

"What if touching it causes something totally unexpected to happen?" I asked. "We're in our afterlife. Remember? This isn't Earth. Who knows what'll happen when I touch it? Maybe it'll take me somewhere else and leave you standing here alone."

I could tell I'd hit a nerve with that one. Liam's eyes bugged out a little, and a look of fear crossed his face.

"Okay, then don't touch the fence." Liam's face relaxed. "Let's just walk in one direction or another and find a gate or that connector clip."

"Don't wimp out on me! Remember how the Guiding Spirit said we need to trust our intuition? The spirit said we'd find a way if we follow our instincts. Well, our intuition led us here, and my intuition's telling me this fence isn't really electrified. I think we can touch it without anything at all happening to us. You need to put aside your fear of being zapped and listen to your intuition. What's it really telling you?"

"Shoot. I don't know. I just don't want to touch that fence."

"I think we both should touch it at the same time in case something weird happens only to the one who touched it." I could tell by the look on Liam's face that he was starting to give in. "That way, we'll be more likely to stay together. If we do things separately, we might end up separated in our afterlife, and I know that would make me very unhappy. I'm glad we're together."

"So am I, but I just don't want to touch that fence."

"Oh, Liam. You can be so hardheaded! Okay. So how about this: you hold onto my arm, and I touch the fence."

"Why can't we just look for a gate?"

"Because we've already been walking forever and we have a long way to go to cross the mountain and get to that ocean. Wouldn't it be nice to save some distance? You're the one who said it's too far to go on foot." I was getting sick of arguing with my little brother.

"Ugh..." Liam exclaimed. "You know that if this fence is electrified I'll still get zapped through your arm, don't you? Remember what Mom taught us about electric circuits when she homeschooled us last year? Well I sure remember it, and I know that even if I'm only holding your arm, I'll get zapped. The electricity's gonna rush through both of us, not just through you."

"Okay. Look at it this way. You were always good at handling pain when you were alive. Right?" Maybe stroking his ego would work. "You dealt with a broken arm, didn't you? And you ran the mile run and the two-hundred-meter dash so fast you felt like your legs were gonna explode. I think you'll be able to handle the shock of the fence if it gives you one. But honestly, my intuition says we're gonna be able to just push it down and walk right over it."

"Okay. Fine. You win. I'll do what you say. But if I get zapped, boy am I gonna be mad at you!"

Liam moved closer to me and wrapped his little hand around my bicep. Then he said, "Go ahead." He closed his eyes tight.

I slowly reached out and touched the fence with my pointer finger. Seemingly of their own will, my hand and arm immediately yanked backwards. Liam felt my fear and jumped away.

"Did you feel anything? 'Cause I sure didn't," I told him with a big grin.

"Then why'd you pull your hand back like that? You scared me!" Liam complained, still startled.

"Sorry. I guess it's just habit for me to test the fence that way. That's how I tested it at home to see if it was on."

"Well let's try again," Liam said. He seemed to be feeling a little braver now that we had done a short test. Once again, Liam grabbed my bicep, and I touched the fence. It didn't hurt at all.

I held the fence for a few seconds, and then Liam relaxed and grabbed it too. Crossing the fence was easy then. We just pushed it to the ground and climbed over like we did back home after Mom or Dad had turned it off.

We were standing on the other side of the fence then. "Which way?" I asked, looking up and down the fence.

"Left. It starts with 'L.' Maybe that'll bring us luck," Liam said with a grin, heading in that direction. I wasn't sure why he was grinning. Maybe he thought there was something special about the fact that both "left" and "luck" started with "L." But, for all I knew, it was because his name started with "L," too. I rolled my eyes and followed him. Honestly, I didn't really care in which direction we turned. And maybe little Liam was having a moment of divine intuition or something. There was no need to argue about it. We walked along the edge of the field beside the trees. I hoped so much that we would come to a trail so as not to be stuck bushwhacking up the mountainside. We walked silently for quite a while with no trail in sight.

"Hey, Solon. Wanna hear my cool British accent?"

"About as much as you want to hear my piano practice."

"Oh. Well then I guess you do, 'cause I actually liked hearing your piano music every night before bed."

"Oh boy," I thought. "Here he goes."

Liam launched into the voice and role of a British man speaking affectionately in his deep, sexy British voice, attempting to lure a prudish American lady out to a fancy dinner. I had to laugh at his silly man's accent and I laughed even harder when he spoke for the American lady, who had a ridiculous, high-pitched, squeaky voice. Of course, as he spoke he used his whole body to punctuate his words in each of his roles: at first, he acted manly and big-chested, and then he rolled his eyes and fluttered his lashes with prissy hands to match. What an actor! He had performed like that when he was alive, but boy was it funny to see him do it again in this afterlife, a partly transparent outline of his former self throwing himself around acting ridiculous.

When Liam's one-man acting sequence ended and I had complimented him with, "That was awesome!", we slipped back into silence again. It wasn't long before I could see something hopeful up ahead.

"Look. See that break in the trees?" I said pointing. "Maybe that's a trail up the mountain." When we reached that spot, we found the beginnings of a trail.

"Yippee. We did it. I'm psyched! I hate bushwhacking!" Liam held out his spirit hand in thumbs up. "I guess the "L" in lucky helped," Liam said grinning with pride.

All I could think to say was "Good thing we followed your intuition."

We hiked silently upward, Liam in the lead with me trailing closely behind. Looking around, I noted we were walking through the same types of trees we used to pass on many of our family hikes—lots of maple, birch, eastern hemlocks, and some fir. In fact, the trail looked similar to the Mt. Hunger trail that Dad and Mom used to hike with us. As we climbed higher, the forest floor became oddly covered in a misty haze. I could no longer see my spirit feet. It made me feel as though we were walking on clouds. Playful Liam kept leaning over and trying to scoop up the mist with both spirit hands. He started humming "More Than a Feeling," one of his favorite songs by Boston, as we hiked. The walk was rather peaceful and, well, felt surprisingly spiritual somehow. I was feeling completely connected to Liam, but also to all the trees and mist that surrounded me. It felt as though I had become one with everything that existed in the space around me. It was as peaceful as climbing into my soft, warm bed at home, snuggled up with my fleece comforter, completely safe, relaxed, and loved.

In time, the trail became steeper. Liam called out to me, "Yo, dude. This is getting old. It's gonna take forever to get over this mountain. We need a horse."

He had a point. It was a big mountain. I wasn't crazy about horses like some of the girls had been three years before, when we were in fourth grade. They wouldn't talk about anything but horses! Liam and I had a bit of experience with horses, though—enough to know they could be quite useful. When we would visit Nanny and Gary in Montana, they would saddle their two horses and let us ride around the ring. Liam and I took turns circling the ring on each horse. I kind of liked it, but it always made my legs hurt, and sometimes other, more private parts would hurt, too, if those parts accidentally hit the horn of the saddle. I always wondered why the powers that be named it a horn? In my thinking, it should have been called the hold-on-for-dear-life part of the saddle. I know. The name is rather long, but honestly, that was the first thing I grabbed when my horse would start to trot or canter. I never felt completely comfortable or at ease up there on a horse.

I was walking along the trail thinking about Nanny and Gary and riding horses and admiring the mist and trees when I collided with Liam. "Oof. What'd you stop for? Warn me next time, would you?!" It took a little doing to separate his misty spirit body from mine after the collision, but we managed. Liam just stood there, pointing straight ahead with his jaw hanging open.

Directly in front of us stood a wall of rock, an enormous ledge with moss and small tree shoots growing on it. The trail took a sharp left at the ledge and continued to snake upward around the ledge. Big deal. We had seen ledges like that hiking on Earth.

"Why'd you stop?" I asked. "What're you staring at?"

"You don't see it? There's a huge hole in that ledge. I think it's a cave or something."

I moved in front of Liam on the trail and made my way straight toward the ledge, unsure of where this supposed cave may have been. As I moved closer, the ledge split open, forming what definitely looked like an opening to a cave. "I think you're right," I said. "That was weird. It just opened up as I walked closer."

"Yep. That happened for me, too. That's why I stopped," Liam said.

"Are you thinking what I'm thinking?" I asked. "This cave could somehow help us."

"Yep. It came out of nowhere, so I bet it's there for a reason. Maybe it holds a treasure," Liam suggested with a smile. No doubt he was thinking about *Treasure Island*, the book Mom read to us every night before bed leading up to our trip to Louisville.

I wasn't crazy about the idea of entering an unknown cave without some guidance or reassurance that bad guys or monsters weren't lurking inside. Fortunately, though, we had explored some caves when our family was with Nanny and Gary in Hawaii. Even though I felt a bit claustrophobic when we came to really tight spaces, the caves were lots of fun to see. One of the caves was a lava tube, and the other was a traditional cave, the kind with stalactites and stalagmites. As I thought about those cave trips, an important point suddenly dawned on me.

"How will we see in the dark?" I asked. I was remembering that when we explored the Hawaii caves, we had flashlights. When we all turned the lights off, the cave was completely dark. We couldn't see a thing.

"Who knows what'll happen inside? Remember. We walked into the Enchanted Castle and found ourselves in a field," Liam said. "So maybe there'll be some light when we get there."

I thought back to the Guiding Spirit's advice, "Trust your intuition."

"What does your intuition tell you?" I asked.

Liam did not hesitate. "Something good will happen in there.

Why else would the cave pop up in our path? I don't think it's gonna swallow us up or anything."

"I guess not." If Liam wasn't scared, I had no reason to stand there overthinking what could go wrong inside.

I started to walk through the opening of the cave, and Liam grabbed my hand just before I hit the entrance. "Remember, we gotta stay together just like we did when we crossed the fence." He had a point. I wasn't crazy about holding my little brother's hand, and I kept imagining what my friends would have said about that. But I felt safer and less alone with him. Besides, I couldn't always be the leader. For the moment, I was happy to let Liam lead.

We crossed into the cave entrance, ducking our heads below the low hanging rocks. We continued to walk into the cave ever so slowly, crouching down and holding hands. By the time we were able to stand up straight again, we were surrounded by nearly complete darkness.

"What now?" I asked, turning around to be sure we could still see back to the opening of the cave. Phew. The light from outside was flowing into the cave entrance. We had an escape route that we could actually see if we needed it.

"Let's go in a little farther," Liam said. I was surprised that he was feeling that brave. His intuition that we'd be safe must have been pretty darn strong.

We tentatively shuffled forward for a few more feet, and then heard what sounded like far-off thunder coming toward us from deep in the cave. More rapidly than I could describe, the thunder grew louder and louder like a herd of elephants running straight at us. Suddenly petrified, I grabbed Liam's arm tightly and turned to run back toward the entrance. The moment I turned around, the entire cave lit up with that same brilliant, soothing light we'd seen at the end of the tunnel that carried us from the fire scene. I turned around again, looking deeper into the cave toward the sound.

What I saw was so beautiful that it nearly brought tears to my eyes. A herd of ponies of all colors and ages was galloping across a giant field of green grass, manes flying. The mothers with babies were bringing up the rear of the herd, trying unsuccessfully to keep up, but clearly enjoying themselves as they ran, throwing their heads in the air.

"You said you needed a horse," I said. "Looks like you've got a whole bunch now."

"Do you really think that's why they're here?" Liam asked me. "These are wild horses." He was right. There were no saddles, halters, or bridles to be seen. "How on earth could we ride one of them?" Liam asked.

"Maybe on Earth you couldn't ride a wild pony," I said, "but I bet we can ride one here." I wasn't sure why I said this. It just slipped out. Maybe it was my intuition.

"We'd have to catch one first and conjure up a saddle and bridle somehow. How do you expect to do that?" Liam asked

"We don't need a saddle," I said. "Remember how Mom sometimes rode horses bareback after the saddles came off?" Mom insisted riding bareback was much more comfortable than riding with a saddle. I remember trying it out and thinking she was right. The horse's body felt soft and comfortable under me. And there was no hard horn to worry about, either.

"Great. Then you catch a horse. Show me how it's done, big bro. Good luck getting on!"

I wasn't sure how to catch a horse. Nanny and Gary always did that. "Here horsey, horsey. Come to Solon." Nothing happened, of course. How could I have been so dumb?

"Hey," I said as an idea came to me. "Remember when we

went to that rodeo in Wyoming with our cousins? Cowboys lasso horses. We could lasso one."

"With what rope, silly?"

"Good point." I had to think about that one. "Wait," I looked around the cave for anything growing that might help us. "I got it! We could make some rope from those leaves back there." I pointed back the way we had come to the ferns and other understory growth that I had seen along the path we followed into the cave. When we were in Hawaii, Liam took a workshop about how to make rope out of Ti leaves. And as a Boy Scout, I'd also learned how to make rope out of living grasses. In fact, the scouts and I had learned all kinds of survival and outdoor skills. Of course, living in Vermont, we never learned how to lasso a pony like the Boy Scouts out west probably did. Still, in this cave in our afterlives, I just had to trust my instincts, and something was telling me that making a rope and lassoing a pony could work.

Liam and I set about collecting greenery and worked together inside the mouth of the cave to create a long rope. It took a bunch of time and energy, but it was fun and brought back lots of fun memories of being with Mom and Dad and our family, as well as with the Boy Scouts. We chatted away as we worked together.

We talked about our weeklong stay at Boy Scout camp near Mt. Norris, and also about the time we hiked Mt. Adams with Mom and Dad and spent the night at the Madison Spring Hut in the Presidential Mountains. Liam and I actually got more sleep at that Boy Scout camp than we had in the Madison Spring hut with Mom and Dad and all those loud snorers. Their racket kept Liam and me up most of the night. The long hike back to the car the next day was total torture, mostly because we hadn't slept a wink.

"So, what do you think?" Liam said, holding up the rope, which was getting longer.

"Let's give it a try," I said, thinking our rope was quite long.

First, I used one of my fancy Boy Scout knots to create the

sliding loop at the end of our rope that would encircle the horse's neck when I threw it. Then, I started to twirl the rope overhead, just as I had seen those cowboys do in that rodeo. Only when I looked up at it, my rope wasn't creating an amazing circle, the way the cowboys' ropes had. "How do they do that?" I wondered aloud. As I twirled my rope and tried to make it create that beautiful loop, Liam and I walked a little closer to the herd of horses. They had stopped to graze in the grass and turned to look up at us just as I released the rope. Not only was there no loop, but it was also then obvious that the rope was nowhere near long enough. It dropped to the ground well in front of the herd. The ponies stood there unfazed.

"Let's move a little closer. Maybe we should both try throwing it," Liam suggested. "Maybe it'll go further if we combine forces."

We took about twenty steps closer, and then Liam stood in front of me and grabbed the rope too. On the count of three, we twirled it above us. When I looked up, I was amazed to see that a perfect loop was circling overhead at the top of our rope ready to lasso a pony's neck.

"On the count of three," I said. "One. Two. Three." We threw that rope with all of our spirit hearts. As it flew through the air, it seemed destined to land on the ground again, but then at the very last minute, it rose up again, twisted its way through the horses, and landed perfectly around the neck of the black pony at the very back of the herd. I was shocked.

Without our even pulling on the rope, the black pony galloped up to us, skidded to a halt, and then lowered its head to the ground in front of us. Maybe the horse was hoping we would take off the rope.

"What now?" Liam asked.

"You're the one who said you needed a horse."

"Let's ride it over the mountain to the ocean and get back to

Mom and Dad. You get on first, and then pull me up behind you," Liam said.

I looked around, trying to figure out a way up onto the horse. "Come this way." I walked with the horse and Liam following me back through the cave entrance. Once outside, I stepped up onto a knee-high rock beside the cave opening and climbed onto the horse. The pony simply stood calmly in place. I pulled Liam up behind me and let him wrap his arms around my waist. The horse began to throw its head around, clearly eager for me to remove the lasso.

I said. "Sounds crazy, but I'm going to take this rope off."

"Okay, smarty. Then tell me. How do you plan to steer?"

"Maybe we can send it our thoughts, just like we do with one another. Maybe the horse'll understand us," I suggested. I wasn't sure where I came up with that one. Intuition again?

"Oh, please!" Liam said, clearly thinking I was out of my mind.

I leaned over and loosened the rope. The horse put his head down, and we watched the rope slide off the horse's neck onto the misty ground. The pony just stood there, clearly going nowhere.

"Let's think of climbing this mountain to the top, then going down the other side to the ocean," I said. "Maybe the horse'll take us there."

"Sure would beat walking that far!"

We both went silent and thought hard about getting over the mountain. Nothing happened.

"Great. That didn't work. Close your eyes as you think about it," suggested Liam.

We both closed our eyes and concentrated. All of a sudden, as if someone had branded his butt, the pony reared up. I grabbed onto his mane just in time to not fall off. Luckily, Liam had wrapped his arms around my waist, and he held onto me for dear life. When the horse's front legs hit the ground, it took off running up the path at break-neck speed, its mane continuously whipping me in the face. I leaned forward and pulled Liam and myself further forward so that I could wrap my arms around the pony's neck.

The trees around us blurred as we flew up the mountain path. "Hold on!" I said. We both nearly fell into the mist as we rounded curves at a speed unheard of on Earth. It even felt much faster than Dad's driving! When we reached the summit, I wanted to stop and enjoy the spectacular view. Hadn't that always been the case when we hiked with Mom and Dad? The climb could be grueling, but all the effort was so worth it at the summit when we looked out across the landscape.

And this heavenly mountaintop view was simply amazing. The whole of the ocean opened up before us, stretching across the horizon, but the pony left us not more than one second to take it in. Without the slightest bit of hesitation at the summit, that horse started barreling down the backside of the mountain. Oh crap. Liam and I were forced to lean back a bit and squeeze with our legs to hold onto the pony's bare back.

After a lightning-quick trip down the backside of the mountain, the pony galloped across the sand toward that ocean, and as it did, yet another bizarre thing happened. I could feel my legs being stretched out to the sides, as though the pony were growing much fatter at an alarming speed. I glanced back to see Liam performing an amazing feat: he was doing what looked like an absolutely painful split with his legs out to his sides. It reminded me of all those girls at the gymnastics studio where I had taken my lessons. When I turned to look straight ahead again, I was startled to see that we were about to hit the ocean water.

"This is it, hold on tight," I yelled. "Don't let go! We're about to break through the water!" As I said that, I yanked with all my might to pull us up further on the pony's neck. I thought that maybe this would help us avoid the splits as the pony's girth expanded. But when we reached the edge of the water, I was surprised that we didn't dive through the water's surface at all. Instead, the pony just ran, feet dancing across the glassy surface, moving so smoothly that it felt as though we were flying instead of running.

"This is incredible. What's happening?" I yelled.

"Look. The pony has wings now! We're flying across the water!" It was truly spectacular to be flying just above the surface of the glistening ocean toward the beautifully lit horizon. These sights and the breeze against my body filled me with a sense of freedom and light. I looked back toward Liam and noticed that every time the pony's wings pumped rhythmically downward, the tips nearly touched the water, leaving behind us a path of circular ripples that shimmered with light. We flew on in silence. My mind wandered back to Earth.

"Don't we have to break through the surface of the water to go back? Last time, the eagles flew straight into the water. We're just flying on top. How can we get there?" I asked.

"Last time we thought together about Mom reading to us in the family room at bedtime. Let's try it again."

We both went silent and thought hard about bedtime reading with Mom. Mom or Dad had read to us almost every night of our lives, so it was quite easy for us each to picture. I imagined the two couches in the family room and Mom seated on one, book in hand, calmly reading to us, Liam sprawled out on his back atop the same couch, with his feet buried under Mom, or his legs tangled in hers. Sometimes I would be on the other side of Mom, or other times, I would lay on my back on the other couch, covered with my fleece blanket, listening intently.

My peaceful train of thought broke when suddenly the pony shot skyward.

"I forgot this part," I yelled. There must be something about rising up, then shooting back down, like we did on the eagles, to break through the surface of the ocean. It seemed that crashing into the water like that was part of what allowed us to return to Earth. "Hold on!"

"I am holding on!" Liam yelled a little too loudly in my ear.

I was gripping that pony's neck with all my might, although I was not sure it was doing me much good. I felt myself slipping backward, and my grip was almost broken. *"Just a little longer,"* I told myself. The pony suddenly dropped toward the ocean, and I felt that familiar elevator-lifting feeling in my gut. We careened toward the water at an un-earthly speed.

When we hit the water, everything went quiet. We were standing in our old family room, Liam's arms still wrapped around me as if his life depended on it. I turned my head around to look at him and discovered his eyes were still closed.

"Look Liam," I said, prying his arms off of me.

We eyed the room in disbelief. The image we had focused on was in front of us then, but with two major exceptions. We were in the family room, but Mom was nowhere to be seen, and neither was Dad. I stood there listening for them in the house but didn't hear a sound.

"Where are they?" Liam asked. "It's so quiet."

"I obviously have no idea where they are. I just got here, remember?" The silence bothered me and made me sad. It reminded me of our final fall alive on Earth. Mom had started her teaching job an hour away, and so I often arrived home to an empty house and then did my homework alone while I waited for Liam to get off the bus an hour later. Mom sometimes made it home before Liam that fall, but not always. If Mom had a late meeting, we'd go to Dad's office and hang out there with him. That sure beat being home alone like we were at the moment.

"You know. It's probably very quiet for Mom and Dad here without us loud boys to keep things interesting," I said.

"Yeah. I bet you're right."

Not wanting to think about how painful that must have been for Mom and Dad, I quickly changed the subject. "Let's go upstairs and see if they're here reading or something."

We headed up the stairs slowly, unlike the way we traveled upstairs when we were still alive, and would race to the top. I realized as we were ascending the staircase that I was floating, not walking. My spirit legs moved as though I was walking, but my feet didn't hit the floor. It was as though I was slowly drifting across the surface of each step. It was pretty cool, but a part of me still longed to have my body back. It felt weird to be home without it.

LIAM

I DRIFTED UPSTAIRS just behind Solon. It felt strange to be home and not know where Mom and Dad were. I yelled to them, but there was no response. Duh! If they had been in the house, they wouldn't have heard me anyway. Shouldn't I have already known that? Adjusting to life as a spirit was taking me some time.

When we arrived at the top of the stairs and looked across the living room, I saw through the large front windows that the sun was beginning to set over the mountain range.

"Sunset alert!" I exclaimed as I headed toward the windows. It was something our family often shared: when one of us spotted a pretty sunset across the mountains, he'd alert whoever was around, and whenever we could, we would each stop what we were doing to sit in front of the living room windows and watch the sun's spectacle before the night arrived. Some of those sunsets over the mountains were absolutely amazing. In fact, the last sunset we saw before we left for Louisville, before that fateful Christmas morning fire, was the coolest I had seen yet. It looked like a volcano erupting from the top of the mountain range, a colorful funnel flowing skyward. As I thought of that sunset, I began to wonder if that funnel pointing skyward was some sort of sign of what would happen to us.

Solon drifted beside me to watch the sunset. We stood there in silence. It never ceased to amaze me how quickly the colors morphed and adjusted as the sky gradually slid into darkness.

Solon and I watched the sunset, but there was no sign of Mom or Dad in the house. When darkness finally arrived, I turned away from the windows and looked around the living room. Everything looked as it had looked before we left for Louisville, except that the Christmas tree and all the Christmas decorations were gone and newly framed photos of Solon and I were propped up all over the room. A cardboard box sat in the corner with six photo albums laying on top of it. I recognized those albums. Dad had created them and given them to extended family members each year, often at holiday time. We kept an extra copy for the four of us because each album was a record of our family's favorite photos taken throughout each year. And there they were in the living room. I could see that Mom and Dad had gathered all the albums and photos of us that they could find in the house. I felt like I had to get out of the room or else I would start looking too closely and long to be back in my life again. I wanted to stay and look around the house some more and maybe see if we could figure out where Mom and Dad were. But I didn't want to be carried off by a storm.

"I'm going back down to my room," I said. "Mom and Dad aren't here, but I bet they'll be home soon. Time to check out my old digs." Solon followed me downstairs and stopped off in his room.

Not much had changed in my room. Many of my clothes sat folded, in a cardboard box in front of my dressers instead of inside the dressers where they belonged. I instinctively went to open my favorite drawer but discovered that my wispy hands could not grab the handles. It seemed like I'd have to find some other way to open the drawer. So I closed my eyes and thought hard about the drawer opening. When I opened my eyes, I was surprised to see that it had magically obeyed my wish, which was pretty cool! I looked in the drawer and found all of my soccer clothes and jerseys still there, neatly folded and clean, as expected. Not surprising: Mom and Dad know how much those soccer jerseys meant to me. I figured that they would keep those shirts for a long, long time and wouldn't give them to the Salvation Army in a box.

The little things I loved collecting were scattered across my desk, and my books still filled the shelf in my closet. Some of my stuffed animals were on the bed, and someone had pulled all of my Pinewood Derby cars out and lined them up on my bed beside the stuffed animals. It seemed that Mom and Dad had not gotten rid of any of my stuff. In fact, they had hardly moved anything I owned, except for those boxed clothes.

While I was exploring my room, Solon must have been exploring his because I heard him say, "Ouch. Ouch. Ouch." Thinking he had somehow hurt himself, I quickly headed into his room. "What happened?"

"Oh, nothing happened to me here," Solon said, "but I expect this is incredibly painful for Mom and Dad. It has to hurt worse than anything has every hurt before." I couldn't help but think of how sad and depressed Mom was after Amanda died in her car accident.

"Can you imagine how Mom and Dad feel now?" He asked. "They lost both children. Both of us!"

Immediately after Amanda's car accident, Mom spent most of five days in the hospital with family members while doctors tried to save Amanda's life. When Amanda died from her injuries, Mom cried and cried and cried. Nothing could console her. I remember overhearing her telling Dad, "I don't know how I could keep on living if anything close to this ever happened to one of our boys." She felt so, so badly for Amanda's parents.

"Mom and Dad must be a wreck," Solon said. "We have to help them. We have to. We don't want either of them to do something drastic." I shuddered at the thought.

"Yea," I said. "Where do you suppose Mom and Dad are?" As I waited for his response, I looked around his room. All of his Pinewood Derby cars were organized on his shelf beside the many trophies he had earned from the hours and hours he spent using his perfectionist ways to make really fast, cool-looking cars. Most of his clothing, like mine, was boxed up in front of his dresser. The autobiography he had written as part of his advanced literacy class lay on his nightstand. Mom or Dad must have moved it there. Just like my room, his room looked almost exactly like it had when we left for Christmas in Louisville.

"Maybe they went to a movie," Solon said, "or to visit Grandma Nancy and Opa, or maybe they went out to dinner." He stood there looking at me. "I wish I knew," he finally said.

I wandered out to the family room and looked around.

"Come here. Check this out," I said. All around the built-in shelf that circled the family room, eight-by-ten-inch framed photos of Solon and I were propped up. The photos showed us doing so many fun things and taking so many awesome vacations in our lifetimes. There were photos of Solon, photos of me, photos with both of us, and photos of us with family. It was a fabulous bunch of memories. Looking at it made me sad beyond words: sad that we were there in the pictures and there in spirit, but not alive still.

"Whatever you do," Solon said urgently, "do not look at these and wish we were back in our old life. We aren't ever coming back for real. We're in some other dimension now. We're just spirits. Pure spirits. Remember the calm and peaceful feeling we have in our afterlives, that feeling that everything is okay and we're at peace. You have to focus on that, and not on missing your old life." Solon was quite worked up, but I knew him well enough to know that he was trying to convince himself as he tried to convince me.

"My, you sure are full of a lot of 'have to's' tonight!" I said. I didn't like my brother to tell me I "had to do" anything!

"Yeah, well I don't want to be whisked away to some dark and dangerous part of our afterlives," he said. "As hard as it is looking at these pictures, we just can't wish we were back in our lifetimes. Okay?"

"I know," I said. "But seriously. Our afterlives feel great to us, but we left Mom and Dad behind. Shoot, I wish we had never had to do that." I thought about the separation from our lives on Earth and the strangeness of being in this new dimension. I was thankful to have my brother with me in the confusing in-between.

"Let's just stay together," I said. "I'd hate to get separated and stuck in different places. Maybe there's some dimension we haven't even discovered yet! We're together now, so let's keep it that way." The thought of the unknown really bothered me.

"We'll stick together," Solon said, "or at least we'll try. I suppose you never know. It's been a little hard to predict the future lately."

As we stood in the family room looking around at all the Lego ships and buildings Solon and I had put together, my eyes settled on my Lego castle. Wait! That castle fell apart when Cameron was with me for that sleepover in November. I fell to pieces too, crying and crying and knowing it would take me forever to rebuild it. Mom held me close, wiped my tears, and told me not to worry, that she would help me rebuild it. We'd do it together on weekends. But then the holidays took all our free time as we made, bought, wrapped, and addressed gifts for our extended family. We were extra busy because we had had to work around Mom's new teaching job, her hour-long commute, and her weekend workload. There hadn't been any time to spare through the holidays. As the days crept on, I asked Mom for help and she told me not to worry, that we would definitely rebuild that castle together. We'd do it during Christmas break. Unfortunately, thanks to that damn fire, I hadn't lived beyond the third day of Christmas break. Yet there my Lego castle sat completed. Looking more closely, I even saw the rebuilt trebu-chet and all the little knights neatly arranged standing guard.

"Look," I said. "Mom must have rebuilt my castle. She prom-ised she would help me."

"Yeah. But everything else is where we left it, and nothing seems to be missing. How long do you think it's been since we died?"

"I don't know. But hey! I got it. Let's check the calendar." I floated rapidly up the stairs and flipped on the kitchen light using only the power of my mind—so cool! A new, 2010 calendar hung on the wall open to January. I yelled down to Solon, "Yo, dude. It's January." Then I raced back downstairs again. I was able to race down those stairs really quickly when I was alive, but it was nothing like the speed I had then, floating without friction and gravity to slow me down. I started to think that my newfound, other-dimension abilities were quite cool. I was actu-ally beginning to like this spirit thing!

"Great. What part of January? Early, late, or middle?"

Solon's face lit up and he ran into his room.

"What're you doing?" I asked, following.

"Shoot. If we had my iPod, I could find today's date, but my iPod was with me in Louisville. It must have burned up. Ugh! My poor iPod! And my cellphone too!" Solon loved those two things.

"Sorry, dude. Mine burned up too," I said, knowing he was right. Unfortunately, there weren't any electronics down there to help us figure out the day's date.

I said. "Let's go upstairs. Maybe we can find some piece of mail or something with a date," I said.

We went up to the kitchen and poked around for a while but didn't find anything helpful. There wasn't any mail laying out on the counter like there usually was. Two eight-by-ten-inch photos of Solon and I sat on the kitchen table beside Mom's PC. On the other side of her computer sat a second computer that I hadn't seen there ever before. It looked a lot like Dad's, but it was a little bit smaller and it wasn't sitting where Dad usually worked on his, at the other end of the table. In my nosiness, I quietly drifted over and opened the mystery computer.

"Look! It's a MacBook Pro!" I was so excited that I began to jump up and down. Solon raced over to look at the computer.

"O.M.G.! That's exactly what we wanted for Christmas!" Solon and I grabbed for each other, jumped up and down, and did a little midair dance around the kitchen, thrilled that we got our Christmas wish after all—well, sort of at least.

"But wait," I stopped jumping and said, "how could it have survived the fire? If we got it for Christmas, it surely would have burned up under that tree."

"You're right." We both stood there thinking about this for a minute. "Well, maybe someone bought it after the fire . . . "

When Solon and I looked at the computer's desktop, it was obvious what the computer was for. There were multiple folders: "Memories of Solon and Liam," "Fantasy of Solon and Liam's Lives in Heaven," and "Dreams Of Solon and Liam." There were even two icons for documents on the desktop. One was called "Memories About the Fire." The other was titled, "Items Lost in the Fire."

"Check this out," I said. "Someone's using it for all things related to you and me and the fire." Solon drifted closer and looked over my shoulder.

"I bet Mom or Dad got this MacBook Pro in memory of us," Solon said, "and I bet each of us really was gonna get one for Christmas from someone. Mom and Dad knew how badly we wanted these computers." He grinned. "It's nice to know we're not forgotten. Like we ever would be," he said, his face becoming more serious. "I just hope we aren't on that list of items lost in the fire. 'Cause we aren't lost. We're right here!"

"I bet to Mom and Dad it feels like we're lost, but you're right. We're definitely not lost. And we're not items, either. Items can be replaced. People can't," I said.

I used my thought-power to open the document "Items Lost in the Fire" and scanned it quickly. It was full of the things we had brought to Louisville for our four-day trip that had burned up in the fire, including clothing, books, and other items. Sure enough, Solon and I were not on that list, and the MacBook Pro wasn't on it, either.

"I think Grandpa Irv and GiGi were planning to give us the MacBook Pros for Christmas. And Mom and Dad have one now to use in our memory or something. Do ya think?" I asked him.

"Probably," Solon said.

Although there was no MacBook Pro on that list, there sure were a ton of other things. I was surprised by how long Mom and Dad's list was, and I couldn't even begin to imagine how long GiGi and Grandpa Irv's list probably was. That fire was so bad that they must have lost their entire home.

Trying to avoid the sadness that was creeping in, I said, "See. You're not an item, Solon. "

"Don't be dumb!"

"Maybe you and some girl were an 'item' once, but you're officially not an item," I said with a grin to bug him.

"Very funny!" Solon said, rolling his eyes. "Be serious for a minute, would ya? Let's look in some of these other computer folders."

I opened the "dreams" folder and discovered that it was empty. Solon moved a little closer to me, and I noticed the computer slide over toward him a bit until it was resting between both of us. He must have done that so he could see it a little better.

"Look Liam!" Solon called out, pointing excitedly. "There's an iPod Touch!" It had been behind the computer all along, and we just hadn't seen it. Solon immediately became excited. "But how could that be? My iPod Touch was in Louisville. I know it fried in the fire."

"Maybe Mom or Dad bought this one. You know, you're not the only one who's allowed to own one in the universe. I know you didn't want me to have one, but don't you think it's possible that Mom or Dad bought one?" I asked him.

"Well, yeah," Solon admitted. "But I wouldn't think that Dad would buy a Touch since he just got an IPhone. Maybe this one's Mom's. On second thought, maybe not, since she hated for us to focus on our DSIs and our iPods and ignore the people around us. She wouldn't want one herself."

"Are you kidding? Mom loves music, and so does Dad. Maybe they decided to get one after seeing how cool ours were."

I wondered what Mom or Dad would have in their iPod play-list. I thought that maybe it would be full of songs they liked and played all the time when we were alive. I decided that it sure would be fun to hear some of those songs again and that we simply had to take a look at what our parents were up to with that iPod. I worked my spirit magic to turn on the iPod and waited for it to warm up. Meanwhile Solon wandered into the living room to look out the window.

"Holy crap. They're coming up the driveway!"

I quickly shut off the iPod, feeling as though I were sneaking around and needed to hide. But why did I feel that way? Solon and I were invisible, so hiding wasn't exactly necessary. Besides, we wanted to communicate with Mom and Dad, and there they were, coming up the driveway.

Solon and I waited and watched at the living room window. "What do we do now?" I asked. "How'll we talk to them?"

"I don't know yet. Remember what the Guiding Spirit told us. We need to follow our intuition."

I heard the familiar and welcome sound of our garage door opening and our car pulling in. Mom and Dad entered the house, removed their shoes, and headed upstairs to the kitchen, chatting about their dinner out. Dad made his way to his computer at the kitchen table, and Mom headed for the kitchen sink and began putting away some dishes that were in the drying rack.

"Do something!" I urged. "Say something to them."

"Duh!" Solon said. "They have no idea we're here, and they won't be able to hear us, remember. Hey! Mom! Dad! Yo! Here we are!" he screamed. There was no sign that Mom or Dad heard him. "See. What'd I tell ya?"

"But try forcing your thoughts into their heads the way we do in the afterlife. Better you than me since you think I'm too loud," I suggested.

Solon went silent and closed his eyes, trying to force something their way. I waited and watched, hoping for some sign that Mom or Dad knew we were present and trying to communicate, but nothing seemed to change.

"You try," Solon urged. "Maybe this is one time where your excessive loudness will be good."

I closed my eyes, scrunched my face up tight, and tried with all my might to yell some positive thoughts into their heads. I told them that we were okay and that we were there in the house trying to help them. I told them how much Solon and I loved them and wanted them to be happy. But nothing I was trying to say seemed to get through.

"It's not working," Solon said, interrupting my focus. "We're just gonna have to wait until something new strikes us. Maybe some intuition will help us figure this out."

As Solon and I continued watching them, Mom began preparing for bed. It was a familiar scene. First, Mom went to the sliding glass door and whistled for the kitties to come in. Spurs and Coco came running, and Mom headed downstairs with a can of cat food and a spoon to the laundry room where their cat bowls were kept. We followed her and the kitties while Dad stayed at the table working at his computer.

After filling the cats' dishes, Mom went into my room and said, "Oh, Bubbins." That was one of her many nicknames for me. "I love you." She bent over and hugged and kissed my pillow in the same way she had kissed me every night of my life. "Night night, Bubbins. Sleep like a pumpkin. I love you so much. I'll see you in the morning."

Holy cow. That was exactly what she said to me when I was alive. Same words. Same order. Same everything. Mom always was a fan of routines. She claimed that routines were what kept her sane when we were toddlers and we needed regularity and predictability. I don't know about Solon, but I sure loved having a routine at bedtime all through my life. It made me feel comfortable when I was left alone in my room at night. I knew it like the back of my hand.

But ... to keep saying "see you in the morning" when clearly she would not? That was hard to take. The only way to see her in the morning would be to stick around 'till then, but she still wouldn't see me again. Overcome with sadness, I began to cry. It hurt too much to see Mom kiss my pillow without me there and to know that she hadn't let go of our nighttime routine. But, it must have brought her comfort, maybe in the same way it brought me comfort. Maybe it helps her feel safer or feel closer to me again. I had to hope that was the case.

Mom took a deep breath and started crying as she left my room and headed down the hall to Solon's. He and I followed along behind. When Mom got there she said, "Oh, Sweetheart, I love you," just as she had done in my room She bent over and hugged and kissed his pillow. I turned to look at Solon. He was crying, just like I had only moments ago. "Goodnight, Sweetheart. Sleep like a pumpkin. I love you so much. I'll see you in the morning." Ouch. Ouch. Ouch.

Mom left Solon's room crying more, but somehow it looked like going through the nighttime routine with our pillows had been helpful to her. She seemed to be walking a little straighter and taller. Mom climbed the stairs, kissed and hugged Dad, and headed to the bedroom. Solon and I stayed to be with Dad. When Mom left, he walked over to where his cellphone lay and flipped it open. A picture of me showed on his phone screen. It was the picture he had taken of me when Solon and I first got our cellphones four months before Christmas. Dad stared at the photo of me holding up my cellphone and smiling. He stared at that photo for a long time, lost in thought and looking sad. Eventually, Dad turned the phone off, set it back on the top of the waist-high cupboard, and headed downstairs. Solon and I floated along behind him.

First, Dad went into Solon's room and looked around, just standing there, looking extremely sad. I wondered what was going through his head. Eventually, Dad sighed, left, and went to my room to look around. He appeared equally sad. Though I could not hear what he was thinking the way I sometimes could read Solon's mind, it was obvious that Dad was thinking of us and no doubt wishing we were comfortably tucked in bed and sleeping in our rooms so that he could kiss us goodnight too. It made me doubly sad. I started to cry again.

Dad continued down the hall into the laundry room and took out a bunch of wet clothing. Then he hung it on the drying racks in the family room. While he did, I went upstairs alone, hoping to ease some of my sadness. Mom had just finished changing into her PJs and was putting her clothing down the laundry chute in the upstairs hallway. When I followed her back into her bedroom, curious about what her room looked like, I saw the urns containing Solon and my ashes sitting on top of her dresser surrounded by photos of us, photos of our friends, and poems.

My panda and penguin and Solon's Pooh and Tigger were on the nightstand next to Mom's side of the bed. We had slept with those stuffed animals when we were a lot younger. She must have moved them from storage to her nightstand because they, too, brought her comfort somehow.

Dad came back upstairs, followed closely by the floating Solon, and as Dad passed by me entering his bedroom, it dawned on me that our parents would soon be in bed and then asleep. How would we communicate with them then?

"We don't have much time," I said to Solon. "We have to find a way to communicate with them before they fall asleep."

"I haven't thought of a way yet. Have you?"

"Well . . . no." I thought about it. I figured that maybe somehow, when our parents were on the edge of sleep and just about to doze off, their brains might have been able to hear us.

"I know it didn't work before," I said, "but maybe if we try to force our thoughts into their heads now they'll hear us better 'cause they'll be drifting off to sleepland," I said.

"I wish I knew how we made this work in our afterlives," Solon said. "I think closing our eyes helps sometimes. Seems like sometimes our thoughts get where we want them to go when we close our eyes." He stopped and thought for a minute. "What should we say? Maybe if we both say the same thing at the same time they'll hear us because we'll both be doing it together."

"Oh geez. I don't know. They think we're dead and gone forever, so we have to convince 'em we aren't completely gone. So what do we say?" I asked.

"How about we say, 'Mom, Dad, we're right here. You just can't see us. We're okay. Really.'" Solon suggested.

"Yeah, but I think we should add that we love them and always will," I said.

"Good idea," Solon answered.

"So, when you say 'go,' we're just going to think really hard 'Mom, Dad, we're right here. You just can't see us. We're okay. Really. We love you and always will.' Then we're going to just hope they somehow hear us, right?" I asked.

"Right," Solon said. We stood side by side watching Mom as she kissed Pooh and Tigger and Panda and Penguin goodnight and set them back on the bedside table. Dad came out of the bathroom and climbed into bed beside Mom. They kissed and held each other for a while. When they were done hugging, they told each other they loved one another and to sleep well, and then Mom turned off the light. All was quiet.

"Let's do it now," I said, "and get to them right before they fall asleep. On the count of three, let's push our thoughts to both of them at once. One, two, three. Go."

We both closed our eyes and silently tried to push the words into their heads. I peeked once to look closely at Mom's eyes. Nothing changed. Solon walked around to the other side of the bed and looked at Dad as he and I both kept thinking those words and repeating them, trying as hard as we could to push them into their heads.

"See anything?" I asked "Do you think Dad can hear us?"

"Nope. Nothing's changing."

We watched and listened as Mom's and Dad's breathing slowed and they drifted into sleep.

"Great. That was a complete failure. What now?" I said.

"Maybe it'll work while they sleep. Let's keep trying. On the count of three. One. Two. Three. Go." We kept repeating those words in our heads for another five minutes or so, but we didn't notice any difference at all. What did we expect? Mom and Dad were asleep.

"I don't know," said Solon, "but I'm not leaving until they

understand that we may be dead, but we're not gone. We're not hurting. We're not forever lost to them."

"So what next?"

"I have no idea," Solon said. He looked at Mom and Dad sleeping and quietly said, "Man, I love you guys. I'm so sorry for you."

"I love you too, Mom and Dad," I said. We made our way back into the kitchen, and Solon went directly to the iPod. No big surprise. When he was alive, he lived with that iPod. If he was separated from it, he'd freak. I could hear it now. "Oh no. I forgot my iPod. Turn the car around. We have to go back."

"Wow!" Solon said. "This thing has all my songs on it. How?"

I slid myself over beside him and looked over his shoulder at the song list. "Let me see. Are my songs on there too?" I used my thoughts to quickly scroll down through the playlist. Sure enough, all of my songs were on there.

"Mom or Dad must've bought this iPod and loaded both of our songs onto it," I said, "'cause my songs are here too."

Solon stood there looking at me for a second and then yelled in a sudden flash of excitement, "Maybe we could control the iPod when it's set to shuffle. If we could, then maybe we could send Mom or Dad messages through our songs."

"How?" I asked.

"Well, lots of the lyrics to the songs we liked talk about things kind of like messages. You know. They speak of some feeling or something. Maybe we could think of some songs that could be useful for sending messages to Mom and Dad," Solon suggested.

"Sounds like a stretch to me," I said, setting the iPod back on the table. "I mean, think about it. First we have to figure out how to make certain songs play on the thing while one of them is listening. What are we gonna do, take it out of the hand of the person listening?"

"Of course not," Solon said, "but maybe we can think about the song we want to have play, and then somehow it'll play next without our having to hold it."

"It's worth a try, but it looks like we'll have to wait on that until someone chooses to use the iPod, won't we? It's kinda hard to use an iPod while dreaming sweet dreams and catching some Z's." Suddenly, this great idea hit me. "That's it! We can send dreams! They're asleep, but maybe we can send a dream message, a visual picture like a film that they'll understand."

"Good idea. If they remember their dreams, maybe we can help 'em. Let's give it a try," Solon said, heading for the bedroom with me close behind.

"I know Mom remembers her dreams," I said, thinking aloud as I followed him. "Remember how she'd tell us her crazy dreams and laugh at them with us. We always looked at her like she was nuts. Dad is such a sound sleeper that I'm not sure if he remembers his dreams, but it is worth a try."

Solon said, "But I'm guessing the only way this can work is if each of us sends a visual image to only one of them. Otherwise, you and I may not be picturing the same things, and the images might get all jumbled up. See what I mean?" I nodded my head. "So, who do you want to send a dream to?" Solon asked. "Wait. You're so darn loud, maybe you should push your visions into Dad's more deeply sleeping head. I'll send Mom a dream. How about that?"

"Okay, let's go," I raised my hand for a high five, and we both started laughing when we remembered that high fives don't work in the spirit world.

We floated back into Mom and Dad's bedroom. I stood beside Dad, and Solon stood beside Mom. I counted aloud to three and we each closed our eyes and thought hard about the pictures we wanted to send to Mom and Dad. We were silent for a long time, and there was no way to know whether or not our dream messages had reached their targets, but we kept trying anyway, focusing hard on the pictures we were trying to send. Finally, I asked Solon, "How are we ever gonna know if it worked?"

"Good question. I suppose if they talk about a dream with one another, we might know. Then again, I don't suppose either of them wakes up remembering all of the dreams they had at night anyway. Did you remember yours?" Solon asked.

"Sometimes," I responded, "but only if it was scary or shocking. I don't think we sent them a scary dream, though. I guess we're stuck just waiting for them to wake up so that we can see if somehow they got our messages."

I floated back into the kitchen to check out that iPod. I never had an iPod Touch when I was alive, just a Nano. Solon never let me explore his, so I took this chance to check it out. The selected wallpaper that showed when I turned on the iPod had a photo of Solon and me grinning at the camera in Vancouver, British Columbia. Dad took it during our trip to ski at Whistler with Grandpa Irv in February of 2009. That was an awesome trip, and Solon and I looked so happy in the photo. It was no surprise that Mom or Dad had selected it as wallpaper on the iPod. I found over one hundred family photos on the iPod, and in the folder marked "favorite photos" there were lots of photos of Solon and me. Seeing these photos made me happy 'cause they reminded me of so many great times, but it was also sad to realize that there wouldn't be any more photos of us.

I scrolled through the song list looking for songs that might help us send a message to Mom and Dad and remembering all those great tunes. Solon floated around, looking in the fridge and the cupboards. Don't ask me why. As spirits, eating wasn't exactly necessary anymore. Maybe he was trying to see what Mom and Dad were eating.

As I fished for songs in the iPod, I could hear the wind picking up outside. In what seemed like no time, the wind began howling, and the rain started striking the sliding glass door in full force. The weather made me nervous. I turned the iPod off and left it on the table.

"Listen," I said, heading for the slider. "It sounds like it's getting pretty nasty out there." I flipped on the outdoor light switch with my mind. The tree branches were whipping about, and sticks and smaller branches were falling onto our deck.

"Oh crap! This is bad. This is very, very bad!" I was becoming more frantic with every passing moment. Solon rushed over beside me. I rambled on in fear. "Looks like one of those hurricanes from our afterlife that could send us to the wrong place. I don't want to get stuck. I don't want to go somewhere awful. We have to get back to our afterlives and stop thinking about the lives we had here before. We have to leave, *now!*"

"You're right. We have to get back, but how?" Solon asked. "We have no eagles. We have no flying ponies. What do we do?"

I thought about it and quickly decided to try calling the eagles the way Solon had called them in the church. Granted the eagles had been flying overhead when he tried, and when we had tried to repeat it in the field in our afterlives, it hadn't worked, but, what the heck? It was worth a try. Standing inside in front of the sliding glass doors, I raised both of my hands over my head, palms outstretched, and pictured those eagles arriving on the deck to carry us home to our afterlives. Solon saw what I was doing, stood beside me, and followed suit. "Let's close our eyes, too," he said. We focused with all our might.

When I opened my eyes, there were two eagles sitting proudly atop the outdoor picnic table, looking directly at us, feathers ruffling in the wind. What a relief it was! "Let's go!" I said as I started moving forward to drift through the glass and out onto the deck. But before I passed through the glass, Solon grabbed my arm.

"We promised to stick together, right?!" Solon said. Boy was I glad he grabbed me, because as soon as we hit that deck, the wind picked us up and threw us over the railing. The eagles watched as Solon and I flew through the air and landed in the grass. The birds didn't budge as the wind gained even more speed.

Solon and I held onto each other for dear life as we struggled to push through the wind and climb the ramp at the front of the deck. We had to will our movement with all of our might. Eventually, we made it to the picnic table. The eagles' feathers were ruffling in all directions, but those smart animals had wrapped their talons around the backs of the picnic table chairs and had not been carried off by the ever-strengthening wind. It was a sight to behold. Eventually, Solon and I were close enough to climb onto the eagles' backs. We wrapped our arms around their necks and prepared for takeoff.

"Picture the door of the Enchanted Castle. We need to travel to the same place in our afterlife!" I yelled over the now howling wind.

"Okay," Solon said, closing his eyes. "Concentrate."

The wind was so strong that I wondered how the eagles could possibly fly in it without crashing. Sure enough, when they took off our flight proved worse than the bumpiest plane rides Solon and I had ever taken in our lives. Yet I felt strangely calm and at peace, and I definitely was not sick to my stomach. Perhaps there was some benefit to not eating in this afterlife and to not feeling every single sensation I had felt while I was alive. As Solon and I flew side by side, the eagles climbed higher and higher in the sky. It didn't scare me at all.

"Hold on tightly," Solon encouraged. "I think the eagles are gonna drop down and break across the horizon into the afterlife now."

When we came to the other side of the mountains, both eagles nosedived toward the Lake Champlain. Well, I thought it was Lake Champlain, but I guess it could have been the ocean in our afterlife. I held on tightly as we crashed into the water's surface and then landed on the doorstep of our Enchanted Castle. The eagles waited for us to climb down. We patted them on the head, and off they flew.

I looked at Solon. "You all right?" I asked.

"Yep. I sure am glad we can call on those two eagles!"

As good as it felt to be back in the safety of my afterlife, I was darn sad to leave Mom and Dad in our old home. I couldn't help but wonder if we would ever be able to help them.

SOLON

I STOOD ON the doorstep of our Enchanted Castle and looked around to get my bearings. So much had happened in our after-life, yet it seemed like not that much time had passed on Earth. Though Liam and I never were able to figure out the exact date on Earth, according to the calendar, less than a month had passed since our deaths. Mom and Dad were still alive and extremely sad to be alive without us, and we still hadn't figured out how to tell them we were okay.

"Now what do we do?" I asked. "We couldn't tell Mom and Dad anything."

"Maybe we pushed visions into their dreams. We can't know that from here, but at least we tried."

"Too bad we couldn't stay longer to send 'em messages with the iPod. That could've been fun," I said.

"Gee, maybe that's why that awful wind came. I was scrolling through the list and we were both wishing we could listen to the songs again to figure out which ones to play for Mom and Dad. But maybe we really just wanted to listen to the songs like we used to. Maybe it was like wanting to go back to our past lives or something," Liam said.

"Yeah, I guess. Maybe. But if we don't listen to the songs, how'll we pick which ones to use as messages?"

"Maybe that's the point," said Liam. "Maybe we should just use our intuition when the time comes rather than try to plan it all out ahead of time. Maybe if we're back visiting and Mom or Dad are using the iPod, we should just think about his or her mood and determine which song to play right then. See what I mean?"

"I guess. You could be right. Right now, my intuition says we should walk back," I pointed across the bridge, "to the field we arrived in when we first came to this afterlife, the one Amanda took us to. I have a sneaky suspicion there's something or someone there to help us."

"Well I don't know about that," Liam said, "but do you think Amanda might be there?"

"Who knows? I am just telling you what my intuition says. Let's go."

I started to float across the bridge, heading for the field. Liam followed me in silence.

When we arrived in the tall grasses, Liam quickly found and picked up our football and threw it in my direction. I caught it. Liam ran off for a long pass, and I threw it directly into his diving hands.

"Great throw!" Liam yelled.

"Good catch!" I yelled back.

We continued throwing and playing for a long while. It was so nice to just throw and catch and not think about anything else. Every time I threw, the ball landed where I wanted it to land. I aimed diving passes, long passes, and short passes, and, amazingly, Liam's hands were always there.

Liam said, "Man! You're on fire!" I cringed at the new irony of that normally harmless phrase.

Liam yelled, "You're a lot better with that football than Mom was the first time she played catch with us while her leg was healing. Remember that?" The image of Mom hobbling around in that half-cast and trying to play ball with us made me laugh. She hit her target maybe one in every ten throws at best and caught the ball almost never. Every one of us, Mom included, ended up rolling on the ground laughing hard at the ridiculousness of it, but we were all grateful to be playing ball again after so many months.

"Yeah, I remember. That was fun," I said. It had been difficult for all of us to have Mom laid up in bed, then on crutches for so long, and then strengthening her ankle for so many months. The only benefit was that we spent lots more time with Dad, and boy, did the three of us have fun playing soccer, doing target practice with Liam's bow and arrow, playing kickball, biking, and hiking.

When Liam and I finally became bored with our game of catch, we sat down in the grass. "You know," I said, "I feel strangely one hundred percent well right now. But, isn't it odd that we're virtually alone here in this afterlife? I mean, on Earth people were always around, or we knew where we could find 'em. Here, we're all alone, just the two of us."

"Yeah. You're right," Liam said. "I loved being around people. I especially loved to entertain them. Now it's just you and me. Not that I don't like being with you or something, but I'd like to spend time with other people, too. Keeps things from getting too boring."

"I wonder if we'll always be alone," I said, "or if someday we'll see other kids here, too. Maybe that's why I wanted to come to this field again, to see other kids. Amanda isn't here now, though." I thought about it for a bit.

"You know," I said after a few minutes, "in this afterlife, there's all this cool stuff we can do that we couldn't do before. I love that, and I don't even miss my body that much anymore, but Mom and Dad sure miss us. Why do you suppose they can't see us or feel us when we're there?"

"I don't know. It seems to me like we're in some completely different dimension that people on Earth can't see or hear," Liam explained. "I have no idea how we're gonna communicate from our dimension to theirs."

"Yeah, but there must be a way. Maybe that's part of why we followed my intuition here—to find someone who can help us, like Amanda." I paused to think for a minute. "It's just so odd that we're here all alone. I mean, seriously. So many other people died before us. Where are all of those people? Why are we all alone?"

"Good question," Liam said. "Man. Think of all the people who died in World War II or in the American Revolution. Where are they?" Liam was reminding me of our love of history and of our studies with Opa Jon about the wars that fascinated each of us.

"I don't know," I answered softly, "but I sure wish we'd meet someone, anyone, here. We need someone to help us to make sense of all of this." As I said those words, I noticed two young girls floating through the field toward us. "Look! Who's that?"

"No idea." We stood up and watched them approach from the other side of the field, their long hair floating in the gentle breeze. They looked very peaceful and friendly in the light of our afterlife, so I was not afraid as they approached. When eventually they were close enough for us to see their faces, I was quite certain I'd never met either of them in my lifetime.

"Hello, Solon and Liam," the older girl said. "Do you remember us?"

"Ah . . . no." Liam said, but then he continued. "Wait a minute," he said as he looked at the younger girl. "You look a little familiar. I can't remember how I know you, though."

"Maybe this'll help," the older girl said. She reached into her pocket and pulled out a red construction-paper cutout heart. The heart was emitting a bright glow, like the glow that we found in the tunnel that drew Liam and I up to our afterlives from Earth. I reached out my open hand, merely wanting to touch the heart she held because it looked so tantalizingly comfortable. To my surprise, she placed it in my hand. It felt warm and wonderful.

110

"Look at the back," the older girl urged.

When I flipped it over, I was shocked to see my own handwriting. "Thinking of you. R-I-P Solon." I looked at her, bewildered.

"You probably don't remember, but we lived in your town, too," the younger girl explained. "We died in a house fire, too. You and your brother and all of your classmates made hearts for us at school the year after we died. This is the heart you made for me." She pulled a heart from her pocket and handed it to Liam. He found his handwriting on the back. It was just so strange.

"I don't get it," Liam said.

"You drove by the burned-out house every week on your way to Solon's piano lessons," the older girl said.

Suddenly, I knew what she was talking about.

"I remember," I said. I remembered how, when Mom realized she was going to drive right past the house on the way to my piano lesson, she pulled over and said a silent prayer for everyone who had died in that fire. Liam and I sat there without saying a word, not sure how to respond because we didn't know any of them and couldn't imagine what had happened. It sure was sad to see the house though, and know so many people had lost their lives there. The next year, at Christmas time, each of our classes made hearts in school in memory of these two girls. I was still trying hard to piece together how we were meeting them in this afterlife though.

"Do you get it, Liam? You know which house she's talking about?"

"I think so. But wait." He was staring at the younger girl. "I think my teacher showed me your picture. You were in my classroom the year before me, weren't you?"

That must be why the younger girl looked familiar to Liam. Liam's teacher had shown his class a photo of the girls before they made hearts in the girls' memory. So Liam had "crossed paths" with the younger sister because of his classroom, and somehow, perhaps because I signed a heart in her memory, I had "crossed paths" with the older sister, too. But, we had never met them in person. So how was it that we could connect with them there in the field? Man, this afterlife was making my head spin.

Liam, always social and up for a game, asked the girls if they wanted to play football with us. They looked at him as if he were a little crazy. "Okay, then," Liam said. "Let's just throw the ball around. That'll be just as fun."

The four of us spread out around the field and started tossing the ball around. It was great fun, and I was reminded of how much I missed my friends back home. Matt and Luke, Dan, and the guys I always ate lunch with at school. We had a great time together. But still, it was beginning to look like Liam and I could have a great time in our afterlives, too, if we could just resolve this nagging need to tell Mom and Dad we were doing fine. Somehow, we needed them to know that they should go on living and enjoy themselves until they died and could come to the afterlife to be with us again. Until then, Liam and I would be okay. I was becoming pretty sure of that.

After a while, the older girl asked, "Have you met your Guiding Spirit yet?"

"Met. Hmm. If you call hearing the voice 'meeting' the Spirit, then yes," I said, "but we've not seen it, if that's what you mean."

"Nope. I know you won't see your Guiding Spirit. But it's good that you've spoken with the Spirit. Just remember that you can ask for help from the Guiding Spirit whenever you need it."

"Well, we have," Liam said. "The spirit only told us to follow our intuition. That hasn't gotten us very far."

"Well, try asking again. It can't hurt. It's not like the Spirit'll get angry at you or anything," the older girl said, "and every time you speak with the Spirit, you'll learn something new about yourselves or something about how this spirit world works. That'll help you figure things out. It's like a giant logic puzzle, only the logic in the afterlife seems so, so much different from what we think of as logic on Earth."

"That's for sure. We should probably get ourselves back to our castle, Solon," Liam encouraged. "That's the only place we've been able to talk with the Guiding Spirit—through that door."

"Yeah. That's true," I said, turning to look at the girls. "Sorry to ditch you like this, but our parents are very upset and sad without us, and we want to help them as soon as possible." They nodded their heads.

"How can we meet up with you again? Where will we find you?" Liam asked.

"We'll be around. There are many, many places to visit in your afterlife. We'll see each other again in one of these places. Don't worry." Though they said not to, I would probably worry about it anyway, 'cause, like Liam, I was enjoying having people my own age around to talk and play with. I sure hoped that after we settled our affairs on Earth, there would be a way to connect with more and more young spirits in this afterlife.

"Go along now," the girls said in unison, smiling. "We'll see you again some other time." And, just like that, the girls disappeared right in front of our eyes.

"How'd they do that?" Liam asked, looking at me. "Here one minute. Gone the next. I wanna learn how! That's straight out of Harry Potter or something!"

"No doubt we'll be performing disappearing acts before long, but right now we have more important things to do. Remind me: how do we get to the Enchanted Castle from here?" I asked.

We both looked over in the direction we had come from, where we had originally found the Enchanted Castle that rescued us from the first hurricane. At the moment, there was no castle perched at the edge of the field.

"It's gone," I said.

"We can do this. We conjured up the Enchanted Castle in the wind before by both thinking of the same thing. It just happened we were both thinking about castles. So you think again about playing "The Enchanted Castle" on piano with Alison, and I'll think hard about my Lego castle. I bet the Enchanted Castle will appear."

We both closed our eyes and thought hard, and when we opened them, the castle sat once again at the far edge of the field looking like it had always been there. We drifted there as fast as we could, crossed the moat, and used the crimson handle to open the massive door. As before, we found ourselves standing in the huge, green field surrounded by flex-net fencing.

"Okay, Spirit," I said. "We're back. What can you tell us that'll help us?"

"Are you there Spirit?" I asked. "Do you know everything that's been happening to us?"

"Yes. I'm here. Always have been," the Guiding Spirit said.

"We're back for some suggestions," I said, "something that'll help us figure out how to communicate with Mom and Dad."

"I don't need to say much," the Guiding Spirit replied. "The two of you are doing great with following your intuition. By spending time alone yet together, you're gaining a deeper understanding of what has happened and what's happening now. Your deeper understanding will help you achieve your goal. My role is to guide you, but only you can reach those understandings through your own thoughts and actions. That's why I say, 'go on'. Pull together all that you've been learning as you do things both here and on Earth, and combine that with everything you just learned from talking with the girls, and you'll figure this out."

"I wish I were so confident," I said under my breath.

"Put your heads together, and it'll come. There's no rush. You have time."

"We have time, but Mom and Dad are back there hurting so, so much. We want to help them sooner rather than later. Don't you understand that?" Liam asked, clearly frustrated.

"Of course I do," the Spirit replied. "You love them more than anything in the whole world, and it hurts to watch them in so much pain. The trauma and the extreme grief they're experiencing is grueling, and it pains me to watch them go through it, too. But they'll be okay. They'll get through the pain, and you'll help them in ways you aren't even aware of yet.

"You know your parents best. You were made from them, were raised by them, and died with them nearby, and you remain connected to them and will forever. You'll be able to figure out the right recipe for helping your parents now."

Liam and I were silent as we let this sink in. It made perfect sense.

"Start by looking hard at what you've tried and what you've experienced here in your afterlife. You can do this. Be confident in yourselves and keep working at it. Don't give up. Only you can determine the right recipe for helping them heal."

I thought to myself that nobody needed to worry about Liam or me giving up. We'd find a way, even if neither of was sure how we would do it.

"Well thank you," I said to the Guiding Spirit.

"Yeah. Thanks," said Liam.

The Guiding Spirit's words reminded me of encouragement from Mom and Dad. In our schoolwork, and in our sports and musical instruments, they always said not to expect perfection or a quick trip to the good result, but rather to keep working at the things we cared about until we got closer to our goals. If learning to help Mom and Dad was like learning to play piano, Liam and I would just need to keep working hard to figure it out. Nobody ever learns to play piano well by simply being told how to play. It's way too complicated.

"So what do we do now?" Liam asked, interrupting my thoughts.

"Let's talk about what we know, and then we'll decide."

LIAM

SOLON AND I walked up the slight rise to our left and sat down across from each other.

"Let's start by trying to figure out what we learned from the girls," I said. "There must be something important in that conversation, or the Guiding Spirit wouldn't have brought it up."

"How about those hearts we made for the girls after they died?" Solon said.

"Yeah. That was weird," I said. "Holding that heart gave me the most peaceful feeling. It was so warm and wonderful in my hand. Did you feel that?"

"I sure did. It felt so amazing to hold that heart. But why? What's it mean?"

Solon and I thought about it for a while.

He finally said, "We made those hearts when we were alive on Earth. Do you suppose the fact we made 'em has anything to do with why they make us feel so good when we hold 'em?"

"I don't know. Maybe it's because the hearts showed our sympathy for the girls. Maybe it's just because it was a nice thing to do." I said.

"Maybe." Solon paused. "I wonder . . . you know how the only spirits we've seen here in the afterlife are ones we crossed paths with on Earth?"

"Yeah. That's true," I said.

"Well, there must be something powerful that connects us

117

to the things we encounter on Earth, some connection that's so strong that it carries into the afterlife," Solon said.

"Maybe. But how do you suppose that affected the hearts we made for the girls?" Solon and I just thought about it for a while, keeping our thoughts to ourselves.

"That's it!" Solon exclaimed. "We touched and interacted with— no, not interacted with—we *created* those hearts and we made 'em while thinking of the girls. Maybe some parts of our spirits are somehow attached to the hearts because we made them. Or maybe our spirit is attached to anything we touched on Earth. I don't know. Does any of that make sense to you?" Solon asked.

"I suppose. Maybe that's why we're meeting up with spirits we crossed paths with on Earth. Part of our spirits are somehow interconnected and attached to one another because of the contact we had with them on Earth." I wasn't sure whether or not we were moving in the right direction, but it was beginning to sound like maybe we were onto something.

"I don't really know." Solon said. Then he was quiet for a while. "You know, if our spirits are attached to these hearts, and if that's what's helping us feel so good when we hold 'em, this could be useful. Maybe we could use this idea somehow to comfort Mom and Dad."

"Maybe." I said. We sat thinking for a while.

I interrupted the silence. "If our spirits somehow attach to objects and bring comfort to the person holding the object, then maybe all the things we touched in our lives that are still in our house will comfort Mom and Dad."

"Maybe that's why Mom hugs our pillows and kisses them good night as if they were somehow you and me. She followed the exact same bedtime routine, but with the pillows instead of you and me. She was obviously sad and crying, but somehow it must bring her comfort to touch those pillows," Solon said.

"Yeah. But how can we use this idea to bring them even more comfort? 'Cause clearly they're still sad," I asked. "Can we somehow add comfort now that we're spirits? And, here's the other thing: we don't just wanna comfort them, like those hearts felt comfortable and warm to us. We want them to know we're doing okay in this afterlife. How can we do that?" I asked.

"I've been thinking about that, too. Remember how we touched their iPod? I wonder if somehow our spirits are now attached to the iPod. Maybe it'll help them. Maybe whoever uses it will find that it's warm and comforting in their hand," Solon said. "But still, you're right. We have to find a way to send them a message, not just comfort them."

Again, we stopped talking to collect our thoughts.

"You know, there is a song on my iPod by Linkin Park called, "Leave Out All the Rest." Solon seemed to be thinking aloud. "There are some key lines in that about remembering the good things about a person after they die. That doesn't really tell Mom and Dad we're okay, though. But, "Halo" is on the iPod, too. I wonder if that song would help them know that we're spirits now and that we're okay. I can't remember all the words to that song, though," Solon said.

"I can't either, but it's a good idea. I'm sure there are other songs with lines that could help. We'll check it out when we get back there next time." I wasn't feeling sure that it would solve our problem entirely, though, and I thought that it might even cause us more problems, so I asked, "What else can we do to help Mom and Dad know we're okay? We need to send that message somehow."

"I'm not sure," Solon said. "The big question, though, is how are we gonna know if they're getting any of our messages? How are we really gonna know if they understand we're okay?" Solon asked.

"Let's go back there and stay for a while and watch them,"

I said. "Maybe we'll see some signs. Maybe we'll hear them discuss a dream, or maybe someone will write about a dream. Remember the MacBook Pro had an empty folder on the desktop called 'Dreams of Boys'? We can look in that and see if anyone added to it."

"Good idea," Solon said. "You know, every time we've returned to Earth we haven't stayed long. The first time we were only there for our Louisville funeral, which couldn't have been longer than an hour or so in Earth time. And the second time, we were only there long enough to see the bedtime routine and then watch Mom and Dad fall asleep. Maybe if we stay longer next time, we'll see enough to know for sure that Mom and Dad are comforted and doing okay and that they think we're okay now, too." Solon's voice trailed off as he fell deeper into thought.

"We have to stay longer. That's all there is to it," I said.

"It'll be risky," Solon said. "We're gonna have to make sure we don't do anything to make the bad hurricane return. We definitely have to remember not to even think about wanting to live on Earth again. You know, it won't be easy to control our urge to be with Mom and Dad for good again."

"That's for sure. I miss them so much."

After a few seconds, Solon said softly to himself, as if midthought, "But we can't. At least, I don't think we can . . . " He sat thinking a bit longer, and then his face lit up a bit. "Maybe there's a way to leave behind a part of our spirit to stay with them for good, to be with them for as long as they live." Clearly, he was excited at this new idea.

I thought about it for a while. It would certainly help Mom and Dad if they could feel our spirits present, and it would even help to comfort Solon and me because we would feel more connected to Mom and Dad from here.

"That's it," I said. "Maybe that's what happened when we touched objects when we were alive. Maybe some part of our spirit stayed with the objects. Maybe we can touch objects on Earth this time as spirits and leave part of each of our spirits with those objects. Heck. Maybe if we hug Mom and Dad in a certain way, part of our spirit will stay with them forever and comfort them," I said.

Solon sounded quite encouraged by this. "That way, we can stay with them for eternity, don't you think? And after they die, then we'll meet each of them in the tunnel, just like Amanda met us, and we'll all be together again," He sat thinking and his face slowly fell. "It's a nice idea, but do you think it's possible?"

"Well, maybe," I said, "and the only way we'll know is if we get on with it and get back to Earth to try it out. Are you ready?"

"But shouldn't we make a plan first? What are we gonna do when we get there?" Solon asked.

"Let's just go. We can't plan out every last detail. We never know what's going to happen until it happens. We'll figure it out as we go, and we have lots of good ideas to help us now. Let's go."

Solon said, "Okay, fine. Let's go now."

I raised both of my arms, palms to the sky, hoping to call the eagles. Solon followed suit, and both eagles appeared out of nowhere and landed beside us. We climbed on, hugged their necks, and leaned forward.

"Think about Dad reading to us during the bedtime routine on the couch," I said. We both closed our eyes and pictured the scene, and the eagles took off.

Before we knew it, we were standing in the family room of our home looking straight at the couch. Mom and Dad were sitting there watching some TV show. If Solon and I were alive, we would have definitely blocked their view. Out of habit, we stepped aside.

SOLON

Cool! Mom and Dad are watching an action flick. I love action flicks!

"Hey," Liam said, heading for the stairs. "I'll race you!"

I definitely wasn't in the mood for a race, but I made my way upstairs anyway, knowing that as much as I wanted to watch that movie, I'd better not because we had work to do while Mom and Dad were focused downstairs and I definitely didn't want to cause a storm.

When I floated into the kitchen, Liam was already sitting at the open Macbook Pro.

"Check it out," he said, pushing the computer over to me without touching it. "The folder of dreams has two new files in it. This one's titled 'Dream of Older Liam'. Read it."

I read:

An older, high-school-aged Liam was beside me in a group of other high school kids. I was eating a Ben and Jerry's Peace Pop. Liam came over and stood beside me, sneaking bites of my Peace Pop and laughing about it and running away. I kept acting like I was upset and he should get his own, but I really was not upset to share with him. I was having fun acting offended at his sneaky thievery. He knew that, and he just kept at it while I pretended to be upset.

"That sure is a weird dream. Is this anything close to what you were imagining and trying to send when we sent dream visions last time we were here?" I asked.

"A little, but not much. I pictured me sitting peacefully on a bench eating an ice cream cone dipped in chocolate. I figured since Mom and Dad know how much I love ice cream they'd know I was okay and doing something I love. I certainly wasn't stealing ice cream in my vision, though it does sound like something I would've done to Mom or Dad while I was alive," Liam said with a grin.

"What's the other dream in the folder?" I asked, hoping that somehow my visions got through a little too.

"It's titled, 'Solon Dream.' I haven't read it yet. Let's look at it together," Liam said.

I was in the basement of a house we were looking at for possible purchase. Chris was upstairs looking around and I was checking out the basement for some reason. This basement was huge with a bike track around the outside edge of it. There were lots of guys down there racing their bikes, and they were encouraging me to race too, but I just watched. The owner of the house came around the corner, and he was all scraped up and on crutches. He was crying, so I went over to him and gave him a hug, and, though I did not know what had happened, I tried to comfort him. I asked him what had happened, and he couldn't really tell me through his tears. I said "It looks like you were down here racing and having fun with your friends and you crashed." He said yes, that a lot of them had crashed. I asked him if other friends were hurt too, and he said yes. Then, from behind the owner of the house, Solon stepped out of nowhere. I said, "Oh my gosh, Solon, come here. I haven't seen you in so long. Did you have fun?" It was as if I thought he had been away at camp or something. He said, "Hi Mom. Yes, definitely. I had fun." I rushed over to him and gave him a huge hug and told him it was great to see him again. He told me it was great to see me again, too. I told him I missed him and that it was great to have him home. Then I asked him if he had seen his Dad yet. "Did you give him a hug too?" I asked him. He told me he had seen him upstairs and had given him a hug before he came downstairs. Then I woke up.

"I guess we know Mom had this dream," I said.

"Yep. Is that anywhere close to what you were visualizing and trying to push into her head?" Liam asked.

"I was visualizing having fun riding my bike in circles in the driveway without falling down and crashing. I figured that might be a good way to show Mom that I'm okay now. You remember how in the summer and fall before we died I crashed in the driveway two different times and scraped myself up pretty badly? My second fall, doing super-tight turns, I hurt my leg so much that Mom took me to the emergency room. Remember that?" I asked.

"Yeah," Liam said. "It seems like what we tried to force into Mom and Dad's heads might have reached them a little, but these dreams aren't exactly what we thought they'd be. Why?"

"Who knows? Mom and Dad have lots of other images and emotions they're dealing with too, so maybe the dream becomes some sort of a combination of what we try to send and how they're feeling. Does that make any sense?" I asked.

"I guess. I suppose the Peace Pop in the Liam dream is like the ice cream cone with chocolate on it. And the whole idea of me being at peace seems to have gotten through if you take that 'Peace' name literally. But isn't it interesting that Mom imagined me at an older age? I was just imagining me at ten years old, the age I was when we died. But in Mom's mind, I was fifteen years old." Liam was quiet again.

"Yeah. In the dream with me, I wasn't the one riding the bike and having fun. Other guys were racing around that indoor bike track, and one of them was severely injured. Then I stepped out from behind him, totally uninjured, telling Mom I missed her and that I had fun while I was gone. I guess Mom might have got the sense from this dream that I'm okay. Don't you think?" I asked.

"Probably," Liam said "but it's another case of what we tried to push into her head changing into something different. I bet you're right that the dreams just became a combination of what we tried to push into their heads and how they were feeling at the time.

"Any other dreams in that folder?" I asked.

"Nope. Only these two. That's better than nothing, though. I think we're making progress on this communicate-with-Mom-and-Dad thing, don't you?" Liam asked.

"Yep. But we still have a long way to go to make sure they know we're okay," I said.

"I'm going back downstairs. I bet the movie's almost over, and I wanna watch what Mom and Dad'll do after it ends," Liam said. I followed him down. He was right. The movie was almost over. The lead actors were kissing and then the credits came on. Mom leaned over and she gave Dad one, big, passionate kiss. Liam and I both said "yuck" and hid our faces at exactly the same time the way we always had when they kissed in front of us before. The timing of our display of disgust cracked us up. I guessed it was good to know that Mom and Dad were still in love even with all the stress they were under.

Dad shut off the TV and pulled out the DVD while Mom gathered the dishes from the coffee table. It looked as if Mom and Dad had eaten dinner in the family room in front of the TV. That's something we rarely did as a family because Mom and Dad felt that eating dinner in the dining room together every night was very important to our family health. Around the dinner table, we talked about our days, shared highs and lows, laughed, and joked around. Liam and I would pull a fair amount of crap every now and then to be sure Mom and Dad were paying attention to us. We would use potty-talk (a funny term from our younger years), throw a pea or two . . . just kid stuff. It was never fun to be sent away from the table, but Mom and Dad insisted that our mealtimes be pleasant for all.

For all the dinners we had upstairs, there was one down-stairs dinner I very clearly recalled because it was *so* much fun. Mom was in a crazy mood one day and decided to throw a Simpsons Movie party for the family. She rented *The Simpsons Movie*, bought some root beer and frosted doughnuts with sprinkles, and made sure there was some beer on hand for her and Dad. She grilled hamburgers and hotdogs, and we ate in front of the movie before consuming our dessert, doughnuts with tons of sugar, just the way Homer Simpson likes them. Mom was so tired that after she finished eating, she fell asleep on the couch. The movie was so, so funny, and Liam and I joked around with Dad for many months, repeating funny lines from that movie with a Homer or Bart Simpson accent. Mom felt a little out of the loop, but she still laughed and said she was glad we enjoyed the party. It was out of character for Mom to share a movie like that with us, but that's part of what made it so fun. And hearing Dad laugh so much . . . that was the best.

Mom and Dad headed upstairs. Liam, always curious, followed. I stayed downstairs to look around my room again. Nothing had moved since my last visit, except maybe the pillow on the bed, but only slightly. I recalled how Mom had kissed it and said good-night to me the last time Liam and I were back to visit. I thought back to how that paper heart felt in my hand in our afterlife, so warm and comforting, and suddenly I was curious if my pillow might feel that good. I stood beside the bed and reached out my hand to touch my pillow. My spirit hand traveled right though it, and my forearm was nowhere to be seen, but the pillow stayed intact as if nothing had touched it. It was weird—I didn't feel that overwhelming warmth and comfort like I had with the heart. Weirder still, I felt a pulsing travel through my arm and extend through my spirit body. It was a slight expansion and contraction as though the pillow was breathing or maybe something was circulating in it. It felt comfortable, like a little massage. I left my hand in place for a while to see if the feeling changed. The pillow gradually lit up as though a dimmer switch were being turned up. As the light brightened, the pulsing of the pillow quickened. It was beginning to freak me out a bit, so I yanked my hand out of the pillow. Suddenly, the light disappeared and both the room and the pillow looked as they had when I entered the room. The pulsing in my spirit arm was gone too. What had just happened? I ran upstairs (well, floated quickly, actually) to find Liam and tell him what had happened.

Liam wasn't in the kitchen or living room, so I went back to Mom and Dad's bedroom to search for him. As I made my way down the hallway, I could hear the water running in their bathroom. Mom and Dad were probably getting ready for bed and brushing their teeth. When I floated through the closed bedroom door, I found Liam standing in front of the wooden boxes that held our ashes. My urn was glowing like the pillow had been glowing only moments before.

"You gotta come see what I discovered!" I exclaimed.

"Check this out. Your urn is glowing. It just lit up while I was standing here," he said.

"Did you touch it?"

"No. A few minutes ago it slowly started to glow. It became brighter and brighter. It's so bright beside mine, you'd think it'd be hard to look at, like the sun. But it's not hard to look at, not at all. It feels good. It kind of reminds me of the light we saw at the end of the tunnel after we died and of the way our afterlife looks with all that comfortable light bathing us." Liam was in awe staring at the urns. "I don't wanna take my eyes off your box. How come mine's not lit up like that?"

"I think I know," I said. "Follow me. You gotta see this. It's amazing!"

We floated quickly downstairs to my room, and I showed him what happened when I touched my pillow. "That's amazing!" Liam said. " I gotta see if it'll work with my pillow." He raced into his room with me following closely and pushed his hand through his pillow. His eyes bugged out as he looked at me. "It's pulsing, and the pulsing gets stronger as the light gets brighter. Incredible! What's happening?"

"Take your hand out and watch," I told him. When his hand came out, the light suddenly disappeared. "Now let's go upstairs and see if your urn's lit up like mine." We raced upstairs, floated though the door into the bedroom, and saw that both urns were shining so brightly that the entire room was bathed in that same comforting light.

Just then, Mom came out of the bathroom. Oh, crap, I thought. She would know we'd been up to something. The room was so bright that it was like the sun had parked itself right inside it! But Mom just went about her business as if nothing at all were different. Clearly she couldn't see all of the light. Liam and I were in another dimension or across some horizon for sure.

In front of her dresser, Mom removed the necklace she was wearing, kissed the locket on one side and then the other, and put it into her jewelry box. It was the same necklace I had seen her wearing the last time we had returned to Earth. She looked down at the children's book resting on the dresser top titled Love You Forever, hummed the tune she used to sing to us, and then placed her hands on each of our urns. She breathed in deeply and slowly twice. Finally, she sat on the side of her bed, said goodnight to Pooh, Tigger, Panda and Penguin, and then turned off the light. A little while later, Dad came out of the bathroom and crawled into bed beside Mom. They hugged and kissed goodnight.

"What now?" Liam asked.

But before I could answer, Mom cursed and climbed out of bed. "I forgot to let the cats in."

"I'll get them," Dad said.

"No need. I'm up, and I want to visit the boys' rooms again," Mom said.

Mom called for the cats from inside the screen of the sliding glass door. Coco came right away, but Spurs was nowhere to be seen. Mom led Coco downstairs with a can of cat food in hand. Liam and I followed. After feeding Coco, Mom went through our complete night-time routine just as she did every night, using our pillows in place of us. It was so comforting to hear it. If it felt anywhere near as good to her as it did to me, it's no wonder she still goes through the motions of this routine every night in our absence. I noticed, this time, she didn't cry one drop. Maybe she was just too tired and ready for bed. Maybe she was getting used to the fact that she had to kiss pillows instead of kissing Liam and me. Or ... maybe ... No, I thought. That couldn't be. Well, I guess *maybe* she could somehow feel Liam and my spirit more now that we put our spirit arms through those pillows. There was no way to know, short of asking her, and we both knew that wasn't possible.

"Notice Mom didn't cry this time? I wonder if somehow she felt our spirits," I said.

"Maybe," was all Liam could say. The downtrodden look on his face told me he was feeling sad.

"Oh, no. Be careful, Liam! Think some happy thought about our afterlife. Try thinking about playing catch with Amanda in that beautiful field, or meeting Misty and the other dead animals you loved so much. Don't start longing for Earth so much that we can't stay longer. Please. We really need to stay for a while longer," I said.

Liam closed his eyes and was quiet. When he eventually opened them again, I was eager to hear what he was thinking.

"That helped," Liam said, looking at me. "Thanks."

On the way back upstairs Mom let Spurs in. We followed her to her bedroom and watched her climb into bed again. Dad was just falling asleep and it didn't take long for Mom's breathing to slow, a clear sign that she also was asleep.

"Let's get outta here and talk about everything that just happened to try to make sense of it," I suggested. The urns were still glowing brightly as Liam followed me into the living room.

"Would you look at that?" Liam pointed to a deck of cards sitting on the end table. "We could play some rummy!" Rummy was, without question, our favorite family card game. We often played it after dinner. Dad's the one who started that tradition. Nana, (Nanny's Mom), taught Dad how to play when he was young. With Dad's instruction, Liam and I had become pretty good players, if I do say so myself. Sometimes we even beat Dad and Mom. Whenever Liam or I won a hand, it wasn't just the luck of the draw, but skillful card selection that led us to victory, we figured.

"Yep. You're always up for a game," I said. "Hate to spoil your fun, but I don't wanna play now. I wanna talk first and see if we can work anything new out," I said.

"What's there to discuss? We touched the pillows and they lit up and pulsed. Then, the urns lit up. Pretty cool, huh?! Seems like we were able to connect our spirits to the pillows." Liam took two cards and propped them up against one another using only his mind. No hands.

"Yeah. But why would the urns light up?" I asked. "That part's confusing." Liam didn't seem all that interested in figuring it out right now. He was more interested in trying to control the cards to build a card house. Of course he had to do this with only the power of his mind, and it was quite the scene. He would get pretty far along, and then the whole thing would collapse into a pile just as card houses had in real life. But I had to hand it to Liam. He kept right on trying.

After a while, I asked, "Do you think somehow there's a

connection between our spirits and the objects we were close to in our lives, like the pillows? Do you suppose that's why the pillow lit up when we tried to touch it—because there's already some connection between our spirit and the pillow from our lifetime?"

"Maybe," Liam answered as he continued to try to build the card house. "That might mean that if I try to put my hand through this card, it, too, will light up and pulse like the pillow did." He reached his spirit arm out, and his hand went right through the card. The card seemed to light up a tiny bit, but it was nothing like the bright light of the pillows. It sure did look strange to see Liam there with his arm halfway through the card.

"Feel anything?" I asked. "Is it pulsing?"

"Nope, no pulsing. And, it's hardly lit up at all. I wonder why."

"Well, I don't know about you, but I sure was more attached to my pillow than to that deck of cards," I said. "My pillow traveled with me to summer camp and sleepovers, and it always felt so good to rest my head on it at night. Maybe somehow more of our spirits are locked into the pillows because we spent so much time with them? You know, sleep is a big part of everyday living for people. Card playing's not."

"True. But why'd the urns light up? Our spirit hands went right through the pillows, and then the urns lit up all the way upstairs without our touching them. What's up with that?" Liam asked. I was glad his interest was sparked and glad that I was no longer be the only one who was curious about the stuff we'd seen here.

"Well, I don't know. That's confusing." I thought for a while. What are urns? What's in them? How might they connect to the our lifetimes and the objects we had been close to?

"Do you suppose it has anything to do with the fact that the body and the spirit are connected?" I asked. "You know. Mom used to tell us that the body and mind are connected, the mind can help the body be healthier, and all that crap. Well, if the body and mind are connected like she said, then it would make sense that the spirit is connected to the body, too."

"Okay. But how exactly does that relate to the urns?" Liam wanted to know.

"Well, the urns hold our ashes, and the ashes are all that remains from our bodies. So, if there's some connection between body, spirit, and the objects we were attached to when we were alive, then it would make sense that our urns lit up when we touched the pillows. It's all connected."

"Yeah. When we were alive, we each had a body, a mind, and a spirit. And now we're just spirits without bodies," Liam said. We both sat quietly pondering all of this.

"But maybe as spirits each of us still has a mind, or something like it, since we're able to communicate with each other and think through things like this," I said.

"Yeah. I guess."

"And I think we're getting closer to being able to comfort Mom and Dad and help them understand we're okay now."

"How?" Liam asked.

"Well, it seems we got through to them a little bit by forcing visions into their dreams. Now we're figuring out a body–spirit–object connection, or at least we think we are. Maybe we can use that to comfort them somehow," I said.

"And how on Earth do you propose we do that?"

"I don't know yet. Give me some time."

Liam kept right on trying to build that card house as I watched and thought, and Mom and Dad slept the night away in the next room. The card house never became as large as the one Liam and I had built together in our lifetimes, but it sure was cool looking. There was no doubt in my mind Liam was feeling proud of himself.

LIAM

SINCE I NO longer needed to sleep, nights on Earth always seemed long but I kept myself busy building for quite some time. When I'd had enough of the card house, I floated into the kitchen to look again at the iPod. I turned it on and looked at the song list again in search of anything that might work to send messages to Mom and Dad or whoever else happened to listen to it. I was determined to keep Solon and me from going back to our after-lives yet, so I didn't listen to a single song. When Solon came into the kitchen, he told me he had gone into Mom and Dad's bedroom again. Apparently, they were still sleeping, and the urns were just as brightly lit as before. It was weird.

"What do you think would happen if we tried putting our arms through this iPod?" I asked. "Neither of us used it in our lifetimes, but the song list is ours. Do you think it'll recognize our spirits somehow and light up even though we never touched it in life?"

"Your guess is as good as mine. We could try and see. Think anything bad'll happen?" Solon wondered aloud.

"Let's each try to put a finger through it at the same time and see what happens," I said, feeling daring.

We each stuck our misty, see-through index fingers into the iPod screen with the playlist on display. Nothing at all happened: there was no bright, heavenly light; no pulsing or throbbing; and no tunes. No nothing. We pulled our fingers out.

"Shoot," Solon said. "It doesn't seem to recognize us."

"Maybe something happened and we just can't see it yet." I said.

"Like what?"

"Well, like maybe it'll somehow choose the right songs for Mom or Dad when they listen to it. That's what we want to happen, so maybe it'll just happen," I said.

"That's ridiculous. How's the iPod gonna know the 'right' song? We haven't even looked at the list to know if there even are any songs there that'll send the messages we wanna send. Come on. Be serious."

"I know. But maybe now that we've put our spirit fingers through it, somehow the music that comes on when they listen to it will comfort Mom or Dad as it plays. Isn't that what we're aiming for anyway? We don't want them feeling so sad and disconnected from us. We want them to feel that we're okay now," I said.

"Yeah. But that sounds like a long shot," Solon said doubtfully. "I'm going back into Mom and Dad's bedroom to see if I can send them another vision for a dream. Come try again with me."

"Okay. It can't hurt," I said as I followed him into the bedroom. When we got there, I was surprised to see that Mom laying awake in bed, clearly agitated and upset. Her eyes were closed, but tears were streaming down her face. I hated seeing Mom cry, and I desperately wanted to cheer her up somehow. But how?

An odd looking contraption—a small, electronic box about twice the size of a matchbox—rested on her stomach. It had a little green light on it that alternately lit up on one side of the box and then on the other. When I looked closer, I could see that there was a black cord extending from the end of the box. The cord split, and Mom was holding something attached to each end of that split cord in the clenched fist of each hand. How odd.

"What on earth's that thingy?" I asked Solon. "I've never seen anything like it. Why is she holding it?"

"I have no idea." We both watched as Mom's breathing slowly changed from very rapid and uneven to slow and steady. Gradually, she stopped crying, and her body seemed to relax. After a while, she unclenched her fists, got up and went into the bathroom for a drink of water. While she was away, Solon and I looked more closely at the round things she had held in each hand.

"It looks like it's some sort of vibrating thingy," Solon said. "It sends a vibration through the cord to this round thing on the end. And look. It alternates from one side to the other. She must feel it vibrate in one hand and then in the other hand when she clenches these in her fists like she was. Why do you think she does that?"

"I don't know," I said, "but it must have something to do with how upset she was. It seemed to help calm her down. Maybe she had a bad dream, and this thingy somehow helped her relax."

"Maybe," Solon said.

I could only imagine the dreams she would have been having after living through that fire. As Mom walked back to her bed, she said quietly under her breath, "I love you boys so much. I'm so sorry we couldn't get you out. I'm so, so sorry." She started to cry. Shocked, Solon and I looked at one another.

"Does she know we're here?" Solon asked with a look of surprise and excitement.

"MOM. We're here! We heard you! We're right here! We're okay!" I said. There was no sign that she heard me, of course. Solon's face showed disappointment again.

Mom turned on her machine thingy again and lay there holding the ends. Gradually, she stopped crying and relaxed. Her breathing slowed. She was falling asleep again, but before she did, she turned off the machine, set it on the nightstand, and rolled over. Within only a few minutes, she was sound asleep.

"Whatever that electronic thingy is, it seems to comfort her,"

Solon said. "She must be having nightmares. She and Dad were trying to help us find a way out of the house, but we both died. It must have been so unbelievably scary and traumatizing for her."

"Do you suppose that's what this electronic thingy is for, to help Mom deal with those difficult fire thoughts?" I asked.

"Probably," Solon said.

We stood there, uncertain what to do since that Mom was sleeping soundly. "Should we try to send her dreams again?" I asked.

"That's a good idea. Let's try." We both went silent and concentrated hard.

Before I got too far in my vision, I started to wonder if Solon and I would confuse Mom by both sending her visions at the same time. Or, on the other hand, maybe we would both end up in the same dream somehow, our two visions merging into one. We continued to concentrate on sending Mom visions for a while, and then we switched over to Dad. We worked at sending Dad visions for a long time. When I finally got bored, I headed over to the Mom's dresser again.

On the way, I noticed a black sweatshirt folded up on the corner of her dresser and a green one on the opposite corner. "Check this out! Mom has my black Vans sweatshirt over here and your green South Pole sweatshirt over here. I wonder why they're not downstairs in our rooms."

"I guess she wants 'em close," Solon said. "I'm not surprised. Remember when she bought 'em for us on our fall shopping trip to JC Penney? We fell in love with them then, and from that day on wore them almost every day. Mine was the first sweatshirt I ever wore regularly to school when it was cold out. Before that, I never really liked wearing sweatshirts. Too warm."

Mom's jewelry box sat in the center of her dresser between

where my sweatshirt and Solon's sweatshirt lay. Seeing it there gave me an idea.

"You know that necklace Mom wears now, the one we've seen her in both times we returned to Earth? I wanna see what's in it." I concentrated hard on opening the top of her wooden jewelry box with my mind. The locket was right where she had left it that night. It took all the strength I could muster to lift the locket out of the box, suspend it in midair, and force it open with my mind.

"Help me out here, will you," I said. "This is really hard to open." We both concentrated, and very gradually, the locket opened up. There were two face shots: one of a smiling Solon, and one of me grinning from ear to ear.

"I guess Mom really wants us to stay close, huh?" Solon said.

"Yep. From what we've seen, it looks like she wears this every day," I replied.

"Hey," Solon said. "What do you think'll happen if we try to touch each of our photos? Do you think they'll light up like the pillow? Maybe it'll be like the iPod, and nothing would happen."

"I bet nothin'll happen just like with the iPod. I don't remember Mom ever having this necklace and these tiny pictures of us before. So if we didn't have any connection to this necklace when were alive, my guess is that we won't feel any connection or see any light."

"I'm gonna try anyway. Do you wanna try with me?" Solon asked.

We each reached out a spirit pointer finger and pushed them through each of our photos. At first, nothing happened. There was no pulse or light. But as I tried to pull my finger out, I noticed that two tiny lights the size of the heads of pencil erasers remained on my photo. The lights covered the sides of my head. Boy, did my photo look funny then.

"Check it out!" I said.

"That's weird. I didn't feel anything, did you?" Solon remarked. He was looking curiously at the tiny lights that remained over his picture, too.

"Nope." I looked over at the urns to see if maybe they were casting an even brighter light in the room, but their light wasn't any different. I looked back at our photos again, and the lights over the sides of our heads remained. I started to wonder if the little lights would ever fade. Uh-oh!

"How do we get 'em off there?" I asked. "What if Mom notices? If we messed up her photos of us, she's gonna be really mad."

"Relax. You're thinking in the mode of a living person. She's not gonna see anything. Remember, she doesn't even notice she's sleeping in a room fully lit by our urns. How do you suppose she'll notice these lights on our pictures?"

"I guess you're right," I said with a sigh of relief. "Let's put it away now."

"Yeah." We worked our mind-magic to close it. After we had placed the necklace into the jewelry box, we closed the lid a little too abruptly. Neither Mom nor Dad moved a muscle, but Spurs, the cat, who was asleep between Mom and Dad, clearly heard it. His head rose as his eyes popped open and his ears perked up. He jumped down from the bed and padded over to the dresser, hoping to hear another noise. I bet he thought some small animal he should chase was prowling around on the dresser. Solon and I both reached out to pat Spurs, but our hands stopped about two inches from him, as if there were a wall preventing us from getting any closer. Solon called out Spurs's name, but Spurs gave zero indication that he had heard a thing. He jumped up onto the dresser top and stalked slowly around, sniffing madly. When finally he was convinced that no small animal was there for the hunt, he tiptoed his way across the second dresser, the one with the urns. It seemed that the cat couldn't see the bright light and had about as much awareness of our presence as Mom and Dad did. He settled back onto the base of Mom and Dad's bed and curled up to sleep again.

Solon and I spent the rest of the dark night in the family room looking at the memorabilia from our lifetimes and reminiscing about the good ole times we had had with Mom and Dad. Whenever we started to get sad or feel the urge to return to our past lives, we gave a signal and started to talk about the wonders of our afterlives. It worked. We weren't carried away by bad weather the entire night.

I was amazed as I looked around at the toys and thought about all the things we each had saved in our rooms—the memorabilia. It was the only "stuff" that Mom and Dad had left of us. That, and photos of our time spent together. It didn't seem like much. I wondered how that must have felt for Mom and Dad. The emptiness must have been awful. If one of them had died when I was alive, it would've been nearly impossible for me.

"Let's go look again at the MacBook Pro and see what other things Mom's been writing. Maybe that'll give us some ideas of how we can help 'em." I said.

We wandered up to the kitchen table, opened the computer, and then clicked on the folder called "Memories of Solon and Liam." Whoever was writing that was keeping a log of the memories about Solon and me and our family times together. It was quite a long file, and reading it kept Solon and me busy for a long time. The sun began to rise and light came into the windows, and then we heard someone moving around in the bedroom. Not wanting to be caught in the act, I closed the file, closed the computer, and waited for whoever was getting up to come to the kitchen for breakfast.

SOLON

DAD CAME OUT of the bedroom and headed straight to the kitchen cupboard. He pulled out the Fig Newtons and the almond butter, grabbed a knife from the drawer, spread the almond butter on two Fig Newtons, and then carried them to his computer. If Liam were alive, he would have been begging for a Fig Newton with almond butter too. I only would've wanted a Fig Newton. As far as I was concerned, those two could keep their almond butter for themselves.

Dad's work laptop, a seventeen-inch MacBook Pro, rested at the opposite end of the table from the thirteen-inch MacBook Pro Liam and I had just been using. Dad sat in front of his computer as he ate his "neutrons," checked his email, and dealt with replies. It seemed he was on the computer for quite some time before he finally got up and made himself his real breakfast—a mix of cereals topped with almonds and raisins.

Eventually, long after Dad was done with his breakfast but while he was still sitting and working at his computer, Mom finally came out of the bedroom and kissed him good morning. She was wearing Liam's black Vans sweatshirt. I wondered if Mom alternated wearing Liam's sweatshirt and my sweatshirt on different days, and I thought that maybe that's why she left them folded on her dresser.

Liam and I hung around watching as Mom and Dad went about their morning routines. When Mom finished her breakfast, she and Dad started to discuss plans for the day. Clearly, this was a weekend day, because Dad was home and ready to do some non-work activity. Or . . . I suppose Dad might have been taking some time off from work after what happened to us. Oh, how I wished there was an easy way to know the date.

It dawned on me that the computer could tell us the day's date. I snuck over beside Dad and looked in the corner of his computer. It said it was Saturday and gave the time, but there was no date. In order to see the date, I would need to open the dashboard icon.

"Hey. We can get today's date off the little MacBook," I said. "There's a calendar on the dashboard. But we'll have to wait 'til Mom and Dad are gone or they'll see the computer open up. Man, that sure could freak 'em out. They have enough to deal with."

"Great idea," Liam said. He extended his hand for a high five. I was happy to give him one, but our hands just passed right through one another. We both chuckled.

Mom and Dad considered what they would do during the weekend without us. They spoke for a while about how sad the evenings and weekends had become because it was just too quiet. Then Mom groaned and talked quietly through tears about how hard the approaching summer would be. As a schoolteacher, she spent her summers with us, working very little. I imagined that she'd really miss us then. Ugh. My heart went out to both Mom and Dad. It felt so frustrating to be standing right there beside them without them recognizing me and feeling me near.

"Ugh! What can we do to help 'em?"

"Shhhhhh . . . listen to Mom."

I listened. Mom was recalling what had happened while she was sleeping last night.

"It was awful, so I used the tappers and thought about my sanctuary. That worked. I calmed down again and eventually fell asleep."

"Dear, you need to wake me when this happens so I can hold you," Dad said. "I want to help."

"I know you do. But, I don't want to wake you up. You need your sleep as much as I need mine—even more than me since you have a job. And I am not sure how much good it would do us to lie awake talking about the fire again and again. I'm worried I'll just keep crying and feeling awful, and, in the process, I'll suck you down and send you back to the fire, too. You don't need that." They were both quiet for a while.

"You know I think of the fire all the time too. I want to help you," Dad explained.

"I know you do," Mom said, and she paused. "And you do help. Believe me. You do help me just by being with me and holding me during the day like you are now. I don't know what I'd do without you. When I was trying to fall asleep after I was calm again, I kept telling the boys I was sorry we couldn't save them." She started to cry again. Dad held her tightly in his arms and kissed her on the side of her head as she buried her face in his chest.

"I know. We did absolutely everything we could have done to save them," Dad said. "They were taken from us."

"I still can't believe it happened. I can't believe they're gone."

"Neither can I."

"What did we do to deserve this?" Mom asked, crying again.

Dad told Mom that it had just been some rotten luck and that there was nothing anyone could have done to change it. We were just in the wrong place at the wrong time.

Sniffling, Mom said, "You know, on a happier note, I had what I think ended up being a pretty good dream right before I woke up this morning."

Liam and I looked at one another. Hopefully, that was because of us...

"All four of us were on a motorboat traveling around a bay. Somehow the boat started taking on water and we needed to put on these special rescue suits, all of us. After we helped the boys put on their rescue suits, we all got into the water. We were climbing onto the side of the boat trying to tilt the boat down so that we could start to bail it out. For some reason, we all needed to get back in the boat at one point to continue bailing. While we were in the boat, we noticed that there were these enormous great white sharks swimming all around us. There were lots of people swimming in the water, but the sharks were completely avoiding them and just swimming around our boat. Then I realized that we had to get back into the water and do something to stop the leak from the outside or the boat would sink, taking all of us down with it. Before we all got back in the water, I remember being totally paranoid that Solon and Liam would get eaten by a shark, and I didn't want to let them out of my sight. We all got in the water because we had to in order to fix it. Even though I tried to keep an eye on the boys when we were in the water, somehow they became separated from us and I became incredibly scared. I thought the sharks had eaten them. At the end of the dream, you and I were sitting in the boat, sad as ever, and the boys came riding back toward us on the backs of two sharks. The sharks had not eaten them at all. Instead, the boys came back to the boat riding on the sharks, happy as can be. I was totally shocked and very relieved. Then I woke up."

When Mom had finished the tale, Mom and Dad held one another tightly. "It sure would be nice if they could come back to us," Dad said, looking sad.

"Did you hear that?" I asked. "Maybe forcing our dreams into their heads last night worked. In the end of Mom's dream, we turned out okay, didn't we? We were safe!"

"Yeah. True. It doesn't seem like they feel that much better, though, does it?" Liam asked.

"No. I suppose not. There's got to be some other, more direct way to tell them we're okay and to help them be less sad," I said.

When they were done talking, Dad sat back down at his computer and Mom went into the bedroom. Liam and I followed her. The room was still lit by this intensely beautiful light from the urns. Mom went to her jewelry box and put on her necklace. That's when I noticed she was crying again. Her sobs got louder, and she held her hands in her face. Slowly, she walked over to the urns and laid her arms over them, and then she put her face in her hands and leaned over the urns. Instantly, her breathing slowed and she stopped crying. She stayed there bent over the urns for a while, silently calming herself. When she eventually lifted her head and stood up, she kept a hand on the top of each urn. That's when I realized she was beginning to glow a little. Somehow the light from the urn was flowing through her and shining from her. As soon as she took her hands away from the urn, the glow around her was gone.

"Did you see that?" I asked. "Mom was glowing!"

"I didn't see her glow, but I sure did see how much she relaxed and calmed down when she leaned over the urns. That was amazing. Somehow it comforted her big time," Liam said.

"I agree. But seriously, you didn't see that? When she was standing there with her hands on our urns, she was glowing a little, as though the energy from the light surrounded her and flowed through her when she touched our urns. I wonder if somehow this connection to that energy or spirit or whatever you wanna call it calms her down. Do you suppose that somehow when she touches our urns, she makes a connection with us and with the energy we see in our afterlives? Do you think maybe she feels more connected to us when she does this?" I asked.

"Jeez. That's pretty big. Who knows? I wish I could read her mind. I always have wanted to, but I can't. Can you?" Liam asked.

"Nope. Not that I know of," I said, "but that's not gonna stop me from trying," I said.

"I wonder if somehow kissing our pillows at night does the same thing. Do you suppose she's comforted by it because the pillows have our energy or spirit attached to them?" Liam asked.

"Good question. Those are the two things we've seen light up with that intensely beautiful light. I wonder..."

"Our photos in the necklace are lighting up a little too. But those lights are so tiny. Do you think they could bring much comfort?" Liam asked.

"I have no idea. We'll just have to keep our eyes and ears open and keep trying to figure it out." I said.

"Well I'm just glad to see there's something that brings Mom comfort in this new world of theirs. I hope Dad finds something that works for him too," Liam said.

Mom opened the lowest drawer of her dresser and removed her running shorts, shirt, and jog bra, clearly preparing to change for a run. That was odd considering we hadn't seen her run since she broke her leg in July. Throughout the fall before we died she was on crutches and visited the physical therapist regularly. If she was really getting ready to run, it meant her leg must have been well healed. Maybe she was just getting ready to go for a walk or something. Once again, I wondered about the day's date. How long ago was that fire? How long had Mom and Dad been trying to adjust to life without Liam and me, and how long had she been running for exercise again? Would she have been well enough to kick the soccer ball around or play catch with us if had still been alive?

Liam noticed what Mom was doing. "I'm outta here," he said. "Mom's about to change. You know the rules. Out we go." We left the room in a rush. Floating quickly down the hallway, we could hear music ahead. Turning into the kitchen, we saw Dad sitting at his computer, chin in hands, staring at the scene while a Ben Harper tune filled the room. Curious as always, Liam and I floated over and stood on either side of Dad checking out what he was up to.

"It's us!" Liam exclaimed. Sure enough, Dad was watching a slideshow of photos of me and Liam set to music. Liam and I watched as the photos and the music shifted. The screen displayed so, so many awesome memories of us growing up all set to some of Liam's and my favorite songs. The photos alternated from littlest and, sometimes, loudest Liam to little me. There were pictures from Wiscasset, Maine, Charlotte, Vermont, Ithaca, New York, Suffield, Connecticut, and Barre, Vermont, and some from our vacations, too. I don't know about Liam, but I was becoming more and more sad looking at the happy shots of our lifetime and thinking about how Dad must have been feeling watching it. Poor Dad. We had to figure out how we could help him know we were okay.

"Let's give Dad a group hug," I said. "He clearly needs one. He probably won't feel it, but at least we'll feel like we tried something. Please. I have to feel like we're at least trying to comfort him. Look how sad he is!" I pleaded.

"No need to beg. I love hugging Dad," Liam said as he reached his arms around Dad's neck. As expected, Liam's and my arms flowed right through Dad. He seemed not to notice and kept right on staring at the computer screen as Sarah McLachlan's "Answer" began to play and scenes of Liam and me on top of New Hampshire's Presidentials appeared. "Answer" always moved Mom to tears when we were alive, and she never understood why. When Amanda died, Mom decided we needed to play that song at her memorial service. And there the song was on our memorial slide show. Ugh.

If I had still been alive, tears would have been flowing from my eyes as the words of this song poured out of the computer. It was torture, standing next to Dad without being able to show him that we were there right next to him feeling sad and missing him and Mom more than ever.

Before I was fully aware of what I was doing, I started to visualize myself alive and well again. In my mind, Liam and I were back in our old bodies, hugging Dad for real. It felt so good, just like the hugs he gave us before we got on the school bus each morning had felt. Oh, how great it would have been to be back in our old bodies living with Dad and Mom again, right back where we were supposed to be in our loving family doing all of our fun family things together.

"Solon! Look out! We have to stop watching, NOW!" Liam yelled as he raced to the sliding glass door. I turned around and watched as a giant branch crashed down onto the deck. Liam and I could feel the whole house shake. When I turned back to look at Dad, he was acting as if nothing at all had happened. Oh, crap.

"It's weather from our other dimension," I yelled. "We have to get out of here and back to our afterlives, NOW!" The wind was whipping outside unlike any storm we had ever seen. I floated rapidly into the dining room, Liam at my heels, to look out over the hillsides at the weather.

"We've really done it now," Liam said with fear in his eyes. "Look! Not one, but two tornadoes, are coming our way. What do we do now? If we go outside, we could be swept away in this wind. Think of something. Quick! We have to do something to get back without being sucked up by the storms."

"Maybe the eagles are waiting for us on the deck," I yelled, running back toward the slider. But as I rounded the corner of the counter and looked out the slider, I saw the eagles lift off of the deck, feathers flying everywhere, struggling mightily against the strong wind.

"Quick! They're about to leave!"

Liam and I grabbed each other's hands, floated through the slider, and were immediately thrown up and over the deck railing into our playground thirty feet away. I turned to see the eagles in the distance flying away.

"Come back, eagles!" Liam yelled. "Come back! We need to go back to our afterlives. Please. Come back!" As Liam begged them, I lifted my arms in the air to call the eagles back, but they just kept flying away.

"Oh crap!" Liam said. "Think. Think. Think. How do we ride back to our afterlives now?" The wind speeds kept getting stronger, and it was making me feel we like we needed to find cover, and fast.

"We'd better get inside out of this wind," I yelled. We pushed hard, struggling against the blowing air to return to the deck. When we finally made it onto the deck, though, the house was nowhere to be seen. It was gone with the wind, or something.

"Where'd it go?" Liam asked with fear in his voice. "Where's the house? Where's Dad?"

"We're in another dimension," I answered. "Think fast before we end up in the wrong place in our afterlife. Quick. How else can we get back to the Enchanted Castle?"

"Maybe if we picture the castle in our heads like we did in that first field. Maybe then it'll appear," Liam said.

"But we're not in our afterlife now. We're stuck in some in-between or something. Let's try, but . . . "

We both closed our eyes, struggling against the wind, and pictured the castle at the edge of the field. "Look around. Do you see it?" I asked. We both looked all around.

"No castle, but look. That twister's almost here. What are we gonna do? I wish the eagles would come back."

"They can't fly in this wind. We'd need something monster-like to carry us out of here and keep us out of the tornados!"

"That's it!" Liam exclaimed with excitement. "We need a dragon! They're incredibly strong. A dragon could protect us."

"Great," I yelled over the howling wind. "And where will we find a dragon in this mess?"

"Remember the *Eragon* movie? Picture Saffira, the dragon, flying toward us. Picture us climbing on her back and riding back to our afterlife. Maybe it'll work!"

Ah, *Eragon*. Liam had been crazy about the *Inheritance Series* in his life. He had read and reread them so often that I lost count. His favorite book was *Brisinger*, the third in the series. He absolutely loved the tale and the dragon-riders and sword-wielding warriors who fought to rid the land of evil. I admit that I wasn't as crazy as Liam was about those books. I preferred mysteries and other, more realistic action stories. But the *Eragon* movie was good, and I have a pretty good picture of the dragon heroine in it. Still, I felt remarkably stupid closing my eyes and picturing a dragon that we could use to ride back to our afterlives. It sure beat standing there in the wind and waiting for the tornado to send us to a horrible, possibly evil part of our afterlives, though.

Liam yelled, "It worked!"

I have never seen Liam so excited. When the dragon descended through the harsh wind and landed beside the deck, Liam struggled over and stood in front of it. The dragon slowly lowered its head so that its eye was in front of Liam's face. As I approached, fighting the wind to stand cautiously beside Liam, it became clear that Liam was having some sort of silent conversation with this giant dragon. It reminded me of the *Eragon* movie. The dragon and the hero communicated with one another without saying a word aloud.

"This is not Saffira. Solon. Meet Baldash. Baldash, this is Solon, my brother," Liam said, as if the weather were totally pleasant and we were at a cocktail party drinking ginger ale.

"Can you take us back?" I asked the dragon. "*Now*, before the wind takes us?"

"He says he can, but we have to go now," Liam said.

"Twist my arm, would ya," I quipped. "How do I get onto this thing?" I asked looking up. Baldash took two giant steps backward in the wind, raised his head, and snorted fire into the sky. I jumped back as the blast of fire and heat washed over the top of me. Thank goodness I was not directly in front of that! As a spirit, I would have been blown to the next kingdom!

"Solon! Show some respect, would you? This isn't a *thing*! Baldash is a majestic dragon due far more respect than you're showing him. He tells me he doesn't like you and doesn't wanna carry you on his back 'cause you're rude. If you wanna stay with me and get back to our afterlives together, you'd better learn to be nicer to dragons, and *now*!" Liam yelled.

"Sorry," I said, looking at Baldash. "I didn't know whether you were a boy or a girl. I'll be nice if you can help me figure out how to get on top of you," I said.

"Solon! Are you losing your mind? You're a spirit now, not a human. Remember! Think about it, and do it fast! We have to go," Liam said. As he floated up onto Baldash's back, he turned to look at the twister just over the closest hill.

"Stop making me feel like a fool! I'm not stupid!" I yelled at Liam as I floated up and sat down behind him on Baldash.

"Hold on tight!" Liam said. Like he really had to tell me that. This dragon was twice as tall as our house (and where had that house gone, anyway?), with a head the size of a Tyrannosaurus Rex. Add the strong wind and the tornado to this picture, and, well, obviously I would hold on tightly to the dragon and to Liam so as not to fall or become separated from my little pest of a brother. We had to stick together.

Baldash took off, wings pumping, flying close to the ground. I looked down, marveling at the amazing wind patterns created in the tall grass of the farmer's field below as Baldash's giant wings worked to keep us afloat.

"Can you tell Baldash to fly a little higher, please?" I asked as we flew a healthy distance from the giant twister that threatened to send us to places we wanted to avoid. "Flying this close to the ground makes me nervous."

"What are you worried about? Dragons do this all the time," Liam said as if he knew everything there was to know about dragons. "It'll be okay. Remember how the horse that brought us back to Earth last time flew just above the water? That felt great, didn't it?"

"Yeah, but that was different. I knew that if we fell off, I might get back to Earth by breaking the surface of the ocean. If I fall off here over land, I'll probably break my spirit, not the water," I replied.

"Just relax, would ya?!"

I tried to settle in and enjoy the ride. It was all hard to believe. First we rode eagles, then we rode a pony, and then there we were, riding a giant dragon. "What's next?" I wondered aloud.

The dragon carried us over the mountains and down to Lake Champlain just like the eagles had done when we returned to our afterlife the last time. We flew along the surface of the lake for a bit, moving out over deeper water until Baldash suddenly shot skyward and then plummeted through the water's surface. Before we knew what had happened, we were standing on the bridge to the Enchanted Castle again with Baldash nowhere in sight. Phew.

If I could have somehow told that story to my still-alive friends, they would have never believed it. They surely would have thought I'd lost my marbles.

LIAM

"Where's Baldash?" I asked looking around and feeling sad that our precious dragon friend had left us.

"How am I supposed to know? I'm more concerned about where Dad and the house went. That was freaky! One minute we were in the house, and then we stepped out of it and it was gone."

"Must be that everything that happened outside the house happened in another dimension," I said.

"That was a really close call," Solon said wringing his hands. "What do we do now? I mean, we just barely made it back here. What if Baldash hadn't come? What then? What if next time we can't control ourselves, mess up again, and end up in that awful place in our afterlives for good? What then? That was so close!"

I was surprised to see Solon so worked up. "We shouldn't try to go back again right now," I said. "Let's take a breather for a bit. Aren't you thinking we should try to figure out what we learned from that trip and make a plan before we go back anyway? You're the one who loves to make a plan first." Solon just stared blankly at me for a bit, lost in thought.

"Besides," I said, "maybe we can learn something here from some other spirits—that is, if we find any." I thought about how nice it was to be with kid spirits my own age in that first field and how nice it would be to meet some other spirits so I didn't have only my brother to keep me company. "Where should we go now?"

"Nowhere. I just wanna sit here, rest, and collect my thoughts." Solon plopped down and threw his feet over the side of the bridge. With his legs dangling down, he rested his arms, one on top of the other, on the lowest railing of the bridge, set his chin on his folded arms, and looked out across the moat to the field beyond. Clearly Solon was enjoying the peace and quiet. It was a picture Mom and Dad would have loved to see—serene Solon deep in thought on the bridge in front of the Enchanted Castle. In some ways, this was a familiar scene: me wanting to go do something with friends, and Solon enjoying his quiet.

"It's so nice to be back in all this amazing castle light. It feels like nothing could possibly be better," he said, swinging his legs a little. "Everything feels nearly perfect now," Solon explained. "Almost . . . "

I sat down beside Solon. We sat still in silence for a long while, longer than I was used to sitting still, each of us in our own little world thinking. Eventually, Solon spoke.

"I know this sounds crazy, but I wonder if these storms keep bringing us back to the afterlife from Earth because, now that we're dead, we need to somehow keep connected to the energy in the afterlife in order for our spirits to continue. Like, maybe wishing we were human again isn't what makes the storm come. Maybe it's something different. Maybe the storm comes to save us, to return us here to recharge our energy so that our spirits stay alive. Maybe being on Earth after we've died is just too much of a drain for our spirit energy or something. Sounds a little far-fetched though, doesn't it?"

"I don't know. This whole experience feels out there. I mean, really: we died in a terrible house fire, we were escorted into our afterlife by our dead cousin, we met our Guiding Spirit, and we've traveled on animals to and from Earth three times now by crossing into some other dimension—or at least that's how we think it works. Last time we came back here riding a dragon! Come on. Does any of it make sense? This is like stuff out of the fantasy novels we used to read." I sat thinking about that and how it really did feel like a fantasy story I would have loved. It felt like some of the many great books we read and the places we traveled to in our minds.

We continued to sit in silence, thinking and soaking in the light. It was so peaceful. We were surrounded by complete silence, and golden light emanated from everything: the moat, the castle, the bridge, and even from Solon and me. I could feel that light filling me with more energy, pouring into me somehow.

"Hey," I said. "Here's a happy thought: maybe Mom and Dad can imagine us in our afterlife. Think about all the fantasies they read aloud with us—*The Dark is Rising* series, some of the *Harry Potter* books, *The Keys to the Kingdom* series, and so many more. I bet they worked up pretty healthy imaginations from all that reading aloud and that their imaginations'll help 'em through this somehow." I sat happily thinking about Mom and Dad imagining us in our afterlives.

"I bet you're right. I certainly hope they can use their imaginations to feel better somehow. I feel so sorry for them," Solon said, another sad look crossing his face.

"Me too." I sat and considered that for a bit. "I think somehow the things we've done on Earth since we died are helping them feel more connected to us. I'm not sure why or how. It's just . . . that's the way it feels. Must be my intuition or something." I said.

"I hope you're right," Solon replied. "My intuition isn't saying anything at all right now."

"Well, it seemed like sending them dream thoughts worked a bit," I said.

"Yeah. I guess. A bit." Solon replied, gently swinging his lower legs.

"And don't forget—that light from the urns seemed to help Mom calm down," I said.

"Yeah. I've been thinking about that. Wondering, really. Do

you suppose we left some added spirit energy with the urns, the pillows, and maybe even a tiny bit with Mom's locket?" Solon asked. "Do you think that our energy stayed there when we returned to this afterlife? Or do you think it's only there when we're there?"

"Jeez. I don't know. Probably we left it behind, but who knows?" I replied.

"Well, I'm thinking maybe that's why we needed to return to our afterlives. 'Cause if we gave away some spirit energy by being back on Earth, it would make sense that we needed to return to our afterlives to get a 're-charge' or something," Solon explained, "Wouldn't it?"

"Yeah, I guess. It seems clear that we can't just go back to Earth and stay there now that we're dead. But I sure do like the idea of leaving something behind there when we come back here," I said.

"Well, at least we left some things behind. All of the stuff we owned, wore, and played with. All the photos, and all the memories. It might not seem like much when our lives used to completely fill up their lives, but the things we left behind can help Mom and Dad, I expect. If any of the stuff weren't helpful, Mom and Dad would get rid of it, right? It sure does seem that photos help 'em. Our photos are everywhere!" Solon said.

"I know all that stuff is there. What I mean is, I like the idea of leaving behind some of this amazing afterlife light energy that is so soothing and comforting. Don't you think it would be good to have that stay with Mom and Dad to comfort them?" I said.

"Of course . . . if it can help them," Solon replied, "but it didn't seem that they saw the light the way we do here."

"True. But don't forget that it seemed to comfort Mom when she put her hands on the lit urns. She calmed right down. So maybe she doesn't need to see the light for it to help her," I said.

"That's true. And she didn't cry when she said goodnight to our pillows on our last visit," Solon remarked.

"I wonder if those little lights on our pictures in her locket necklace will give her any comfort. If she wears it every day, maybe," I thought aloud.

Solon was quiet for a bit. "Does any of this matter if the light doesn't stay behind when we go? I mean, seriously. We're trying to find ways to show Mom and Dad that we're okay here and bring them some comfort. And even if the light does stay behind, light doesn't really tell them that we're okay, does it? I mean, it isn't words." Solon was getting a little agitated. "I hope that light is as comforting for Mom and Dad as it is for us if it actually stays behind when we go," Solon said. "but it surely isn't a direct way to tell them that we're okay now." I could tell he was getting more and more frustrated by his inability to talk to Mom and Dad and tell them we were all right.

"I'm beginning to think that there may not be any direct way to show them that we're okay," I said. "But given Mom's reactions when she hugged the pillow goodnight and touched the urns, I do think that the things we did somehow helped them to feel more at peace."

"You might be right," Solon said, looking sad again. "I give up. This is all just so hard to figure out. I hope that the light helps them know that we are all right, but I am not convinced that's the case," Solon said.

"Well, maybe we can find the Guiding Spirit again and see if we can learn more somehow. It's worth a try," I said in an upbeat tone, trying to cheer him up.

"I think I would rather go back and visit Amanda and the girls from Barre. They might be able to help us," Solon said.

"Okay, whatever makes you happy bro'," I said, thrilled. "When do we go?"

"Give me a minute," Solon suggested. "I need more energy."

We rested on the bridge bathing in the light of the castle for what could easily have been another half of a day on Earth for all I knew. I was itching to get up and go but Solon, who must have totally exhausted himself on Earth this last time, just did not want to leave that bridge. Since he mentioned going to the first field, my thoughts were filled with small animals, Misty, my football, and games of toss with our Barre friends. I knew better than to push him to go before he was ready. That never worked.

When Solon was finally ready, we crossed the bridge over the moat heading to where this whole adventure had first begun. The golden grasses swayed as the light of the afterlife shone down on us. We walked forever, it seemed, without seeing Amanda, the girls, or any other forms of life for that matter. I was beginning to wonder where everyone was hiding.

"This is odd," I said. "Amanda and the girls aren't here anymore, but neither are the animals. Where'd everyone go?"

"No idea," Solon said. We walked and walked, unable to see or find anyone that might have been able to play catch with us, much less help us figure out the afterlife. I was beginning to feel rather lonely.

"This is pointless," Solon said, putting words to what I already felt. "Nobody's here, and nobody is magically appearing. Let's go back to the castle and try to talk to the Guiding Spirit again."

We turned around and walked forever back to the castle, entered the monstrous door, and found ourselves in the large, green field surrounded by the fence once again.

"Welcome back," the Spirit said. "I was beginning to wonder if you'd ever make it."

"You've been waiting for us?" I asked.

"Yes. It seemed you were going to sit on that bridge forever. Then, when you got up instead of coming to visit me, you wandered back to the land of tragic entrances. Pah! I understand. You'd rather be with spirits you encountered on Earth and are now seeing again for the first time in your afterlives. Those familiar faces are far more inviting than me, a spirit you've only just begun to talk to here in your afterlife. That's okay. I'll try not to feel insulted. This is typical of those new to this realm—always wanting one foot in your past life and one in your afterlife. But I sent all of your earthly acquaintance spirits away for now so that you'd come visit me here."

"With all due respect, Guiding Spirit, this is all so new to us, and we really miss our parents, family, and friends. Isn't that to be expected?" Solon said.

"Ah, well, you've already broken many of my expectations. My newbies usually take their time to figure out the connection between their afterlives, their lives on Earth, and their lives beyond, but not you boys. You're quite the pair. I tell you to go forth and use your intuition to solve your problem of trying to comfort your mother and father, and you not only figure out how to solve your problem, but you also unlock the secrets of your afterlife faster than I've ever witnessed."

"Really!?" I was becoming rather excited and was feeling as proud as I had felt the day I won the Dragon Cup at my favorite soccer camp in 2008. Winning that mug was complicated because I had to work with lots of different teams and combinations of players to accumulate my "points" in that friendly competition. But I'm still not sure how I ended up being the highest scorer that summer. It was some combination of my goals and my assists, the total goals scored by the teams I was on, and my wins and losses. I had the same feeling now as I did then, unsure how Solon and I actually did it or what secrets to the afterlife we had unlocked.

"We've figured out some important stuff then?" I asked.

"You could say that," the spirit answered.

"Like what?" Solon asked.

"Oh, Solon. There you go again," the spirit answered. "You know I will not tell you outright exactly what you've figured out. I am excited for you both, though, because you're onto something big. It's going to help you achieve your goals on Earth and accomplish amazing things in your afterlives."

"Ugh. All this secrecy is enough to drive me nuts," Solon remarked. "Why can't you just tell us?"

"My dear child. We've already discussed this. I am *not* your tell-all teacher. I want you to keep a mind of your own and make your own choices. Your mind, your body, your spirit, and the things you touched in your lifetime. They're all yours, not mine."

"I get that part," I said, "and I get that we're in control of solving our own problem with our own tools. But what, exactly, have we unlocked? You said we unlocked some secret to our afterlives. What could that be?"

"Boys. I've already given you plenty of hints about that, and I'll say no more. I simply wanted you to know that you're on the right track. Now, go. Figure it out."

"Liam, we need to go some place where we can talk and figure this out," Solon was forcing thoughts into my head again. That made sense since the Guiding Spirit was always nearby in the field.

"WHERE?"

"The bridge. Let's go back and sit on the bridge and talk."

"OKAY. PROBLEM IS, WE'VE NEVER TRIED TO GET THERE FROM HERE. WHAT DO YOU SUGGEST?" I asked.

We both looked around behind us. There were no castle walls and certainly no door to the castle to pass through to arrive at the bridge.

"Hmm," Solon said out loud. "Remember how you conjured up a dragon last time we were on Earth and needed a sturdy ride home in all that wind?" Solon said. "Well maybe you can conjure up a castle door and we'll find the bridge on the other side."

"Shoot, why don't you try that. Do you think I have some sort of special power?"

"Fine. Let's both try it. Picture the castle door and the bridge on the other side," Solon closed his eyes, so I did too. When we opened our eyes and looked around, there was a large door on the other side of the fence just behind where we were standing.

"Wow. Looks like we did it. Let's go!" In his excitement, Solon had already started walking toward the castle door. To get to it, we would need to cross the electric fence again.

"Do you think it is electrified?" I asked.

"Probably not, but we better both touch it at the same time again just in case it sends us somewhere else," said Solon. He extended his arm, and I clasped my hand around his wrist.

We were totally unprepared for what happened next. The moment Solon touched the fence we catapulted quicker than lightning over the castle door and landed on the wooden bridge.

"Solon," I yelled. "Get off of me!"

SOLON

"ARE YOU OKAY?" I asked, concerned because I had landed right smack on top of him, which meant that our spirit bodies became entangled as my body passed through his. That felt so bizarre— like somehow he and I had become one. I can't say that it hurt, but it sure was different.

"Yeah. I am fine." Liam said. "I didn't feel a thing," I wondered how that could possibly be true given how strange it felt to me.

As we worked to separate ourselves, Liam said, "Flying through the air like that was way cool! I hope we can do it again."

"That's what eagles, ponies, and dragons are for, right?" I replied. "No doubt we'll be flying again soon."

"You're probably right," Liam replied.

"So . . . here we are." I sat down on the bridge, legs dangling, happy to be back in that familiar glow of the castle. "What was our Guiding Spirit getting at? What have we figured out?"

"I don't know. Let's go through all the stuff that happened last time we were on Earth and what we talked about when we were trying to figure out how to help Mom and Dad. It's sure to come to us, right?" Liam said.

"We've already talked about it a ton. What's your guess? What have we figured out?" I asked.

"Well, I bet it's got something to do with us thinking there's a connection between our spirit selves, the objects that we touched in our lifetime, our bodies, and our minds."

"Probably. That makes sense, especially since the other stuff we've been thinking about revolves around that connection. You know, we've been wondering if the light that came from our pillows and the urns after we touched them would stay behind when we left, and whether or not the light comforts Mom or Dad the way that it comforts you and me," I said.

"Yeah. That connection must be it," Liam said. "Do you suppose there's more to it though? If we have a body, mind, and spirit that are somehow connected to the objects we touched in our lives, how can we use this idea to help Mom and Dad?"

"That's it!" My intuition must have been speaking to me, because suddenly it all made perfect sense. "Mom and Dad have those things too, right?! They each have a body, mind, and a spirit that are connected to the objects they touch. Just like you and me. Think about it. When we came into this afterlife, we found spirits we'd connected with on Earth, and we've felt our spirits attached to the objects we touched in our lives. That's our proof. That's proof! That's it!" I was so excited and relieved that I threw my arms in the air and looked upwards.

"Hold on! I don't get it. Proof of what?" Liam asked.

"Mom and Dad have a connection with you and me forever and ever!" I said, turning to face him. "That's the secret of the afterlife. Really, it's also the secret of life, too."

"I still don't understand. Say it in plain English, please."

"So, here's the deal: every spirit, like you and me living on in the afterlife, is connected to many, many other spirits—all those we crossed paths with in our lives. But also, the spirit's connected to the body that it used to be inside on Earth, and to the objects that the body had contact with. Proof of that lies in the way the light of the afterlife flowed through the pillow to our urns—from an object we were very attached to in our lifetimes to our remains." I said.

"Yeah. I get all of that, but how does that prove we're connected forever?" Liam asked.

"Think about it this way. All of these connections between body, mind, spirit, and the objects we touch existed when we lived on Earth—we just didn't realize it. It means that Mom and Dad experience the same connections between body, mind, spirit, and the objects they touch, and they just don't realize it. Their spirits are connected to the people they interact with and to the objects they care about."

"So," Liam interjected, "if we can find a way to help Mom and Dad realize this secret, they should feel comforted? Is that what you're saying? It'll help them to see that we'll always be connected to them, even though we've died. Our spirits will always be with them. Is that it?"

"Yes," I replied. "That's exactly it. Do you understand how big this is? It means that Mom and Dad are spiritually connected to you and me forever. This'll be true from now until the end of time, if there is such a thing."

"Yeah, but how do we help them feel the connection? Hold it. My intuition is telling me they should be able to feel it by touching the objects we touched, right? I mean, their minds key into memories of us. Even if they don't see the light like we do, their minds can bring up images of us, and they can feel our spirits. Right?" Liam asked.

"I think so. The Guiding Spirit told us we'd already figured out a bunch of important stuff. Could be we've already found a way to comfort Mom and Dad without realizing it. Maybe now that we understand the secret, when we go back to Earth, we'll see some evidence that Mom and Dad understand this connection too," I said.

"Wow. Let's get back there and see what we can find," Liam said, standing up in preparation to leave. "It sure would be nice to know they're gonna be okay without us someday."

"I guess it's time to call Baldash, unless of course you'd rather hike," I stood up, recharged by the light and excited to take another trip home.

"Are you kidding me? Hike verse ride a dragon. Hmmm . . . let's see . . . hard choice." Liam was grinning ear to ear. He closed his eyes, and it wasn't long before we felt the wind of Baldash's wings as he slowed his descent and landed beside us on the bridge. We climbed aboard, pictured Mom and Dad at home, and, much to our surprise, Baldash flew straight into the closed castle door. It didn't hurt a bit. As we held on tight, Baldash kept right on flying over the green field. Soon we were high over the Green Mountains and then over the ocean, and before long we had crashed through the water's surface and landed on the snow-covered back lawn of our Barre home.

The moment we landed, the kitchen light flicked on.

"Baldash, you wait here please," Liam said, "in case we have to make a quick exit again." Good idea, I thought, considering we were left scrambling for a ride in that terrible storm during our last visit.

Liam and I entered the house through the sliding glass door and found Terry, our next-door neighbor, climbing the stairs. Not realizing we were there, she entered the kitchen, grabbed a spoon from the drawer, and headed back downstairs.

"Mom and Dad must be on a trip. Terry's here to feed the cats. What do we do now?" Liam asked.

"Let's figure out where they went. Maybe we can follow 'em on Baldash," I suggested.

Liam's eyes lit up again in anticipation of another dragon ride, no doubt. I looked around the kitchen counter and saw Mom's long list of things to bring on the trip. It included her swimsuit, shorts, T-shirts, and sundresses. Based on the snow we had seen when we landed, those items were clearly meant for a trip somewhere far away.

"Look at this," I said, sliding the list toward him. "Where are they?"

At first, a sad look crossed Liam's face, but it quickly changed to excitement. "They're on that sailing trip we were gonna take with Grandpa Irv. I'm sure of it."

It made perfect sense. "Do you remember where that is?" I asked. "Where should we tell Baldash to fly?"

"Don't you worry," Liam said with confidence. "We'll use the secret of the afterlife for this one. We just need to imagine an object we know Mom or Dad are attached to, one we know they wouldn't leave home, and we'll find 'em."

"Like what?" I asked. "Something from Mom's list?"

"Nope. I've got a better idea: Dad's computer! He has to take it wherever he goes since he's in charge of so much at the office. He needs it to check his email and keep communication rolling. Don't you see? He uses it a ton when he's in the office and at home, so his spirit must be strongly attached to it. You know he has it with him. He has to. It's the best way to find them. Just imagine Dad sitting at his computer," Liam said.

"That's perfect," I said. "Let's go. We don't wanna miss that sailing trip!"

"Awesome!" Liam replied. We floated through the sliding glass door and found Baldash perched on the deck, watching us as we approached. We floated up onto his back, closed our eyes, pictured Dad at his computer, and, just like that, we were off to the Caribbean.

LIAM

Riding a dragon to the Caribbean sure beat flying there by plane. Yeah, we didn't have a flight attendant giving us soda and snacks, but the views were so much better. We flew about one thousand feet above the Earth's surface, entirely exposed to the open air, at an amazing pace. I could not believe how fast entire cities came and went. Of course I didn't know how, but I was able to quickly absorb the glory of the sights below us—everything from cities to mountain ranges, to lakes, ponds, and rivers, as we raced by at what seemed like the speed of light. I was definitely beginning to love this spirit life and all these new experiences. Seeing our past world this way was truly amazing.

After a speedy flight over some ocean and then over some islands, Baldash descended and soared in small circles about eighty feet above and slightly to the side of a forty-foot sailboat anchored in a small bay.

"Look, there's Dad!" I said, pointing to the deck. Sure enough, Dad was sitting toward the back of the boat, looking out over the harbor, and drinking something from a can—probably a soda, but possibly a beer. Grandpa Irv wasn't far from Dad, covering the boat's instrument panel with a grey plastic, box-like thing.

I could hear Baldash speaking into my head insisting he was tired and needed a place to rest.

"Wait!" I said silently to him. "Solon and I need to get onto that boat. You're too big to land there to rest, aren't you? Could you drop us safely down on the deck if you flew directly over it? Then you can go rest."

Irritated, Baldash snapped back, "Don't ask me!" but he kept circling in the same spot. So I asked Solon.

"Well," he replied, "our Guiding Spirit would tell us to follow our intuition. What do you think?" Solon asked, leaning a little to the right to look beneath us at the crystal clear water below.

I didn't like the looks of it. The boat seemed so far down there, and all that water around it made me nervous.

"I don't wanna risk floating down there on our own. If we miss the deck and hit the water instead, we could cross the horizon again and end up back in our afterlife. Water seems to have a way of doing that to us."

"Good point," Solon said.

I was busy looking around for a solution when I spotted two extremely cute black and white birds flying toward the boat. The birds landed on the back of the dinghy that was hitched about six feet off the sailboat's stern. Mom and Dad noticed the birds too, and as they watched them, Mom started talking to the birds just like I would have.

"Hey! Maybe those birds can help," I suggested. "Yo, birdies! Fly up here and help us!" To my surprise, both birds rose up and flew circles around Baldash, gracefully soaring. Solon and I chuckled, watching them turn circles and peer at us through their little eyes. The birds seemed to be smiling and teasing us, as if to say "Look at me. I can fly down there and you can't." But no. The birds had come to help, I decided. Feeling excited, I carefully stood up on Baldash, and then, when one of the birds flew close enough, trying to ignore the uncertainty I felt, I leaped onto its back, landing not so gracefully on my weightless, spirit stomach. I quickly wrapped my arms around the bird's neck. Phew! I could ride this bird the same way I had ridden Baldash, the eagles and the horse to get where I wanted to go. I looked down at the water below, relieved, and then turned to Solon.

"Check it out! That's how it's done, big bro," I smiled and gave a thumbs up. Solon just sat there on Baldash's hovering back with his jaw hanging open. My bird kept flying in circles around Baldash until I remembered I had to tell it where to go. I thought hard about the dingy, and, right away, my birdie descended and perched on the side of the little boat, calmly walking to and fro, looking up for his buddy.

As I float-climbed down, I yelled up, "Yo, Solon! You gotta try that! It's awesome!" I watched for what seemed like a long while as Solon worked up his courage. When he finally took his flying leap, he missed his bird entirely. He started plummeting toward the ocean like a dropped rock. Fear coursed through me. I envisioned us separated in our journey by the water's surface, he in the afterlife, and me in this peculiar in-between on Earth.

I screamed at the second bird, "Save him! *Now*. He can't fall in the water!" The bird banked around, and, in a full-on nosedive, streaked for the water's surface. Solon was screaming, "*Liam! Help!*" as he fell faster. Just as his right foot began to penetrate the water, the bird squeezed in below his spirit body traveling so fast Solon had no time to grab its neck before it shot skyward. He was hanging from its tail. I couldn't believe my eyes!

"Hold on!" I yelled. I had no clue how, but somehow Solon managed to cling to that bird's tail by only a feather until the bird descended to the dinghy and landed safely beside me.

"Crap! That was close!" Solon said, looking scared.

"You scared me," I said. "Don't do that again!"

"Like I'd ever want to!"

"Hey. We just learned another thing by following our intuition. Not only can we call on make-believe creatures like dragons to take us places, but it seems that we can also talk to birds." I was thrilled. "I mean, we haven't been able talk to Mom and Dad, but did you see how easy it was for me to make those birds come help us? All I did was ask 'em, and they came." What an amazing discovery!

Solon said, "I wonder if somehow this ability could help us comfort Mom and Dad."

"Shhhh . . . listen to Mom," I said, somehow having heard both Solon and Mom at the same time. Mom was telling Dad, "Look, there are two. Two birds. Makes me think of the boys. They're so cute, looking at us like that." Mom and Dad sat quietly watching the birds walk around on the dinghy. Solon and I watched and waited to see what would happen.

After they had had enough bird watching, Dad said, "I'm going for a swim before we set sail. Wanna join me?"

Mom and Dad changed into their swimsuits and dove off the back of the boat. The birds were startled and flew off, but Solon and I remained safely on the dinghy. Mom and Dad finished their swim and pulled up the anchor, and Grandpa Irv motored the boat out of the little bay before he and Dad put up the sails. We floated along behind them on the dinghy within earshot of the sailboat. There wasn't much conversation, except for the banter necessary to sail the boat. Grandpa Irv and Dad talked about their destination, a little island called Anegada. Mom made her way to the front of the boat and sat beside the mast, looking across the sun-covered ocean to the distant horizon. I floated up beside her, and Solon followed. It wasn't hard to see that she was feeling sad. Tears welled up in her eyes.

"Mom and Dad seem to have loved seeing the birds on the dinghy. Do you think we could send some other animals that could cheer up Mom?" I asked.

"We could try. But what?" Solon asked.

"Dolphins. I wanna send dolphins. They're the cutest ocean

animals, and they just love to play. Maybe dolphins could cheer up Mom."

I don't know how it happened. I hadn't even called them, but Mom suddenly turned around and yelled to the guys, "Dolphins! There are dolphins over there!" She was pointing off the right side, toward the bow. Dad quickly walked up the deck, looking where she was pointing. As he did, we could see the dolphins' fins bobbing in the water, coming closer and closer to the bow. Mom and Dad parked themselves at the end of the bow, standing and watching the water intently. The dolphins started swimming just off the front of the bow, crisscrossing in what seemed like a playful dance right in front of Mom and Dad. Mom and Dad were loving every second of it.

Mom cried out, "That's amazing! I've never seen anything like it! Two. There are two." Grandpa Irv had come up to the bow and just caught a view of the dolphins playing at the bow before they swam off. He walked to the back of the boat saying, "I've never seen anything like that. Amazing."

"Well," I said, "That seemed to work. Look at Mom's smile. She seems much happier now, and Dad and Grandpa Irv clearly enjoyed it, too."

"Yeah. Let's hope it lasts and that Mom doesn't start crying again," Solon remarked.

"Maybe crying isn't such a bad thing, you know. When I was upset about something, I always felt better after I cried. Maybe it's good Mom cries. Seriously." I said.

"I always felt like a wimp when I cried. It makes me so mad," Solon said.

Mom and Dad sat down holding hands at the bow of the boat. Mom laid her head on Dad's shoulder and closed her eyes. "That must have been a sign from the boys," she said quietly.

"I miss them so much," Dad said. "They should be here."

Mom leaned into Dad and put her arm around him. "Yep. And I'm sure they miss us as much as we miss them," she said, breaking into tears as she buried her face in his chest. He held her, gently kissing the top of her head.

When Mom's tears had passed, they rested silently holding hands and staring across the water to the horizon. Anegada lay across that horizon, but Mom and Dad couldn't see it. Not yet, anyway.

SOLON

MOM AND DAD sat arm in arm at the front of the boat for quite a while until Dad said he needed to get up and move around a bit. While he headed to the back of the boat, Mom stayed at the bow, staring out at the horizon. I wondered what she was thinking. After quite a while, she got up and wandered back with Liam and I tagging along behind. She descended the staircase to a little galley kitchen below deck. I was expecting to see a smaller space, like the one below Grandpa Irv's boat in Maine, but this room was much larger and had a kitchen surrounded by three tiny bedrooms, two in the back of the boat and one at the front. Cool! Liam and I always loved to go below deck on the lobster boat, and this "below" was way cool.

Mom dug around in her carry-on bag for a while, a bit frustrated that she couldn't quickly put her hands on whatever she was looking for. Eventually, she pulled out a blank pad of paper and a pen. After carrying it to the seating area on deck, she sat and scribbled a few pages, looking rather unhappy the whole time. She didn't cry, but I could tell she was upset. While she shifted this way and that, trying to get more comfortable as she wrote, I moved closer, hoping my presence would somehow comfort her. Liam floated over to hang out with Dad, who was then steering the boat from the stern.

"Solon, this is SO cool!" Liam yelled over to me. "Dad's sailing the boat. I bet we could've sailed it if we were still alive." He gave me a sad look.

Just then, Mom got up from her seat, and told Dad, "This is useless. Absolutely useless. I can't write without the computer. It takes too long."

"Try just jotting down your ideas, and then you can write more of the details when you get home," Dad said.

"I'll try, but...ugh. Writing it by hand takes forever. I can't get my thoughts down fast enough." She descended the staircase again and then came up empty handed.

"Shoot," I said. "I wish I'd seen what she was writing."

Liam had no idea what I was talking about. He was too busy looking forlorn and dejected and pouting as he watched Dad beside him. "This is so unfair. We're here, but we're not. I want to sail this boat with Dad, darn it! I want to be alive again!"

Knowing what was about to hit after that willful outburst, I closed my eyes and said to myself, "Please, please. Let us make it out of there and find a safe route back to our afterlife." Sure enough, when I opened my eyes Liam had that bugged-out look again and was pointing toward the bow of the boat.

"Oh, darn it! I've done it again. Here comes another tornado," Liam yelled. He floated up beside me as the funnel approached. I started to shake as I realized how rapidly this tornado was approaching the boat. It was so much faster than the tornadoes at the house last time had been. We'd need to think extra fast to outpace this one.

"Quick!" I yelled. "Call Baldash! We need to leave now!"

From out of nowhere, Baldash rapidly approached the stern and hovered there. Wind and rain began to pound down on us as we held tightly to one another and the boat rail. Nobody else on the boat noticed. Nobody was running for raincoats or battening down the hatches.

"How're we gonna get up to Baldash? He says he can't come any closer," Liam yelled out.

"We'll have to float up. But no. In this wind, we could be thrown into the water."

"Maybe Baldash can land on the bow and we can climb on there," Liam said. Not likely. The dragon was huge! There wouldn't be enough space. Yet I could see Baldash struggling against the wind to get closer to the bow of the boat. Not knowing what else to do, Liam and I pushed through the wind toward the bow to meet him.

"He can't land," Liam yelled to me when we were taking our final steps. "We'll have to float up there and grab on." But the wind was whipping so fiercely then that we were holding on for dear life to the bow ropes to avoid being carried off. How could we have expected to go anywhere but into the water if we let go?

"Quick! Grab his feet!" Liam said, looking up.

"Are you outta your mind? You know what'll happen if we let go. You think I'm gonna fly over the water holding onto only the dragon's foot? What if we fall off? What then?" I asked, remembering the close call I had just had trying to jump onto the flying bird.

"We have to!" Liam yelled. "The tornado's RIGHT THERE." He was right. There was no other option.

"Jump up, NOW!" Liam yelled as he shot skyward and grabbed Baldash's foot.

"Don't . . ." I yelled as I jumped up and grabbed Baldash's other foot, "leave me here!" In that instant, the tornado hit hard. I heard a loud crack, and Baldash shrieked as the tip of his left wing wrenched back in the wind.

"Holy crap! Hold on tight, as tight as you can," I yelled as Liam and I were whipped around by the violent air currents.

"Think about the Enchanted Castle, NOW!" Liam yelled. "We can get there. Don't think about the worst. Picture the castle!" It's a good thing Liam was thinking straight, because in my fear,

I sure wasn't. I closed my eyes and pictured the castle and the bridge over the moat, which was my favorite resting spot.

"Close your eyes. It'll help," I yelled.

Just then, Baldash shot skyward through the storm at a rate unheard of to humans. Maybe it was the tornado throwing us skyward, but no matter the cause, it sure was frightening. Our surroundings became black as night, and we were spinning at dizzying speed. Then, as fast as we had shot skyward, we suddenly reversed direction and plummeted toward the earth, spinning and spinning. With only faint light surrounding us then, I looked up to see if Baldash was there.

Gone. Baldash was gone.

Fear overtook me as I looked around for Liam. He, too, was nowhere to be seen. I was falling rapidly, holding onto what felt like the foot of Baldash, yet I couldn't see him above me. Surprisingly, feeling entirely alone, I began to pray. I had never been religious in my life, but at that moment I understood that there was so much more than meets the eye in life, and boy, did I need some help.

"Please, Guiding Spirit, help us get back to our afterlife safely and together. Please help us!"

I hit the ocean surface hard, and that time, it hurt like heck. My butt, my legs, my arms—they all throbbed like they would have throbbed if I had still been alive on Earth and had fallen hard. And my eyes, which I had squeezed shut harder than ever before, throbbed too. It didn't feel anything like the familiar and comfortable part of heaven that Liam and I had been aiming for.

"Where am I?" I wondered. Slowly, I opened my aching eyes, but my arms were still straight up, clinging to who-knew-what. I hoped it was Baldash, but it was impossible to know. I couldn't see a thing in the complete darkness. The wind had died completely. I listened, hoping to somehow get my bearings again in the dark. Below me, I heard the faint trickle of water over rocks, as if a stream were flowing about ten feet below me. In the dark, I couldn't see it, but I heard it for sure.

"Liam? Are you there?" I whispered, not knowing if unseen creatures might be lurking nearby, ready to attack me. Liam didn't answer. Shoot. I hung there, determined not to let go and fall into the water that I imagined was flowing below me in some sort of stream. I shuddered to think what creatures might live in it. My arms hurt worse and worse, as if I were still using muscles to keep my grip—as if I were alive again.

As I hung there scared to death and with burning arms, it dawned on me that I might be able to avoid making any noise at all if I just sent Liam my thoughts. I figured that Liam could hear me wherever he was and answer me.

"Liam—where are you? Are you all right?" I waited for his response.

"WHAT THE HECK JUST HAPPENED?"

"I have no idea. Where are you?"

"HOW AM I SUPPOSED TO KNOW?! IT'S PITCH BLACK. I CAN'T SEE ANYTHING. WHERE ARE YOU?"

"I am hanging in the dark from something that feels like, well, I don't know what it feels like. Maybe Baldash, but I don't think so. I can't see, but there's a stream or something running under me. Do you hear that?

"YEP. I HEAR IT. WE'RE HANGING OVER A RIVER," Liam said.

"Don't be so sure of that."

Oh thank goodness! Our Guiding Spirit is here!

"Guiding Spirit. Am I happy to hear your voice!" I said. "Please tell us. Where are we and what's going on. I can't find Liam, but I can hear him."

"Remember how Amanda told you that there are some places in your afterlife you don't want to visit?" The Guiding Spirit asked. "Well, you've landed in one because you keep wanting to go back to your past lives. You're gonna have to get over that sometime soon, you know. It's kinda dark and dreary here, huh?"

"Yes. Help us to get out of this place," I pleaded. "Please."

"Find one another. Don't try to do this alone. It'll be hard enough to survive what comes at you from below. You need to stick together and support each other. Waste no time."

"Solon. I'm scared. Where are you?" Liam cried out. It paid to be loud, cause I actually heard him calling to me from what sounded like the other side of the stream or river.

"I'm over here. Can you hear me?" I screamed at the top of my spirit lungs, throwing aside all caution about animals possibly lurking in the darkness. I desperately wanted to be with Liam again before anything arrived from below. Still unable to see, I struggled with my fear as it seemed to swallow me up, threatening to completely freak me out.

"Yes. I hear you," Liam yelled. "I am moving your way now."

"I'm coming toward you, too," I said, moving in the direction of his voice. "Let's meet in the middle," I yelled.

"Keep talking to me so that I know where to go," Liam yelled. "It is so dark!"

Wanting to keep the conversation going, I asked, "What do you think's below us?"

"I have no idea. This is too scary. Maybe something's in there that'll eat us up if we fall in!" he answered, panic in his voice. I held on a little tighter as I moved in his direction.

"Try to think positively," I encouraged. "Hold on tight and come to my voice. We'll get out of this mess. The Guiding Spirit said that if we're together, we'll be okay. Didn't the spirit tell us that?"

"Yeah, I guess. But I can't see a thing now in the dark," Liam said. The proximity of his voice told me we were a lot closer to each other. We soon bumped into one another. At that moment, it was as if someone flipped on the lights, and they shined in the water below us. The water started to glow, and we suddenly could see again. It was funny. The sound of water running over rocks was gone then, too—gone with the darkness.

As Liam and I hung silently beside one another, I looked more closely into the water below us. It was definitely flowing like a river with rapids in certain spots, and calmer flowing water in others. But looking more closely, I realized that the rocks in the riverbed weren't rocks at all. They were round and shaped like rocks, and water flowed over them, but they were nothing like the rocks I'd seen on Earth. And the water wasn't making any noise anymore.

"Look closely at those rocks. What do you see?" I asked.

He studied the rocks below carefully, then exclaimed, "Holy cow! There's my best buddy Tim."

"Where?" I asked. "I don't see him." I was too busy focusing on other faces.

"Over there!" He said, pointing toward a rock on the right. We sat there studying the "rocks" for a while.

"Do you see Grandma Nancy and Opa Jon?" I asked him, pointing toward the middle of the water.

"Yep," Liam said, studying the water more. We both just hung there and stared for a while. We could see Grandpa Irv and GiGi, Papa Bill and Karen, Nanny and Gary, and every single one of our aunts, uncles, and cousins. In fact, all of our living family members' faces were in separate rocks, but they were all down there in that river. All the faces of our friends were there too. Rocks upon rocks upon rocks of them. All of my friends and classmates from school and camps, and all of Liam's, too, and also the faces of friends and classmates from our younger years were there. There were so, so many rocks, I couldn't believe my eyes.

"Look at them all!" I said. "There are so many. The whole

riverbed, or whatever it is, is covered with the faces of the people we were close to in our lifetimes. It's amazing, don't you think?"

"Yep. It's pretty cool to see them all at once," Liam said with a smile.

As we hung and stared below, however, I watched as the expression on Grandma Nancy's face gradually changed. She had been smiling before, but she was beginning to cry, which made me sad. Her crying became louder and louder, and it wasn't long before she was wailing. As the intensity of her sadness increased, I felt this pain growing inside me that was unlike anything I had felt on Earth. Soon, I realized that every single one of the faces in those rocks, every one of the people we had known and loved and cared about in our lifetimes was simultaneously crying. The look and sound of their sadness filled my heart with an intense, empty feeling like none I had ever felt before.

"What's going on? Why is everyone crying? How do we make it stop?" I asked.

"They're shocked and sad because you died so unexpectedly." The spirit answered my first question before Liam could. "Every one of them is missing you beyond words. They each express it differently on Earth, but each of their souls is hurting from losing your living presence." What a surprise. The Guiding Spirit actually answered one of my questions directly!

"We have to get out of here. I can't take this anymore," Liam screamed. The crying and wailing crescendoed below us, and before long, Liam and I could hardly hear one another, much less think, over the din. It was ear piercing and heartbreaking all at once and more disturbing than anything I had ever experienced, even the fire that took our lives. I desperately wanted to clamp my hands over my ears, but I was quite certain I would fall if I did.

I screamed to the Guiding Spirit, "How do we get out of here?" There was no response.

"We need to get back to our afterlife!" I forced this fear-filled

statement to Liam as loudly as I could without speaking. The crying and wailing beneath us was unbearable, and it seemed to be penetrating deeper and deeper into my soul. It filled me with an intense urge to get back to Earth and help not just Mom and Dad, but also everyone of our sad friends and family members. The thought was overwhelming me.

Liam yelled into my head, *"I BET WE'RE HANGING FROM A BRIDGE. COME ON. LET'S PULL OURSELVES OVER THIS WAY AND TRY TO GET AWAY FROM THE NOISE."* I still hadn't the foggiest idea what we were holding onto and hanging from, but Liam was already beginning to move away from me, so I followed.

"Stay alert," I yelled. *"Don't fall! Look for anything that'll help us get out of here!"* We started to float across, grabbing at whatever was suspending us over the rocks. As much as I wanted to escape from the noise, I felt this intense attraction to all the people below us. I could not ignore them as I moved over, trying to keep up with Liam. Hearing their combined grief was just too much to bear. We had to find our way back to our afterlife proper, and then maybe we could make a plan to go back to Earth and help all those people understand we were okay. (Well, I guess we were okay, if feeling intensely sad for the ones we left behind could be considered "okay!")

"LOOK!" Liam exclaimed, holding on with only one hand and pointing in the direction we were moving in. There was a faint but warm and comfortable light out there. I thought that maybe we were hanging from some sort of bridge that spanned this river and that if we could get out from underneath the bridge, we'd find our way back to the safe and light-filled part of our afterlife.

Then it dawned on me. "We're over the moat! That's light from the Enchanted Castle out there! We're hanging from the bridge over the moat. We need to climb on top of it again." Oh, was I ever looking forward to resting on that bridge.

We slowly worked our way to the edge with Liam leading the way. As he pulled himself up and over the side of the bridge, I could sense his excitement. Moments later, I knew why. The instant I pulled myself out from below the bridge into the light, the warmth of the Enchanted Castle's light flowed into me, instantly making me feel comfortable, safe and loved. Liam was lying beside me looking up at the sky and the castle wall with a look of complete relief across his face. Neither of us said anything. For the longest time we just stayed still, me with my legs dangling over the side of the bridge, and Liam lying flat. I realized that, except when Liam slept, I'd never seen him lay still for so long.

"Are you okay?" I finally asked.

"Not really," he answered. "That's more than I can take. They're all miserable. What're we gonna do? It's been hard enough trying to help Mom and Dad know we're okay. How can we help everyone else too?"

"I don't know. I just don't know."

I lay there, resting. Surprisingly, Liam stopped talking, too. As I lay there trying to trust my intuition, I thought about our peculiar state of being. We seemed to be stuck in some sort of in-between, wanting to stay in the afterlife, but also needing to stay connected to people we knew in our lives. Hanging from the underside of the bridge and witnessing so many of our friends and family upset about our deaths made everything seem so much worse and harder to deal with. What began as a desire to help Mom and Dad understand we were okay had turned into much more—a desire to tell everyone who knew and cared about us that the afterlife's not so bad and that we were doing well.

I wondered how we could accomplish that?

I thought back to all the times we'd been carried back to our afterlife from Earth by violent storms. Each storm had been more severe than the last. This one had been so severe that it snapped Baldash's wing and landed us in a dark and really scary place, which totally depressed me. I wondered what would happen if we tried to return to Earth again to help everyone, not just Mom and Dad, and ended up getting swept back to our afterlife. I figured that we might never make it—or worse, we could get stuck dangling from the bridge over the moat forever. Maybe, I thought, we should just stay on this comfortable bridge, enjoy the afterlife, and forget about going back again. What good were we doing returning to Earth anyway?

I got up. "Let's talk to the Guiding Spirit."

LIAM

"WHAT'RE WE GONNA ask this time?" I wondered aloud as I got up too. "I know what you're thinking. We're not gonna be able to help everyone by going back to Earth, you know."

Solon started walking toward the castle door. "Fine. Let's just go have a little chat with our spirit. Maybe we'll figure out something that'll help."

It was just like I figured: Solon wanted to save everyone from their pain. It sounded dangerous.

"That wasn't what I had in mind," I said, "but, whatever. Let's find the spirit."

When we got to the castle door, we yanked it open, crossed the threshold, and found ourselves standing in the middle of the green field surrounded by the sheep fence again. Exhausted, we sat down facing the mountains.

Before we had time to think, much less ask a question of the Guiding Spirit, we heard, "I see you're back again." That voice was a welcome sound. "Looking for more advice?"

"We'd love some. What should we do now?" Solon asked.

"That depends on what you want to accomplish."

I said, "Well, first off, it'd be nice to know that the things we did on Earth already helped Mom and Dad know we're safe."

Solon nodded his head and then added, "And we want to find a way to be sure that everyone we cared about on Earth knows we're safe, too." He was really shooting for the stars.

"You boys set high goals, don't you? I can tell you that through using your intuition well, you've already completed your job and accomplished your goals on Earth. You don't need to return anymore. It's done."

"What?" Solon and I said in unison, looking at each other.

"What do you mean? How are we supposed to know Mom and Dad understand we're okay?" I asked, confused.

"Are you saying Mom and Dad already know? How can we trust that from here?" Solon asked.

"Your intuition led you to witness things on Earth that should help you know your goals on Earth are already met. Your job now is simply to stay here and adjust to this afterlife. The lure of your past life is strong because the afterlife is so new to you. But, every time you return to Earth, your attraction to your past life grows stronger, and so the danger increases too."

"I don't get it," I said. "Sure, we have some ideas floating around between us that say maybe Mom and Dad are gonna be okay. Maybe, somehow, they know we're safe now, but we didn't see anything to prove it."

"Yeah," Solon chimed in. "We witnessed the connection between body, mind, spirit, and objects, and we suspect that Mom and Dad might be comforted through these connections, but there's no proof they know we're okay. Where's the proof?"

"Proof would be nice. Then maybe we could feel okay about not going back," I said softly. Of course, the spirit heard me.

"If you return one more time in search of proof but you don't see it, what then? Will you continue to return over and over again at great risk to your spirit selves?"

Solon and I looked at each other, uncertain of our answer.

"If I grant you one more visit to Earth now, and this time you find proof that your mother and father understand the eternal nature of their connection to you, you must promise that you'll stay put here in your afterlife and adjust to the peace and tranquility. Your talents are needed here."

Solon and I looked at each other and nodded our heads in unison.

"Yes," I said, staring at Solon to be sure he agreed. "If we have proof that Mom and Dad get it, we won't return again, at least not in the near future." There was no way I was gonna commit to *never* returning at some later time, but I didn't think it smart to tell the Guiding Spirit that.

"But wait a minute," Solon interjected. "What about everyone else? They may not get that we're safe. Can we just leave them suffering? Or should we maybe go help them after we see that Mom and Dad get it?"

"My dears, as much as you would like to, you cannot save everyone from their grief. Each of your friends and loved ones will find their way through their pain in time. The ways they adjust to and cope with your deaths will be different for every one of them. But if you find proof that your mother and father are connected to your forever, you should feel confident that this is the case for every one of the people you care about. Returning to Earth won't take away the pain that exists for those you love in your past world. But your connections to loved ones will remain strong in your physical absence. The connection will help them. You'll see."

Solon looked at me and forced a thought into my head.

I sure hope the Guiding Spirit's right about that. What should we do?

I managed to yell directly into Solon's head.

LET'S MAKE ONE MORE TRIP TO EARTH TO SEE MOM AND DAD. AFTER ALL, THIS ADVICE IS ALL WE HAVE TO GO BY NOW, AND THE SPIRIT'S ADVICE HAS NEVER LET US DOWN.

Solon looked like he was about to die (again!) as he held his head.

"Okay, spirit. For now, we'll only take one trip back to Earth to find proof. Then, we'll stay put for a while in this afterlife dimension. Do you have any suggestions for us?" Solon asked.

"To begin, don't ride the dragon." Wow! I was surprised that we got some more straight-up advice from the spirit! "The dragon emerged from your thoughts in your past life. Ride the eagles. They came from your afterlife. Therefore, they'll be your safest transportation. Second, when you get back to your past life, seek out the places you've already investigated and explore them more deeply. You're sure to uncover some helpful surprises there. Lastly, *hurry back*. This is where you're meant to stay now."

"Thanks," I said.

Solon added, "Yeah, thanks a lot."

"What now?" I asked Solon. "Do we head for the hills?"

"Didn't you listen to a word he said?" Solon asked, irritated.

"Of course I did!" I answered harshly. "We should head for Earth, get the proof we need, and not stay long."

"Yeah, but the spirit also told us to ride the eagles," Solon said.

"Okay, then we head for the hills on eagles instead of hiking. Either way, we have to head for the hills, right? Why are you being such a pain about it?" I asked.

"I'm bothered, that's why. This could be our last trip to Earth to be with Mom and Dad, maybe for a long while. Doesn't that bug you?"

"Yeah. That's gonna be hard. We'll have to say goodbye or something," I answered. "I'm not ready for that."

"Yeah, but that's what we have to do. We just promised the Guiding Spirit that once we have proof that Mom and Dad'll be okay, we'll stay in the afterlife," Solon said, "at least for a little while."

"Shoot. I don't know what to say." We both sat there silently for quite some time. I thought maybe we should postpone the trip since it might be our last. The Guiding Spirit, who must have been listening in on our conversation, began to speak in the most soothing voice I had heard yet.

"Boys. It's okay. Staying in the afterlife doesn't mean that you'll lose your connection to your parents. You'll always be connected to them, even when they're there and you're here. You'll see."

There was no way to know what the Guiding Spirit meant or how it could possibly be true. I suggested to Solon, "We're gonna have to get on with it and trust that this'll all be okay. Let's call the eagles and go see Mom and Dad now."

"Remember," the Guiding Spirit said, "On this last visit, avoid wishful thoughts about returning to your past life. The consequences will be worse if you do that again."

I didn't like the phrase "last visit" one bit, but I decided to let that one pass, assuming that if we really needed to travel back to Earth again after this visit, Solon and I would find a way.

"We will do our best to keep our thoughts in the afterlife," I said.

Neither Solon nor I had called the eagles, but I could see them from a distance flying in our direction. They landed on the hilltop, and we climbed aboard. We wrapped our arms around their necks as they took off at the same time and flew beside one another with just enough space between them that their wings didn't touch. It was simply beautiful to ride the birds again.

I turned to Solon and yelled, "Amazing!"

He hollered back, "Yep. I've never felt better."

We flew on, close to the surface of the field, until we approached the mountains. The birds gracefully climbed higher, and we crossed the summit quickly. As before, beyond the mountains we saw the beautiful blue ocean stretching out as far as we could see. The birds headed downward over the backside of the mountains with amazing speed and began soaring over the ocean. The look on Solon's face was a sight to behold: it was total happiness and peace. He looked the way I felt.

We flew just above the surface of the water for a long while, enjoying every moment of the exhilarating ride in this light. It suddenly dawned on me that the eagles hadn't a clue where we wanted to go. I worried that they might just fly on forever like that.

"We need to think simultaneously of the same place back home or the eagles won't know where to take us. That must be why we're not crossing the horizon."

"You're right. Let's head for the family room, only this time, let's think about Dad reading to us," Solon suggested. We both closed our eyes. In my mind, Solon and I were sitting on either side of Dad on the couch, snuggling into him as he read aloud. As predicted, suddenly, the eagles shot skyward in unison, and Solon and I held on for dear life. We both knew what was coming, so when the eagles bee-lined toward the surface of the ocean, Solon and I held on tightly, looked at each other, and smiled. When we crashed through the water, we found ourselves exactly where we had planned—in the family room back home.

"Yes! We're back!" I was psyched to be there.

SOLON

I COULD HEAR Mom and Dad talking upstairs.

"Let's go up."

"Okay"

Liam flew to the stairs grinning. "I'll beat you!"

"Oh no you won't!" I said racing to the bottom of the staircase. We floated up neck and neck, pushing and shoving each other as though we were still alive. Of course, our misty bodies became entwined, which only slowed us down. I looked at Liam with a grin.

"Old habits die hard, don't they?" I asked. He let out a chuckle as we untangled our spirit bodies and proceeded calmly to the top of the stairs. Mom and Dad's voices were coming from the dining room, so we headed toward the light streaming in the front windows. When we rounded the corner, I was surprised to see Mom sitting in my seat at the table as she and Dad talked while they snacked. I paid little attention to what they were saying. How could I have? Mom was in my seat! It made the dining room look all wrong. If Liam and I had been alive and eating, we'd probably be in our customary dinner chairs, seated across from one another with Mom and Dad at the far ends of the table. If the current seating arrangement felt odd to me, I could only imagine how terrible it must have felt to Mom and Dad.

"Yo, Solon," Liam said, waving his wispy hand in my face. "Earth to Solon. Are you catching any of this conversation?"

"No. I was thinking about the empty chairs," I explained.

"Well that's nice, but you oughta pay attention. They're discussing some memorial fund or something. Listen up!" Liam said.

Mom was explaining to Dad that she was happy to have a memorial fund to keep our memories alive by donating funds to non-profits that would help other kids who needed it for educational stuff. She also was glad that their friends and family had a way to show their love and support for our entire family by giving to the fund. But then she said, "I can only think in limited doses about how to gift from the fund. It's just too painful. Solon and Liam should be here doing these things too."

Dad reached over and held Mom's hand. "I know. They should." Liam and I gave one another a sad look.

After a minute, Mom got up. "I need to tackle more of the fantasy while you're out for your ride." Must have been Dad was planning to go for a bike ride.

Mom and Dad headed into the kitchen with their lunch dishes.

"You did the breakfast dishes. I'll get these," Mom said. While she loaded the dishwasher, Dad quickly checked his email before heading into the garage, probably to pump up his bike tires. When Mom was done doing the dishes she left the room and headed down the hall.

"Follow her. She said something about 'tackling a fantasy,'" Liam said. We trailed along behind Mom as she headed through her bedroom into the attached office.

"Look, Liam," I pointed to the desk. "It's the MacBook Pro." Mom sat down at the computer and opened it. We stood on either side of her and stared at the desktop. I could see all the same folders I had seen the last time I had looked at this screen. She opened the folder titled, "Fantasy of Boys in Heaven," and then opened a document called "Fantasy of Where the Boys Went." She scrolled down the screen until she came to the end of the document.

When she started to type, I turned to Liam and said, "I guess we know who's been writing this. Do you think she's been writing all the stuff on here—the dreams, the memories of us, and the memories of the fire?" I asked wishing I could just turn and ask Mom. Mom, oblivious that we were there, just kept right on typing.

"Probably," Liam said. "I mean, Dad has his own computer, right? If he wrote anything, I bet he wrote it on his computer, not on this one. Maybe we should go take a look at his. He might have some files like this."

"I don't think that's such a smart idea. We'd never, ever think about doing that if we were alive," I said, "What if we mess something up? We'd feel terrible, and we might not be able to fix it. That could really mess Dad up."

"You're right. Besides, if he does have any files about us, we wouldn't find them anyway. They'd be buried somewhere with the zillions of other files he has on there. Unless, I suppose, if he put the files about us onto the desktop in plain sight," Liam said.

"Well, even if he didn't put them on the desktop, I can find them. I can find anything on the computer."

"Right! Sure you can," Liam said. "I bet you'd just mess it up." That really irked me.

"Wrong!" I argued. "It's easy, and it doesn't mess up anything. You just have to know some words in the title, then you can push 'control F' to find the file using that word. Trust me. It works."

"Well, what words would you use then, smarty pants?" Liam asked.

"Well, duh! I would type in 'Solon' and 'Liam.'"

"Be my guest," Liam said. "I bet you don't have the guts to do it!"

He was acting like such a twerp! "I don't have any guts at all anymore, but I'll do it." I smirked, frustrated with his attitude and feeling the need to prove my point. After all, he knew so much less than me about computers. "Follow me."

We floated into the kitchen to where Dad kept his laptop.

Unfortunately, just as we made our way into the room, Dad returned from the garage. Liam and I stood at the threshold to the kitchen, waiting to see what Dad would do. He headed straight for the bedroom, probably to change into his cycling gear.

"Let's wait until he leaves for his ride, and then we can look at the screen and not worry that he'll catch us," I suggested.

"Okay," Liam said. While we waited, I sat down in the kitchen chair Mom always sits in. Spurs, our beloved house cat, was sound asleep on the table, lying next to the two eight-by-ten photos of Liam and me. I wanted so badly to pat him that I reached my hand out again, only to be stopped by an invisible wall. It felt like my spirit hand pressed into one of those foam walls behind the basketball net at our old school. The "wall" felt soft but hard at the same time. It didn't hurt, but for whatever reason, no matter how much I wanted to, I just couldn't touch Spurs. I wondered then if I could force my thoughts into his head, but then I laughed at the idea since I didn't know how to speak kitty language. Whatever. I decided to try anyway.

"Spursie, kitty," I pushed in his direction. "How are you? I miss you!" Spurs remained fast asleep, but his little eyelids and his feet began to twitch as I spoke to him. When I stopped, his movements did too. How interesting. I tried again. "Spurs, Liam and I are here. You know that now, don't you?" Again, Spurs twitched as I spoke to him and stopped twitching when I stopped.

"You gotta come see this!" I said. Spurs didn't budge as I talked to Liam. "I am pushing thoughts into Spurs's head while he sleeps, and he twitches every time. Watch!"

I pushed into Spurs, "Show Liam that you know we're here," and as I did, the cat's eyelids and feet twitched.

"Cool!" Liam said, "Let me try." He went quiet and took on the look of concentration I had only seen when he was trying hard to force his thoughts into my head. All of sudden, Spurs twitched spastically, awoke with a start, jumped up onto all fours, hissed loudly, and then threw himself off the table as if running from something terrible. Oh, duh! Of course. Loud Liam startled the cat. I should have expected that he'd wake up Spurs and freak him out with that voice-in-your-head thing. Poor Spurs. I followed him in an attempt to comfort him, but I couldn't figure out where he'd gone.

Dad emerged from the bedroom in his cycling gear, picked up his cycling shoes, and headed out the front door. He was gone on the bike within a few minutes.

"Now's your chance," Liam said. "Show me your computer magic, big bro."

I sat down and opened Dad's computer. Liam and I looked at the desktop. A file marked "memorial slideshow" was there. I figured that that was the slideshow Dad had been watching the last time we were there. Better not open that one, or we'd risk being carried away to our afterlives again by our desire to return to Earth. Using only my mind, I pushed the command key and "F" and then typed "Solon" and "Liam" in the search bar and clicked return. No big surprise: there were tons of files with "Solon" and "Liam" in them. I scrolled down through photos, travel information, letters Dad has written, information about the memorial fund, and much more. Eventually I saw a file titled "Poems For Solon and Liam." According to the date beside it, it was written after we died.

"Bingo," I said proudly as I pointed to the computer. "I told you I could do it. Looks like Dad's been writing poems about us."

"Cool!" Liam said. "Let's read it!"

"No way!" I said. "I want to, but we can't risk being yanked away from Earth again. If we read his poems, we might get so sad that we'll have to leave again. We have to find proof that Mom and Dad know we're okay while we're here. We're not gonna find it in the poem 'cause it's the first time we've ever looked at Dad's files. Remember, the spirit told us we need to look more closely at things we already saw in our other visits."

"Yeah, but how do you know that proof is not on Dad's computer in the poems?" Liam asked.

"Because we only had one short encounter with Dad's computer before, and it was watching a slideshow that whipped us back to our afterlives faster than a speeding bullet," I said. "I won't risk that again now, not when this might be our last visit. My intuition tells me we need to look somewhere else."

"I suppose you're right. We did spend more time on those other visits with the smaller MacBook Pro, the iPod, and the three bedrooms in this house. The proof must be there," Liam said, "but I'm glad to know that Dad has been writing about us too."

"I agree. You know he misses us a ton. It's hard to imagine how difficult this is for both of them."

"I know," Liam said. "I know."

We both were very quiet for a while. I sat contemplating what to do next to find proof that what Liam and I had done on Earth in our past visits helped Mom and Dad somehow. Suddenly, my intuition began nagging me. "Liam, we need to go see what Mom's writing now." Without listening to his answer, I quickly floated to the office, and he followed. Mom was busy typing very fast. I floated up beside her, and saw that she was typing a quotation.

"Life is eternal. Love is immortal.

Death is a horizon and a horizon is nothing

save the limit of our sight."

Spoken by Rev. Robert T. Jennings

Mom put in a page break and then stood up and left the room.

"Check this out. Who is the Reverend Robert T. Jennings?" I asked. "Do we know him?"

"Look around," Liam said, pointing to the right side of the computer at the desk. "That's the program from our memorial service in Louisville, Kentucky. Maybe it's in there." Sure enough, when I opened and studied the program, I found the quote embedded in the Reverend's benediction.

"It must mean a lot to Mom if she memorized it," I said.

"Think about it," Liam said with that excited look on his face. "It says we've crossed a horizon and life is eternal. So maybe Mom does get it! Maybe this is proof that she knows we're okay!" Just then, Mom returned to the room with the iPod in hand. She sat down at the computer and put the earphones on.

"*Holy crap!*" I exclaimed. "She's using the iPod! Do you suppose that's because we touched it that one time?" I was feeling as excited as Liam looked.

"Who knows? Just watch her, would you," Liam said impatiently looking over Mom's shoulder.

Mom kept listening to whatever played on her earphones without typing anything new. Instead, she sat staring into space, lost in thought, or maybe listening to the words of the song. It was not long before she started to shift in her seat then began to cry. She turned off the iPod, closed the computer, and then flopped down on the bed and grabbed that weird, handheld, electronic thingy she had used in the middle of the night during one of our last visits, clearly to try to calm herself. She held each end in each hand and then turned the machine on and closed her eyes just as she had last time. It didn't take long for the crying to stop and for her body to visibly relax. Wow! It was clear to me she must have been thinking about the fire again. I wondered if maybe the song had upset her or if it was just something that she dealt with at random moments in her days and nights.

"Pretty cool that Mom's been listening to our iPod, huh?" Liam said, "Too bad it didn't keep her from getting upset, though. We thought it would comfort her."

"Yeah. She seems okay now, though. Let's just watch what she does next." Although I still wasn't sure yet that we were helping her and Dad, I certainly was hoping the fantasy would tell us more—if we ever got to read the rest of it.

After turning off her machine thingy, Mom got up and went to her dresser. She pulled her running shorts, jog bra, and a T-shirt from the lowest drawer of her dresser. I looked at Liam. "Guess we need to head out of here," I said. Mom closed the dresser and then stood and stared for a bit at the photos of Liam and me that sat right above the urns on the dresser top. Quite obviously, she couldn't see the bright light coming from the polished, wooden urn boxes, but to our surprise, she rested her right hand atop my urn and her left hand atop Liam's urn and then closed her eyes and breathed deeply. "I love you so, so much boys. Thanks for being so wonderful. Daddy and I miss you more than words can say."

"Do you think she knows we're here?" Liam asked me.

"Nope. She seems to be comforted by touching our urns, though, and she seems to find comfort in talking to us," I said. Mom backed away from the urns and grabbed the bottom of her shirt, clearly about to pull it off. Liam and I bolted for the door, hiding our spirit eyes on the way out. Memories of Dad's voice echoed in my head: "Stay outta there, boys."

"What now?" Liam asked.

"Maybe after she leaves to run, we can look closely at the fantasy," I suggested.

LIAM

"LET'S SWING ON the tire while we wait for Mom to go," I suggested, itching to go to the playground set and do something fun rather than stand around waiting.

"I'd rather play Guitar Hero."

"Are you nuts? That sounds fun, but she might hear it. Then what?"

"Yeah, but she might see the swing moving, too."

He was right. Shoot. That would be just our luck, wouldn't it? With us so close to learning more from Mom's writing, I wasn't willing to risk anything. "I guess we need to just lay low and wait here." I sat down at the kitchen table.

"That's probably the safest idea," Solon said. "Remember. This may be our last visit. I'd hate to leave without feeling that Mom and Dad know we're okay. Seriously. Don't you think swinging on the playground or playing Guitar Hero will make us miss life?"

"Probably," I said. "Let's find that evidence and get back to the afterlife where we're safe." As much as I loved being in our house and near Mom and Dad, I missed the light of our afterlife and how safe and secure it made me feel.

Mom wandered out of the bedroom clothed in running gear and then put on her shoes at the entryway door. "Oh shoot," Mom exclaimed as she headed up the stairs again. That was a boo-bad for Mommy. She didn't even bother to remove her running shoes. We weren't supposed to do that in our lives. "Leave your shoes at the door," she would say, but sometimes we sneaked too.

Mom came back down to the entryway with the iPod in hand, turned it on, and stuffed the ear buds in. Solon stood next to her, spying on her.

"She set it to shuffle the purchased songs." Solon said. "I wonder what it'll play."

"It's nice to know Mom's listening to our tunes as she works out. I hope she likes 'em. I sure do!" I was feeling glad I couldn't hear them—if I could have, I might have had another bad run-in with a tornado.

Mom exited through the front door, and as soon as it was closed, we sprint-floated upstairs to the office, racing each other for the chair. Luckily, a second comfortable office chair was at Dad's desk, so, when Solon beat me to the one in front of the MacBook Pro, I just used my thinking powers to drag the other chair beside his. That was a lesson I had learned in my lifetime: don't get in Solon's way when he's headed to the computer.

Solon opened the folder marked "Fantasy of the Boys in Heaven," and then the document "Fantasy of Where the Boys Went." At the top of page one, the quote by Reverend Robert Jennings that we'd just seen Mom type stared back at us. No big surprise there. When Solon scrolled to the next page, however, we found something entirely unexpected.

At the top of the page, in boldfaced italics, Mom had written *"From Solon's Point of View."* That was beyond odd.

"What about my point of view?" I asked, concerned that I'd been left out.

"Oh, come on. She'd never leave you out. Just read, would ya?"

I kept quiet and began to read, hoping that what Solon said would prove true. Before long, Solon and I were deeply engrossed in reading what Mom had written. I finished reading page three slightly more quickly than Solon did, and then I looked down at the bottom of the screen.

"Holy crap! This thing's fifty-one thousand, five hundred twenty words, and it's one hundred nineteen pages long right now. We're never gonna finish it before Mom gets back. She'll only be gone for an hour or so at most. It's not like when Dad rides his bike, you know. He can ride for three hours. "

"So . . . just be quiet and read! If we don't finish now, we'll find a way to finish later," Solon said, flipping to page four.

Solon and I buried ourselves in reading as much of the fantasy as we could as quickly as possible. We read in total silence. That was kind of how things had worked in our lifetimes too. When each of us got into a book, nothing would disturb or distract us. At the top of the ninth page, we discovered that Mom had written in boldfaced italics, *"From Liam's Point of View."* Solon was right again. Mom hadn't left me out.

"See? What'd I tell you?"

We continued to read quickly, soaking up as much as possible before we'd have to stop. We were surprised when we heard the front door open so soon. Solon quickly clicked out of the fantasy file and then closed the computer.

"We need to go somewhere and talk *now*," I said, my brain cranking a mile a minute.

"We can talk anywhere, silly," Solon said. "She can't see or hear us, you know."

"Yeah, but we can see her. She's gonna come in and get ready to shower. Let's go someplace we can focus," I said.

We headed out of the office, through the bedroom and past the glowing urns, down the hallway, and then downstairs to the family room.

"That totally freaks me out!" I said. "It's like Mom was with us during the fire. But we know she was downstairs in the entryway below the balcony, and then screaming bloody murder out front. Still, she knew exactly what happened from our point of view.

She even knows about the tunnel, meeting up with Amanda, and the Enchanted Castle. Everything! How could she know?"

"I have no idea how, but she seems to know what was happening from our point of view. There's ... like ... nothing she wrote that didn't actually happen to us," Solon said. "We've only read part of the story, but so far it totally fits, doesn't it?"

"Yep. It does. Now we know: Mom understands that we've been trying to comfort her and Dad from our afterlife," I said. "Do you think the rest of her story will just keep following along what has happened since the fire right up to now? Does she somehow have a connection to us that allows her to know everything that's happening to us still?"

"I don't know. There's something strange about all of this." Solon paused, deep in thought. "Maybe Mom really does still have some sort of connection with us and writes things down after they happen 'cause somehow she sees them or feels that they happened. But maybe it's the other way around. I mean, what if she's been writing this story all along, and it's her story that led these things to happen to us. Maybe the connection works in the other direction. Do all these unbelievable things happen to us for real on their own in this afterlife, or did they only happen after Mom wrote them?"

"Geez. I hadn't thought of that," I replied, mulling this over. "I guess the good news is, whichever direction it's happening from, it's clear Mom's still feeling connected to us!"

"True," Solon replied. He was quiet for a long while. "I bet she just somehow knows what's happening to us. I think her story couldn't be directing what happens to us in the afterlife. I mean, think about it. The Guiding Spirit and our intuition guide us now, not our mother and father."

"I guess. That does make more sense. But how does she know?" I asked.

"I think we should ask the Guiding Spirit when we get back,"

Solon answered. "There's a lot we still don't know about life after death. The spirit said we need to stay in our afterlives to adjust. I suspect it will all become more clear when we return this time."

"Let's hope so anyway," I said. "When can we finish reading what she wrote? I don't wanna leave 'til we read through the end. If we figure out for certain that Mom's writing about our story after these things have happened to us, we'll know for sure that Mom and Dad are still connected to us, that they know we're all right, and even that they know we're doing everything we can to help them."

"It's kind of bold, but we could wait for Mom and Dad to fall asleep and take the computer into the kitchen to finish reading it there," Solon said. "Think about it. We can't read it where it is, or it'll wake up Mom."

"True, but moving the computer sounds risky," I said. "We better be careful not to drop it."

"We'll be careful," Solon said.

The rest of the afternoon and evening passed uneventfully. After stretching and showering, Mom read the newspaper. When Dad returned from his bike ride, he stretched and cleaned up, and then he and Mom teamed up to make dinner. It was pasta with tomato sauce and sweet Italian sausage made by Vermont Smoke and Cure. That had been my favorite. Solon used to love it too, but with cheese instead of sauce.

"Careful now," Solon said. "I know you love this meal. Don't go thinking you can have any. No spiritual salivation, you hear, or we'll get tornado'd."

I wasn't exactly sure what a drooling spirit might look like, but the thought of it made me laugh. It was enough to distract me from longing to return to my lifetime. Instead, I kept focusing on Mom and Dad. I was surprised when the meal ended and Mom didn't get the ice cream out of the freezer. If Solon and I had still been alive, we probably would have had it for dessert. After,

Solon would have practiced his piano, I would have practiced my drums, and then Mom or Dad would have read aloud to us on the couch. Oh, how I missed that. I went to the kitchen to take my mind off of my sadness.

Soon after, Mom and Dad came into the kitchen with their dishes and cleaned up, and then they headed downstairs with a movie.

Solon said, "Awesome. We're in luck. Let's read the rest of the story while they're watching the movie." We went into the office. Solon opened the computer and quickly scrolled down to where we had left off. We read, transfixed by the story that we both knew so well already.

"This is amazing!" I said to him at one point.

"You can say that again," he said. Of course, I didn't. Just like when we read novels in our lifetime, we buried ourselves in the story, and time flew. Before we knew it, we came to the end of Mom's writing, to the exact moment she had closed the computer and left for her run.

"Looks like it ends with this visit," Solon said. "Damn. She's written about everything that has happened in our afterlives up to about four in the afternoon today. There's the proof we wanted. Somehow Mom's connected to us still, and she's not dictating what happens to us, either. If she were, she would've already written about you and I sitting here on this visit reading her fantasy while she and Dad watch a movie."

"Holy cow!" I answered. "If she's writing about these things happening after they happen to us, that's proof that she knows we're okay and she knows we love and miss them."

"Yes," Solon said. "She definitely knows we've been trying to comfort her and Dad. Amazing, really, when you think about it. I can't wait to hear what the Guiding Spirit has to say about this. We did it!"

"I'm not ready to leave yet, though." The thought of it upset me. "Are you?"

"No, but we need to."

"I wanna say goodbye to everything first: my room, the cats, and of course, we have to say bye to Mom and Dad. I'm not going anywhere 'til I do that," I said.

"Good idea. Who knows when we'll get back here again or...if..." Solon said. We both were quiet and looked at each other as we thought about that. "I'm gonna miss seeing Mom and Dad, aren't you?"

"For sure," I said. "That's why I want to say bye now and not mess up and get hauled away before we do. Shoot."

"You know, though," Solon said, "the Guiding Spirit told us we should stay put in our afterlives to adjust. That doesn't mean we won't ever come back here once we've 'adjusted,' whatever 'adjust' means. The spirit also said we'd stay connected to them forever, even from our afterlife." We were quiet for a moment. "I can't say goodbye forever. I'm just not willing to think that way right now. We'll see them again sometime, don't you think?"

"I sure hope so," I said, feeling unsettled. "I'm gonna go hang out in my room," I said, heading for the stairs. Solon, knowing I was bothered, followed me a spirit's distance behind without saying a word. We could hear the movie as we descended the stairs. Mom was leaning into Dad, who had his arm around her.

I said in a warning tone, "I'm hiding my eyes from that movie, man, or I might wanna watch it, which could mean trouble with the weather and a quick exit. I'm not goin' there!" I wanted Solon to avoid it too. Fortunately, he headed into his room as I continued down the hall to mine.

When I entered my room, I could see that absolutely nothing had moved since our last visit. How long ago had that been? I wondered. Though I was happy to see that Mom and Dad had not been meddling with my stuff, I couldn't help but think about how sad it all must have been for them. The bed was still covered with my favorite stuffed animals and the cars I had worked so hard to make for the Pinewood Derby. My eyes stopped on the pillow, and I found myself wondering if it would pulse and light up again were I to stick my hand through it like Solon had shown me during one of our last visits. When I tested it, I felt the exact same pulsing that I had felt before, and the light shone from the pillow with intense brightness.

I heard Mom's voice, "That was good, wasn't it?" I heard the clinking of dishes. Mom and Dad must have been getting up. Boy was I glad I'd heard Mom's voice. That was my warning that their nighttime routine was about to begin. I walked quickly into Solon's room and told him we'd better hurry up. We didn't have much time left to say our goodbyes.

Sure enough, Mom went upstairs whistling for the cats. Spurs ran up the stairs when he heard her whistle. Coco was nowhere to be seen. I wondered for a minute about where she could be and then heard Mom open the sliding glass door and whistle outside.

"Mom's coming down here to feed the cats," I said. "I'm gonna meet the kitties as they come downstairs and grab each of them and give 'em a big hug as they run down the hall."

"Oh, that oughta be interesting," Solon said with a smile. "Good luck. Remember, every time we've tried to hug them it's been as if a wall formed between them and us and stopped us."

"We've never tried grabbing and hugging them when they're running," I said. "It might work. At least I can say I tried. Try with me. Maybe the power of both of us at once will break through that wall, and then we'll actually be able to hug 'em."

"Okay. Let's try," Solon decided. "It can't hurt." I wasn't so sure that was true, but I was willing to take the risk.

When Mom started down the stairs, the hungry, speedy cats flew down ahead of her, Coco in the lead and Spurs trailing close behind. Right before Coco hit the bottom step, I said to Solon, "NOW!" and we both dove toward her, moving in the same direction she was headed in. "We love you Coco!" I yelled as Solon and I tried to grab and hug her. She kept right on running and slipped through our arms. Spurs was upon us before we knew it, and, as we tried to grab and hug him, Solon yelled out, "We love you too, Spurs!" Like Coco, Spurs slipped through our arms. Then, when the cats neared the door to the laundry room, a strange thing happened. They simultaneously stopped in their tracks, turned around, and looked straight back down the hallway directly at Solon and me. I was shocked. Just then, Mom, who we hadn't heard coming up behind us as we focused on the cats, walked right through Solon and me. Literally straight through each of us.

"Did you feel that?" I asked.

"Sure did."

When Mom's body and mine intersected, it felt as if a strong breeze were passing through me, and that breeze left me feeling utterly peaceful. It felt like I was one with Mom, a part of her, and not a separate spirit. The feeling was completely connected, peaceful, and warm.

In a rush of inspiration, I yelled to Solon, "Quick. Get in your bed before Mom comes in to do the nighttime routine." It must have been that Solon's brush with Mom's body left him feeling as spectacular as mine left me because his eyes lit up and he turned and floated as fast as he was able toward his room and his bed as I raced to get into mine.

I was lying in my bed when Mom quietly padded into my room. I looked at her eyes as she walked up beside the bed, talking to me. She wasn't crying, as I had seen her do before, and I was reminded of all the times she had done this very thing while I was alive.

"I love you so much, Bubbins." She leaned over to kiss me, but, of course, her head went right through mine to the pillow behind me, which she kissed three times. It was a different feeling than being kissed by Mom when I was alive, but I decided that I would take it. That same experience of utter peace and connection flowed through me. Mom reached her arms around the pillow and hugged it, saying, "Sleep like a pumpkin, small-fried potato." That was another one of those silly names Mom used for me before bed. I thought it was quite funny, and I liked to try to pretend to look like a small-fried potato. I'd curl up with my knees close to my chest and roll from side to side a bit with a childish look on my face. Mom always laughed and gave me another big hug.

"I love you, Mom. Goodbye for now," I said to her, hoping that she somehow could hear me and feel my love the same way I could still feel hers coursing through me. Mom stood up and said, "Tomorrow we're going to pottery and piano. I'll see you in the morning, Bubbins." She left the room.

She said she would see me in the morning? How? I wondered. She mustn't have heard me say goodbye. Of course not. What did I expect? A little discouraged, I got up and headed for Solon's room. I could hear that Mom was still in there.

"I love you so much, Sweetheart."

"I love you too."

"Sleep like a pumpkin. I'll see you in the morning. Tomorrow we're going to pottery, then piano . . . Goodnight, Sweetheart."

"I love you too, Mom. I'll see you in the morning. Bye for now."

As Mom left the room and I pushed through the doorway, Solon climbed out of bed.

"How can you say that to her?" I said, horrified. "We're not gonna be here in the morning."

"I guess it's habit, or maybe wishful thinking on my part. I'd love to see her again in the morning, wouldn't you?"

"Of course. But you'd better be careful, or we're gonna be

blown away to a bad place before we say bye to Dad. He's the only one left to see before we go back," I said.

"Okay. Calm down. I am not wishing I was back here for good. I was just wishing somehow I could see Mom and Dad upon waking in the morning like we used to. Nothing unusual about that," Solon said.

"Not unusual, just dangerous," I replied. "We have to go find Dad now before you mess everything up." I headed for the door. From behind me, I heard Solon quietly say, "Goodbye room. You've been good to me." Solon had always loved his room during his life. He kept things neat and tidy, and sometimes liked to hang out there alone. During those quiet times in his room, he wouldn't even let me in to visit. Being shut out drove me crazy.

When we got upstairs, Dad was busy putting away a bag of tortilla chips and the salsa that he and Mom had been eating as they watched the movie. He opened and looked at his cellphone, before turning off the lights on his way to the bedroom. Solon and I followed close behind.

When Dad pushed open the door to the bedroom, Solon and I were shocked to see a bright yellowish-green light pouring over the threshold into the hallway. It reminded me of that warm, welcoming, and comforting light of our afterlives. The glow was similar to the light that had flowed from the urns before, but it also had a stronger quality that made it feel even more vibrant and full of life. When we entered the room, it became obvious that the yellowish-greenish light was shining from our urns.

"Does that light seem different to you?" I asked.

"It sure does," Solon answered. "I wonder why?"

"I have no idea," I answered.

"Maybe it's because things are changing somehow now," Solon said.

"What do you mean?" I asked him, curious.

"I'm not sure. Mom's grief seems different this time around, doesn't it? You know, when she said goodnight, she said she would see us in the morning and then told us what she'd be doing tomorrow, as if we'd be along with her somehow. That was different."

"Do you suppose she really believes she'll see us again in the morning? That we'll be with her at pottery and piano? How could she?" I asked.

"Who knows? Maybe somehow Mom feels we're with her even though our bodies are no longer there. Maybe the quality of the light is changing because Mom's grief is changing, and she and Dad are finding ways to feel more connected to us even though we've died. Does that make any sense?"

"I suppose. Yeah. I mean, we haven't really changed in a lot of ways since we died, at least I don't think we have. But . . . I think you're right. Mom somehow is coming to understand that she and Dad are still connected to us. I mean, look at that fantasy. Do you suppose she knows that all of those things have really happened to us and somehow she's writing it all down? Do you think she realizes it all really happened as she says?"

"I have no idea, but the writing must be comforting her and helping her feel more connected to us. Maybe that's what's changing. She feels more connected, and maybe Dad feels more connected, too, and so now we see that the light has more life-like qualities than it had before."

At that moment, Dad came out of the bathroom, ready for bed. Mom was already there reading a novel.

"I think we should both hug and kiss Dad goodnight as soon as he gets in bed. I would hate for him to be asleep for our hugs and kisses," I said.

"Good idea."

When Dad climbed into bed, I floated just over the top of

him and lay down beside him on his right side. Solon lay down beside him on his left, just like when Dad read to us with all three of us on the bed. "Now. Let's hug him," I said. We both leaned into Daddy, wrapped our spirit arms around him, and in so doing, passed right into him. Our bodies merged. That exact same feeling I had gotten when Mom passed right through me filled me again. It was a feeling of the utmost peace and comfort, like laying in a hot tub and being caressed by the gentle massage of water jets and the love of everyone and everything in the whole world. I felt as if I would be one with Dad forever.

God, how I loved my Dad. "I love you, Dad," I said. "Goodnight and goodbye for now. We'll be around." This was not goodbye for good. I wasn't sure how I suddenly knew that, but in that moment, I was absolutely certain of it.

Solon said, "Night-night Dad. I love you. Sleep like a pumpkin. Goodbye for now." I could tell he was feeling as much peace and comfort from that hug as I had.

When Solon and I released Dad and stood up beside the bed, Dad's breathing slowly began to change. He was falling asleep. Recognizing this fact, Mom leaned over from the other side of the bed, kissed him gently on the check, and whispered, "Goodnight, lover. I'll see you in the morning." She closed the book she was reading, turned out the light, and settled into her side of the bed.

"Good call. I think we just snuck that in before Dad fell asleep," Solon said with a smile.

"What now?" I asked. "We already said a goodnight and goodbye to Mom, to the cats, and to our rooms. I'm thinkin' it's time to get back to the afterlife."

"I guess you're right," Solon said. "Something tells me we'll be back again. This won't be our last visit. We may have to stay put in our afterlives for a while, but that doesn't mean we can't come back after we 'adjust.'"

"Yeah. My intuition says so too." The hope of returning someday made it easier for us to leave.

We wandered out of Mom and Dad's bedroom and then floated through the sliding glass door to the deck.

"I forget. How do we call those eagles back?" I asked grinning. When I turned to look at Solon, the house we had just left behind disappeared. Fortunately, the weather was still calm. Solon raised his arms in front of him with his palms open.

"Like this!" He said. Soon, the eagles landed on either side of us on the freestanding deck. We float-climbed aboard and embraced their necks, and the birds took off.

"Picture the Enchanted Castle," I said. "We'll be there in no time." The birds flew through the night sky over the well-lit city of Barre and westward over the Green Mountains to the water beyond. After performing the amazing elevator-like ascent and rapid descent through the water's surface, we found ourselves once again at the door of the Enchanted Castle bathing in the comfortable light of our afterlives.

"There's no place like home, is there?" I asked.

SOLON

I TURNED AWAY from the door and sat on the bridge, wanting to collect my energy and my thoughts before moving anywhere.

"Oh, great. Here we go again," Liam said rolling his eyes. "How long will you sit here this time? I'm sick of waiting forever for you to budge. Let's go."

"Relax, would ya?" His desire to always be on the move drove me crazy. Too bad. I was determined to rest and make a plan. "And where do you wanna go?"

"To visit the Guiding Spirit. Where else?"

"Well, there are lots of other things we could do, you know." I said. "We're safe now, so stop rushing. I'm gonna soak in this light for a while and think about everything that just happened."

"Fine," Liam said as he lay down on his back beside me and closed his eyes. "Suit yourself. Wake me up when you're ready to move."

I finally had some time to myself with my brother peacefully resting beside me. What a gift. As I sat gently kicking my legs back and forth over the side of the bridge, I couldn't help but feel amazed by all that had happened to us since we died. I thought about Mom and Dad, but then I thought of all the family and friends we had left behind. I felt sorry for them. They had no idea how amazing this afterlife really was. I suppose I was wishing that each of them could know before dying all that Liam and I had learned about the connectedness of life and death and what lies beyond.

Of course, if someone had tried to tell me before I died that all of this was awaiting us, I couldn't possibly have believed it, much less understood it. Mom liked to say, "Some things are like having a baby. You just never know what it'll be like until you do it yourself." In the same way, it suddenly seemed impossible to me that anyone would understand what happens after death until death takes them away, like it had done to Liam and me.

It suddenly struck me as interesting that my thoughts seemed very in tune with what our Guiding Spirit was trying to tell us. In order to understand this afterlife, we couldn't just ask for explanations from the Guiding Spirit, or even Amanda, for that matter. We had to learn it all by ourselves through our intuition and actions. Hmm . . . I started to wonder whether maybe, just maybe . . . no. That couldn't have been possible.

"Liam," I said to him as I stood up. "Let's find Amanda."

"Man! You set a record. That's the shortest rest you've taken on this bridge. Congratulations," Liam said. "I'm proud of you."

"Oh, knock it off," I said, heading back in the direction of the first field we arrived at in our afterlives—the field with spirits who died sudden deaths.

But before we reached the end of the bridge, the spirit called out to us, "You won't find her there." I looked at Liam. That was strange. I'd never heard the Guiding Spirit speak to us anywhere except inside the Enchanted Castle—except for that dreadful time when were stuck hanging under this bridge.

"Then where should we look?" Liam asked.

"Try entering the castle again. You might be surprised."

Liam and I looked at one another, equally curious.

"We have a whole bunch of questions," Liam said. I turned to him, wondering what questions he meant. Was he referring to the big question I wanted to ask? Could he have been reading my mind while we sat on the bridge?

"Come in. We can talk."

Liam and I walked to the front door, grabbed the crimson handle, and pulled as hard as we could. For some reason, opening the door was more difficult than before, so we only yanked on it long enough to create a crack big enough to slide our spirit bodies through. After we crossed the threshold, the giant door slammed shut with a mighty bang much louder than you'd expect from a cracked door. The noise scared the living daylights out of us.

"What was that?!" Liam asked.

"That sure sounds final. I hope it doesn't mean we can't ever go back," I said, worried.

"Oh, crap," Liam responded. "I hope not!"

We had become accustomed to seeing green grass and a farmer's field surrounded by sheep net fencing every time we entered the castle door. What we saw the was a remarkably bizarre variation on the usual scene. The grass in the field was royal blue, the sky was forest green, and the mountains beyond were lavender. The white fence was black.

"What the heck?" Liam exclaimed. "What happened here?"

"Oh. Isn't this cute? The artwork of a three year old who hasn't learned his colors!" I remarked. Liam chuckled.

"Congratulations, boys. You've graduated!" The spirit boomed, sounding excited.

I looked at Liam.

"Um, with all due respect, Spirit, what on earth do you mean?" I said.

"That's just it. You've graduated from your lives on Earth, so you no longer see objects in your afterlife as they appeared on Earth. Now, you'll see everything in a whole new light." The spirit paused. "Impressive, really. What you've done to this field. It's cute, in fact."

"Whoa. Hold on a minute," Liam exclaimed. "What do you

mean? Are you saying we'll never go back to Earth again, ever?" It was nice to know Liam and I had the same concern.

"Yeah," I added, "'cause if we're never ever going back to Earth, I wish someone would've told me that ahead of time. I might have chosen to do some things differently during that last visit." That's for sure.

Like what? Liam wanted to know. He was forcing his thoughts into my head, hoping that the spirit wouldn't hear him. Lucky for me, this time Liam had not yelled into my head like he always had before. Somehow Liam had finally figured out how to talk into my head at a reasonable volume. I wondered if that was part of a change that happened when he "graduated"?

"I might have visited Matt and Luke, Dan, or Grandma Nancy and Opa since they all live in Vermont too. Come to think of it, maybe I would have tried to visit every single one of the people we knew and loved on Earth to make sure they're all okay and know we're okay." I was feeling a little worked up by the idea of having graduated from life on Earth. What exactly did that mean?

Liam looked overwhelmed and shook his head a little, apparently not sure how to respond.

"Have no fear, child," said the Guiding Spirit. "You'll be able to return to Earth again."

Phew. That was a relief!

"But not until you spend some time adjusting to your afterlife. Turn around and look in that direction." Since we couldn't see the Guiding Spirit, we had no way to know, but somehow I knew exactly where the spirit wanted us to look.

We were standing in the field gazing in the direction of the mountain range that looked so much like our view from home (but with totally mixed up colors!). The spirit wanted us to turn around and look over the fence, not in the direction of the castle but to the back of the field beyond the fence. I couldn't recall ever

having looked that way before. We'd been so focused on getting somewhere—back to Earth or back to the bridge—that we'd
always looked in the direction of the familiar Green Mountains
or straight behind.

A nagging discomfort about the unknown caused me to reach
out and hold Liam's arm as we slowly turned around together.

"Holy cow!" Liam exclaimed. I stood there, dumbfounded.
What a remarkably different view, and a crowded one at that.
Turning around had transported us into an enormous room with
twenty-foot-high ceilings decorated with ornate chandeliers, fres-
coes, and gold trim. Only moments ago we had been standing in
an oddly colored field, but at that moment we stood on a beautifully finished wood floor. I wondered if this was the real inside
of the Enchanted Castle. Spirits were everywhere, floating every
which way at all levels in front, beside, and behind us. Some were
clearly human spirits, and said "hello" or "welcome" to us as they
passed. Some were animal spirits—deer, squirrels, rabbits, and the
like. The animal spirits didn't say a word, but some rubbed up
against us on their way past.

"Do you suppose Amanda's here somewhere?" I asked, still
wanting to speak with her.

"Probably," Liam said. "It looks like everyone and everything
that has ever lived and died might be here!" The room certainly
was packed.

As we spoke, Amanda floated toward us from out of the crowd.
"Hi guys. You did it! You made it! It's great to see you again."
She gave each of us a huge spirit hug, so it took us a while to
untangle ourselves. That didn't matter. The hug felt great!

"Boy, are we happy to see you!" I said, and, one after the other,
Liam and I gave her those rather funny high fives. We all laughed
as our hands passed through each other's.

"No time to talk. Follow me," Amanda said as she turned and
darted into the crowd. It was all we could do to keep up with

her as she whizzed toward who knew what. I felt like a slalom skier working my way through the crowd, not wanting to blend my spirit body with any of those other spirit bodies and have to slow down to untangle myself from someone I'd never met before. That would have been too weird.

"Where are we going?" Liam asked. There was no doubt in my mind that he was loving it.

"We're going to your ancestors," Amanda explained. "They're waiting to meet you, congratulate you, and welcome you to your afterlife. It's a big welcoming party for newbies. My ancestors threw one for me too when I made it here. It was a blast!"

"How come we see all of these other spirits now, and not just the ones we connected with in our lifetimes?" I asked. All of this racing through the crowd was making me feel like I had in my lifetime when I was around lots of people I didn't know: a little overwhelmed. Not Liam. He loved crowds. For him, it was the more the merrier. I bet he didn't mind racing through the crowd one bit.

"I have lots of questions for you, Amanda." I said. "Can we go someplace to talk alone?"

"That would be rude. Everyone's waiting." Amanda said, whizzing just as quickly through the spirits. "C'mon. This is your party. Don't be late for your own party. But don't worry. I'll answer all your questions later. I promise." As I followed along behind, I couldn't help but get a little excited about the upcoming party. I wondered what and who it would include.

It gave a new meaning to the term "surprise party," that's for sure.

LIAM

COOL! A PARTY! I floated along behind Amanda and Solon, wondering what this one would be like. In life, if we were having a birthday party Mom and Solon or I would make a big plan together beforehand. The anticipation was half the fun! Mom would bake us a cake and serve it with our favorite ice cream. When we were young, she took a cake decorating class and then spent loads of time making and decorating our birthday cakes with her fancy tools. When we were older and invited our school friends, Solon and I tried out those popular, store-bought cakes with a commercial frosting job (like Pokémon, for example, when we were crazy about Pokémon). Those cakes looked cool, and our friends thought so too, but the flavor of the store-bought cakes was nothing like the cakes Mom made.

As we floated along, I wondered what we would do at this party. Would we break open a piñata? I thought back to the time Solon and I used papier mâché to make our own piñata for Solon's birthday. We planned it out together and made it well ahead of the party and had tons of fun in the process. The piñata turned out awesome, and we were so proud to share it when Solon's friends and my best friend came for the party. That party was going great, but then Solon made me furious and I whacked him hard in the butt with the bat for not letting me take my rightful turn to break open our piñata. How dare he try to leave me out after we had built it together! As soon as I hit him, Solon started crying (I must have hit him much harder than I had realized!).

Solon ran after me so mad that I thought he would kill me, but Mom chased him and grabbed him before he could hit me back, and then she sent me to my room. Of course I had to apologize after he and I had calmed down, but I was allowed back to the party later. By that time, I had missed the breaking of the piñata, and Solon and his buddies gave me my fair share of the piñata candy in a bag. How boring that was!

But dead people didn't need candy or cake. There'd be no piñata or cake at our afterlife party. I wondered again what would we do. Just sit around and talk like adults? I prayed there'd be something fun to do. Anything.

Amanda, Solon, and I continued working our way through all the spirits floating this way and that until eventually, Amanda turned left and lead us through a side door. When we passed over the threshold, the world suddenly changed again. We were surrounded by woods, and we were floating along a well-established trail through evergreens that reminded me of home. It was just Amanda, Solon and I. No other spirits to be seen. We continued silently on this wooded trail until it spilled out into a large field surrounded on all sides by trees. It felt like a secret field within the forest, a special little hiding place meant only for us.

But as I looked around to get my bearings, I noticed many spirits milling around at the far side of the field—and I noticed something else, too.

"Check it out, Solon! Soccer nets. Over there!" I said, pointing, excited beyond belief.

"Yeah. And mountain bikes too, in that rack over there," Solon said pointing in the opposite direction. A smile spread across his face.

"Follow me, boys," Amanda said, "it's time to meet everyone and get things started."

We followed Amanda to the far side of the field, looking around to soak it all in. I saw a drum set and a piano sitting atop of a stage, a baseball diamond, and a giant pile of what looked to be sticks and old wood.

The closer we came to the spirits floating on the far side of the field, the more eager I was to meet them. When we were close enough, I could see that all of them looked to be about Solon's and my age. Strange.

"Amanda," I said. "Are we in the right place? They're all kids. These aren't our ancestors waiting to meet us."

"Yep," Amanda answered, "These are your ancestors. Really."

"I don't get it," Solon said. "They weren't all our age when they died. Most of them lived long, full lives. Unlike us. So shouldn't they look as old as when they died or something?"

"That's one of the benefits of dying," Amanda said. "You get to be whatever age you want in your spirit form. That is, whatever age you want to be that you've already lived on Earth. So, in your case, Solon, you can be any age from zero to twelve and a half years old. And Liam: you can be any age from zero to ten years old. Pretty cool, huh?"

"That's so weird," Liam said. "That means you can be any age from zero to seventeen and two-thirds then, right?"

Amanda nodded.

"I'm not gonna complain. We have lots of people our age to play with now, Solon, and they're all family members to boot!"

"So, all of these ancestors just appear to be our age now for this party, but they can change to be older or younger whenever they want?" Solon asked.

"That's right," Amanda said, "and you'll see that this has definite advantages."

We were approaching the group of ancestor spirits, and I didn't recognize a soul. How could I have? It's not like we'd seen them in photos as kids. Most of the photos we'd seen of our ancestors showed them as adults, and those we knew in person had been old during our time with them on Earth.

"How will we know who's who here?" Solon asked. "Will they be wearing nametags or something?"

"See for yourselves," Amanda answered. "Hey everyone!" She yelled in the direction of the spirits gathered in this field. "We made it!" The spirits floated rapidly in our direction and surrounded us in a crowd.

I still didn't recognize anyone, until a young girl floated over and stood in front of Solon and me. "Hello boys!" she said. Her eyes were familiar, with a bright and cheery quality I knew I'd seen many times before, but I could not for the life of me figure out which one of our ancestors she could be.

"It's great to see you again, Nana!" Solon said as he floated over and hugged her in a spirit hug that merged their bodies for a minute.

"Solon, how did you know..." I started to say but stopped when I realized that our dearest Nana, Dad's grandmother, was wearing a baseball hat that said "Nana" on it. I, too, went over and hugged her. Our lives on Earth—Nana's, Solon's and mine—had intersected, but during that time, Nana had been in her nineties and approaching the natural end of her life. We had visited her, and she had visited us many times until she became too old and ill to travel. Then we would go see her in her nursing home.

"Nana, it's great to see you again!" I said.

"You too, boys," Nana said. "Though you're here much too soon. Children aren't supposed to die before their parents and grandparents. It is not the natural order of things. But, sorry. You and Amanda already know that, so the rest of us thought that, for this graduation party, we should be kids again and play with you and do the things you so loved to do in your lives. How about it?"

"Sounds great," Solon said. "Where should we start?"

"How 'bout we get to know all these ancestors a little first," I said.

"All of their names are on their hats," Amanda said. "I think you should just play first, and get to know them later. After all, this afterlife is eternal. They're not going away, and you're not, either. There's plenty of time to get to know everyone here later."

Though my curiosity was piqued, I decided that having a little fun with people my own age was too good to pass up. I missed it even more than I had realized.

"Okay then. Let the party begin," I said with a grin.

SOLON

"So, who's up for some kickball?" Liam asked the crowd of ancestral spirits. I figured that that was a great idea and would be a fun way we could get to know everyone.

Liam and I both enjoyed playing kickball at recess in our school days, but probably for different reasons. Liam played for the joy of kicking, running, or catching the ball to get someone on the opposing team out. He was extremely competitive about his kickball and very good at it, but I know he also liked to cheer on other kids and teach his teammates how to do things better. Whenever Mom asked Liam about his day at school, the first, and often the only, thing he spoke about was the recess kickball game, complete with details about who won and how and, of course, the number of homeruns he had kicked. I wasn't totally in love with the game itself. At school I mostly played because I wanted to visit with my friends and be part of the team.

Oh, and Liam and I liked to play kickball at home with Mom, games where Liam and I each were a one-man team and Mom was our designated pitcher. I admit that playing outfield with only one person and a pitcher led to some interesting and heated arguments. Liam's competitiveness could be a serious drag. But in the end, with Mom's encouragement and her often silly and ridiculous behavior, we always ended up having a ball. When Dad, or Grandma Nancy and Opa Jon joined us, it was even more fun. And there we were, ready to play with all of our ancestors. I couldn't wait!

"Where's the ball?" I asked, and like magic, a kickball appeared in my spirit hands. I guessed that somehow I, too, had developed the ability to summon things to appear. Now that was cool!

"Let's play Mom's side of the family versus Dad's side of the family," Liam suggested. "That way, we won't need to pick teams. Picking teams always takes forever."

"Fine," Amanda said, "but we're the only ones who know how to play. Most of your ancestors have never heard of kickball, although I bet they know baseball. You'll have to tell 'em the rules."

Liam's eyes lit up as I handed him the ball and suggested he explain the game to everyone. He loved to explain stuff to people. Since Amanda and I already knew how to play kickball, I pulled Amanda aside.

"Can we talk over here?" I asked her. She followed me a short distance away from the crowd, and we sat down facing Liam, watching as he explained kickball in his typically animated way.

"What's up?" Amanda asked.

Must have been that I had let too many emotions build up inside of me without realizing it since we left Earth the last time, because before I knew it, enormous sadness came rushing outward in a torrent, dragging me to the edge of tears. I knew graduating to our afterlife was making me a little nervous, but, until that moment, I had had no idea how mixed up I felt.

"So," I said through my tight, spirit throat, "I need to know...is it forever, or is it gonna end?" I said, struggling to express myself.

"Gosh. You seem really upset. What's wrong?" Amanda asked.

"Well, you know . . . " I said as the dam broke and the weight of my greatest concern came pouring out. "I need to know that our connection to Mom and Dad will last forever—that it's eternal, just like our afterlives are eternal." I paused, trying to collect myself.

"Go on," Amanda said. "Is anything else bothering you?"

"Well, our lives weren't forever. Not yours, not mine, and not

Liam's. I suppose, for that matter, nobody's life is forever. Everyone dies eventually, right? So maybe that's why I am so scared. I don't want the connection between Mom and Dad and us to die too. I want to know that it'll last forever and ever and not disappear."

"Solon," Amanda said in a soothing voice, "I can only tell you what I know from experience. My connection to my parents hasn't died. The Guiding Spirit tells me it never will. And when their lives end, I plan to meet them here and welcome them to their afterlives, just like I welcomed you and tried to help you find your way in this very different place."

"Last time Liam and I went back," I explained, "we saw proof of the connection we still have with Mom and Dad. Mom's writing about us. It's like she knows what we're doing and saying but I just want to be sure it'll last forever. For Mom and Dad's sake. For my sake. For Liam's sake." I paused to collect my thoughts. Amanda just waited patiently for more.

"Going back to Earth every now and then helped us see that Mom and Dad are gonna be okay, but now the Guiding Spirit wants us to stay here. I need to know that this connection Mom and Dad still have with us isn't gonna go away if we don't visit Earth as often as we have been since we died. See what I mean?"

"Yes, I do," Amanda answered, "Have you learned how to look back on Earth to look at what's happening there without going back yet?"

"What? You can do that from here?" I asked.

"Yep. I can teach you. Looking back without taking the risk of going there will help you know your family's okay. I look back at my family and friends a lot, and I continuously send messages to comfort them. You will too." Amanda explained. "Your family misses you guys as much as my family misses me, and they'll need to rely on their ongoing connection to you to get through that pain. Please know—and I mean know it deeply, in your heart and in your mind—that each and every person who was connected to you during your lives will keep their connection to you forever. You know that feeling you had when your mother passed through you in the hallway during your last visit to Earth? Do you remember how intensely comforting and warm that felt, and how connected you were with you mother in that moment? Well, you have to have faith that your connection with everyone you love exists forever. And, in time, your parents and everyone else will learn to feel it too. The connection lives on, even though you've died and moved on to this afterlife. You'll continue to communicate with them. You'll see."

"So is our connection to our parents is like an eternal living connection then?" I asked her.

"Yes. It's eternal, and it's still alive," Amanda said. "So I guess we could call it an eternal living connection because it'll never die. And your connection to your grandparents, your other family members, and your friends, those are eternal and alive too. Do you feel better now?"

"How can Mom and Dad feel a connection to me from here and be comforted by it?" I asked her, needing to understand this all more fully.

"I have the perfect example, and it involves your mother. You remember how I said you'll keep this living connection not only to your parents, but also to other family members and to your friends? Well, here's proof of the connection I have with your mother still. Maybe it'll help you feel better."

"Here's what happened. When your parents were staying overnight in a hotel at the boat docks in Tortola, waiting to collect the sailboat they were going to take for vacation in April . . . "

"The sailing trip that Liam and I missed because we died?"

"Well, yeah, the one you missed while alive, but visited as spirits after your death."

"How did you know we visited that boat in our afterlives?" I asked.

"Because I have an eternal living connection to you too, silly," Amanda said.

I thought about that and then said, "Go on."

"Well, before your mother, father, and grandfather were allowed to take the boat out on the water, your father and grandfather needed to go to a mandatory training about the charter company's policies and procedures. Your Mom slept in late, but then she woke up, crying and alone. With all the travel, she hadn't remembered that date was the anniversary of the day I died. She assumed her tears were related to yours and Liam's recent deaths, and not to mine."

"I don't get it. How does that prove your connection with her? I mean, so she was sad about your death. I already knew that," I said. "I wouldn't doubt that she remembered the date and that that's what made her cry."

"Well, it's what happened after she got up that shows the connection," Amanda said. "You see, she got up and got her iPod, hoping that listening to some of your music would help her feel closer to you. When she turned on her iPod and started to scroll down to select a song, an instrumental tune named "Amanda" started to play without her having selected anything at all. Before that day, she had never heard the song, and she had no idea what it was. When she looked and saw that it was titled "Amanda," she suddenly remembered that the date was my death day."

"Are you telling me that you played that song for her somehow?" I asked.

"I didn't consciously play that song for her. The living connection between us made that song play. It's what she needed to recognize why she was even more upset than usual when she woke up."

"Whoa. That's wild!"

"That's not all," Amanda said. "You see, when your father returned to the room, your mother told him of the "Amanda" song playing and reminded him that it was the date of my death. They hugged, and your Mom cried some more, and then they went to breakfast. After breakfast, your Mom and Dad had an hour to kill before they were allowed to take the boat out for their week-long sailing trip, so they went for a walk. They kept taking random turns on unfamiliar roads, and then they walked up a hill beside town. Toward the top of the hill, they saw a sign beside the road. It said, 'Amanda's Gifts' and had an arrow pointing up the hill. They followed the road in the direction the sign pointed and came upon a little rundown building. It was the 'Amanda's Gifts' shop. Quite amazing, really. Your mother told your father that it was a sign that I was with them."

"Wow. That's so cool! So this stuff just happens for people on Earth because of their living connection with loved ones who've died," I said. I felt like I was beginning to understand.

"So you see, even though you're not necessarily there like you used to be, your living connection with everyone is . . . well . . . alive, and it'll bring all of those you left behind comfort in your absence," Amanda said.

"Thank you!" I said. "I feel much better. We'll have to share that story with Liam after the games."

It was looking like the kickball game was nearly ready to begin. I stood up and reached out my spirit hand. "Let's go play," I said.

As Amanda and I rejoined the crowd of youngsters, I could feel the excitement in the air. Everyone appeared eager to play. It was no wonder that Liam's infectious attitude about kickball rubbed off on them. Liam, of course, was in his kickball element out on the mound preparing to pitch.

"Solon," Liam yelled, "since you and I could play for either Mom's family's team or Dad's family's team, let's just split up. I am gonna start by pitching for the Emberley side. You go to bat with the Baileys."

Not caring who I played for, I headed toward home plate, quietly contemplating all that Amanda had said as she walked to the outfield to play for Liam's team. My team gathered near home plate. The boy standing to my right leaned over to me and said with a grin, "This oughta be fun, huh Solon?" Uncertain of his identity, I looked to his hat and was shocked to see that it read "Solon Irving Bailey." Holy cow! He was my triple-great grandfather, the one Mom and Dad named me after.

"Wow," I said. "Nice to meet you, Triple Grandpa Solon!" I felt a little foolish calling someone my age "Grandpa," but that's who he was.

"Just call me Solon Irving or something. Whatever you do, don't call me 'triple grandpa' again during the game. How do you expect to win with a triple grandpa on your team?"

"Good point, Solon Irving. No. Scratch that. It's way too long," I explained. "How 'bout I just call you SI, as in 'sigh'"

"Deal," SI responded. "This is your party, so you go up first."

"Okay," I said, turning to address all my teammates. "I look forward to meeting all of you."

"We'll do that later," SI said. "Let's play!"

I walked over and stood about five running steps behind home plate and yelled, "All set, Liam!"

Liam pitched the ball, and I ran hard and nailed it. The ball sailed through the air, out of the field, and into the woods.

"Yeehaw! My best kick ever. Did you see that?" I said, turning to my teammates who stood there as if nothing had happened. What was wrong with those old people? On Earth, my teammates would have been roaring with approval had I kicked it out of the park like that. All of my spirit teammates just shook their heads, not knowing how to respond.

"I expect the ball went exactly where you wanted it to go," SI explained, "but we didn't see it, and we don't know where that is. Was it a good one?"

Oh dear. It seemed like kickball in our afterlives wouldn't be anything like kickball in our lifetimes had been. If the ball always went where you wanted it to go, and only you, the kicker, could see it, what fun could that possibly be?

"Liam." I headed for the pitcher's mound. "We have to talk!"

Liam floated in my direction, "What's wrong? That was a perfect pitch."

"I know. That's the problem," I said. When we came together I explained it to him. "You see, I kicked the perfect kick, too, a homerun into the woods. Did you see it?"

"Nope," was all Liam could say.

"See the problem here, buddy?" I asked. "You'll forever make perfect pitches, and each person up will forever make perfect kicks. We're gonna be here all day running around homerun after homerun with nobody every getting out. That means that your team will eternally play in the outfield, and mine will be up to bat forever. What fun is that?"

"No way! You guys can't bat forever! No fair," Liam complained. "We need a turn too." All of the ancestral spirits were watching us, wondering from afar what we were arguing about.

"How about we just do something completely different? I mean, seriously. This type of kickball would make for a pretty boring party," I said.

"What about soccer. Can we try soccer?" Liam said.

"I suppose, but I bet the same thing'll happen. The person with the ball will have an easy time keeping it from the other team because the other team won't even see the ball, and the kicker will shoot and score. Then the other team will have their turn, we won't see the ball, and the same thing will happen. They'll shoot and score. That would just go on and on all day. Sounds kinda boring to me."

"So what are we gonna do that's fun but not competitive?" Liam asked. Small wonder that he asked that question.

"Well, we could just hang out and talk with everyone like I used to at recess while in the kickball line. You know, get to know them better. Or . . . hey, I got it. We could play the piano and drums to entertain them. That'd be fun, kinda like playing Guitar Hero together at home. Who knows what cool music we would create together if we put our spirit minds to it. Seriously! If every time I kick the ball I hit an amazing homer, I bet as spirits you and I could make some pretty rockin' music with that piano and drum set," I said pointing to the stage.

Our ancestral spirits were patiently waiting for Liam and me to finish our conversation, but each of our teams had drifted into groups, Liam's near first base and mine near home plate.

"Let's make a decision and get on with it," I said.

"Okay. Fine," Liam said, clearly disappointed that we would not be playing kickball. "Let's try playing some tunes," Liam said.

"Everybody in!" Liam and I yelled simultaneously, and, in a matter of seconds, all our ancestors crowded around us.

"Kickball's not much fun here because the ball always goes where we want it to go," Liam said.

"Yeah," I said. "In life, we weren't perfect, and the things we were able to do with a ball weren't perfect either, which kept the game interesting. So instead of playing kickball now, we've decided to play you some music."

"You might already know this, but in life I played drums, and Solon played piano," Liam said. The spirits surrounding us nodded their heads.

"We thought we'd see what happens when we play music here

in our afterlives. No guarantees, but we hope it sounds good and that you enjoy it," I said.

"Go ahead. This'll be fun to hear," Amanda said.

Liam and I made our way to the stage with everyone following. They all sat down in the grass in front of the stage as Liam and I floated up and settled into our instrument chairs. Liam fiddled with arranging his drum set so that everything was where he needed it, and I plunked on individual keys, listening to the piano's tone. It sounded remarkably like the Steinway piano I had used during lessons in life.

When Liam was all set he gave me the thumbs up sign, and on the count of three the two of us began to play. In our lives, we had never tried to make music with our instruments at the same time. In truth, I had never wanted Liam's loud drums banging along as I played my piano. So even if we had talked about what to do musically on the stage, it probably wouldn't have helped us one bit.

But there we sat, playing our first ever duet. At first, our cacophony of disjointed sounds hurt every spirit's ears, including mine. Our ancestors clapped their hands over the sides of their heads, avoiding the din. I couldn't have said why Liam and I just kept right on playing in the face of such a racket, but we did. It definitely was not normal behavior for me. If I had made such awful noise on Earth, I would have definitely stopped immediately. But Liam and I just looked at each other and kept playing. As we continued playing, the tunes gradually became more and more pleasing. In time, our tunes were downright amazing, if I do say so myself. I guessed that that was another one of the beauties of being in heaven: we could create soul-touching music together. It felt great.

"That was cool," Liam exclaimed when, after a long while, we decided to stop. The crowd of spirit ancestors clapped, rose to their feet, and clapped some more. SI came up onto the stage then and put his arms up to quiet the crowd.

"As you can see, we have two connected young spirits here. Thank you boys for bringing us such joy," SI said. Liam and I nodded in unison. "Welcome you to your afterlives. Every spirit gathered here can say from experience that you have many great adventures ahead of you. Your afterlife, which will be uniquely yours, possesses an endless array of paths for you to explore. If you wish, you can invite any of us to join you in your travels. You are not alone."

As SI stood there speaking, I was overcome by an intense desire to know and understand each and every one of the spirits that sat in the audience. It felt like a magnet was pulling at my insides, begging me to look at every spirit ancestor out there and get to know everything possible about them: their history, their lives, their special talents, the web of connections woven in their lives, the living connections that still existed in their afterlives, who they knew and loved, and what made them tick. I turned to Liam.

"Do you feel that?" I asked him.

"You mean that pulling feeling?" he asked. "The one that makes me feel completely connected to all these people, including those I've never met in my life? The one that makes me want to know each and every one of them like I know the back of my hand?"

"Yeah. That one," I said smiling. "I guess we really aren't alone, are we?"

"Definitely not." Liam responded.

In fact, in that moment I was overcome with the realization that the living connections, the forever bonds that Amanda and I had just talked about, existed everywhere—not just in the after-life but also in life. The bonds were so strong that even though we had not met most of our ancestors until that party, Liam and I feel drawn to and comforted by our connection to them. Was it because the love within those bonds had been passed down through generations from mothers and fathers to daughters and sons, and from grandparents to grandsons and granddaughters?

"Liam," I said, suddenly overcome with an amazing thought. "It's love!"

"That's right," Liam said, still deep in thought.

"The living connection that lasts an eternity. It's love. That's it. That's what connects us to everyone we care about on Earth. That's what connects them with us. That's what connects us to all of these ancestors, most of whom we've never met 'til now. The love that is passed down through generations in the family. That's what this living connection is made of. It's gotta be love," I said.

"That's right. I'm thinking the very same thing. The love we share with family and friends never dies!"

Liam and I hadn't realized that, as we had been having our own little focused discussion, all of our ancestors had floated up onto the stage with us. They surrounded us then, and I guessed that they must have been eavesdropping because they formed a sort of giant crowd around us, and before we knew what was happening, they were giving us the biggest group hug I had ever been a part of. I could feel their combined love flowing through me, and, in that moment, I realized that the hug had the same quality as the hugs we used to get from Mom and Dad. It wasn't exactly the same, but it was full of as much love and comfort as any human could have possibly imagined.

"Welcome to heaven!"

ACKNOWLEDGEMENTS

I EXTEND MY deepest gratitude to my husband, Chris (Solon and Liam's father), whose unwavering love and strength enables me to continue to put one foot in front of the other. I love you with all my heart.

I also thank the many professionals who helped me continue to live in the absence of our sons. Thank you, Ginny Frey, for your ongoing guidance. Without you, I have no idea how I would have found a way forward. Thank you, Lois Morse, for helping me remove myself mentally from the fire using Eye Movement Desensitization and Reprocessing (EMDR), and for suggesting, as Ginny did too, that I use creativity on my path toward healing. Ellen Fein, thank you for your gentle and sensitive yoga therapy. You've helped me feel safe in my body again through my breath, living each day more peacefully, and feeling connected to our sons. Thank you, Abby Dreyer, for your expert guidance in the pottery studio. With you, I etched this tale more deeply in my mind through clay[1] and experienced the emergence of beauty from intense heat. Thank you Alison for helping me explore my musical connection with Solon and Liam at the piano. And thank you Carl and Gina Hilton-Van Osdall for helping me look east through my pain. Every one of you contributed to the emergence of this story.

Chris and I extend enormous gratitude to our family and

---

1 * Visit www.crossing-the-horizon.com to view the ceramic tiles that I carved while grieving and writing.

friends. In particular, thank you to Katherine and John Paterson for all of their love and to Katherine for contributing her beautiful forward to this story. There are far too many family and friends to mention here, but please know that Chris and I thank you all for your loving support. I would also like to extend a special thank you to my brother, David, and his wife, Susan. Amanda will always live in my heart and mind beside Solon and Liam.

Last, but certainly not least, thank you to my editor, Diane O'Connell, whose sensitive and expert advice enabled me to improve while leaving whole this healing story that poured forth during the year after the boys died. I appreciate your assistance and the assistance of your talented publication staff. You helped me to show readers our sons as they were, and as they will remain in our minds forever.

Made in the USA
Middletown, DE
25 January 2016